THREE WISHES

A Journey of Self-Discovery and Untold Desires

ECHO SABLE

Table of Contents

CHAPTER I

Hitmen, Entrepreneurs, And Mysteries

The night was cloaked in an unsettling silence, broken only by the soft rustle of velvet curtains swaying gently in the dimly lit room. Iron Smith sat poised like a sentinel on the plush embrace of a large, soft sofa, his eyes fixed on the world beyond the glass. A golden hue emanated from the aged brandy beside him, its aroma mingling with the tension in the air. But it was another instrument that commanded the room's attention—the meticulously assembled long-range rifle resting within arm's reach.

This was no ordinary weapon. Its telescope, capable of magnifying distances tenfold, was Iron Smith's eye on the world. Through the eyepiece, delicate crosshairs formed a precise target—a silent promise of what lay ahead. Yet, the rifle's lethal precision was a mere extension of Iron Smith's own capabilities, for the rifle demanded more than technological prowess; it required the unerring steadiness of a master marksman.

From the nondescript box, Iron Smith unveiled this masterpiece of engineering — a rifle crafted with such precision that it could be disassembled into several parts, each fitting seamlessly into the next.

Once assembled, it became an extension of his will, a testament to human ingenuity and craftsmanship.

Time seemed to blur as he sat on the sofa, the minutes slipping into the shadows of the dimly lit room.

He remained there, fingers splayed, palms turned towards him, scrutinizing the unwavering stillness of his hands. They were like sculptures, carved from stone, devoid of the tremors of life, as if time itself had paused in reverence to their steadiness. It was a ritual, this communion with his own stability—a dialogue between mind and muscle, until satisfaction was achieved.

Only then did Iron Smith allow his fingers to curl around the rifle. The motion was deliberate, each movement calculated. With the silencer affixed to the muzzle, the rifle promised a silent discharge, its report no louder than the gentle pop of a wine cork being eased from its bottle.

In that moment, Iron Smith and the rifle were one—a symbiosis of man and machine, ready to whisper fate into the night.

With the muzzle, Iron Smith nudged the curtain aside, revealing a small, round aperture in the glass—his own handiwork from the moment he'd entered the room.

Perched on the twelfth floor of one of the city's most opulent hotels, Iron Smith prepared for his task in a suite that exuded luxury. The rifle's muzzle extended with precision, and the telescope's lens pressed firmly against the glass, transforming the window into a portal of calculated intent. Leaning forward, Iron Smith placed his eye against the eyepiece, the world beyond the glass coming sharply into focus.

Through the scope, the opposite building loomed—a sleek new structure that stood out even amidst the bustling skyline of Tokyo's most vibrant district. Its facade was a tapestry of glass, revealing the ceaseless rush of people within its corridors. Iron Smith's gaze was unwavering, the crosshairs of his scope settling on the eleventh-floor corridor, tracking a young woman in a vivid red top. He followed her every move, the crosshair lingering on her figure until she vanished around a corner.

In those fleeting seconds, Iron Smith's fingers caressed the trigger with a lover's touch, the promise of finality electrifying. He was the arbiter of fate, the master of life and death, wielding power that transcended the divine or the infernal. It was he, Iron Smith, a killer whose precision was unmatched.

Unmoving, Iron Smith maintained his vigil, the crosshair poised at the corridor's bend, where an unremarkable height marker was etched into the wall at 164 centimeters. His target, he knew, stood at 168 centimeters. The instant the figure emerged, Iron Smith would unleash the bullet, delivering it with unerring accuracy to the target's forehead.

Every detail had been meticulously planned. At precisely 1:00 p.m., the target would leave her office, destined to turn that very corner. Iron Smith's watch ticked with anticipation, and at 1:07, the moment crystallized. The target emerged, the crosshair aligned, and Iron Smith's finger fulfilled its deadly promise.

In a fluid movement, Iron Smith leaned back, his hands a blur as they disassembled the rifle into seven precise components, each piece finding its place within the exquisite box. With a final flourish, he drained the glass of brandy, savoring its warmth before striding from the room.

Iron Smith's precision and confidence were such that he didn't spare a glance to confirm the outcome. To him, the equation was simple and immutable: two plus two equals four. In his world, when the Iron Smith fired, the target fell. It was a certainty as natural as the sun rising in the east.

As he emerged from the elevator, he effortlessly blended into the normalcy of hotel life. He passed through the lobby, acknowledging the courteous nods of hotel staff with a detached professionalism. Once outside, the bustling streets of Tokyo enveloped him, the anonymity of the crowd a comforting cloak.

On the eleventh floor of the gleaming building behind him, a life had been extinguished. Yet, there was no thread linking Iron Smith to the fallen; no suspicion would ever cast a shadow over his presence. The only witness to the truth was the silent bullet, and it would never betray its master.

Meanwhile, Itagaki Ichiro exited his office, his mood as dark as the storm clouds gathering on the horizon. Unbeknownst to him, fate had already marked his path, orchestrated by an unseen hand—a hand as steady as steel, belonging to a man who had already slipped into the crowd, leaving nothing but whispers of the wind in his wake.

Itagaki Ichiro epitomized the successful middle-aged businessman. As the chairman of a prosperous medium-sized enterprise, his life was a tapestry of luxury, woven with threads of wealth and influence. His suit, a seamless blend of sable and wool, was the handiwork of Tokyo's finest tailor, and it only added to his commanding presence. Yet, beneath the veneer of success lay a man entangled in a web of clandestine desires.

Yunko, Itagaki's captivating mistress, was a singer whose fame flickered modestly on the outskirts of the limelight. Her age, precisely half that of Itagaki's, added an intoxicating layer of allure to their clandestine affair.

Yet, it was this very relationship that seeded discontent in Itagaki's otherwise meticulously orchestrated life.

Their meetings were conducted with the precision of a covert operation. A discreet phone call would set the wheels in motion, arranging a rendezvous at their secret hideaway—a sanctuary of quiet and comfort far removed from prying eyes. Punctuality was paramount;

Itagaki insisted on arriving ten to fifteen minutes ahead of Yunko, a testament to his unwavering discipline and the importance he placed on these encounters.

Once Yunko arrived, the world outside ceased to exist. Their secret meeting place transformed into a private universe where time seemed to stand still. They reveled in their shared moments until the clock's hands nudged towards midnight, signaling the end of their stolen hours together.

On rare occasions, business trips offered a legitimate guise for their escapades, allowing Itagaki to whisk Yunko away with him. But barring such opportunities, the unbreakable rule was that he would return home by midnight, slipping back into the facade of the dutiful husband.

Sadagumi, Itagaki's wife, hailed from a distinguished family in Kanto, and her family's influence was a cornerstone of his business success. The stakes were high, and maintaining the secrecy of his affair with Yunko was paramount. This hidden world of rendezvous added an illicit thrill to his otherwise structured life, a tantalizing escape from the rigors of business.

Their clandestine meetings unfolded with regularity, one to three times a week, in a location known only to them. It was a sanctuary that lay dormant in their absence, a secret world accessible solely with their keys.

But last night, as Itagaki happened to pass by their secret haven around 11 o'clock, something was amiss. A light spilled from behind the curtains, triggering a wave of suspicion. Who could be there? He hadn't arranged to meet Yunko, and she would never venture there alone. The thought gnawed at him—could Yunko be entertaining another lover in their sacred space?

Jealousy flared, urging him to uncover the truth. Yet, with Sadagumi beside him in the car, he was forced to mask his turmoil. His mind raced, but his face betrayed him, prompting Sadagumi's concern. "Are you feeling uncomfortable? Your face is very ugly," she inquired.

He deflected her worry with a practiced excuse. "I have a slight headache, maybe I drank too much just now," he replied, hiding the storm within.

Upon returning home, he found a private moment to call Yunko's residence, knowing that the rendezvous site had no phone to disrupt their privacy. If Yunko was home, it would imply that a thief might have entered the rendezvous place.

However, the phone at Yunko's residence rang incessantly, with no one answering.

Restless and agitated, Itagaki's mind churned with scenarios, robbing him of sleep.

The next morning, his anxiety persisted. As soon as he arrived at the office, he resumed his attempts to reach Yunko, dialing her number every half hour until one o'clock. But still, the calls went unanswered, leaving him in a state of heightened suspicion and frustration, the mystery gnawing at the edges of his carefully maintained world.

Itagaki's mounting anxieties propelled him out of the office during his lunch break, his mind fixated on the mystery at their secret rendezvous. In his haste, he left his briefcase behind, a testament to his distraction and urgency. He moved swiftly down the corridor, intent on reaching the corner, where his female secretary caught up with him, his name echoing in the hallway. "Mr. Itagaki! Mr. Itagaki!" her voice called out.

As he turned the corner, an unexpected scene unfolded, one that would etch itself into the secretary's memory with chilling clarity. Later, in her statement to Detective Kenichi, she recounted the surreal moment: "First, there was the sound of glass shattering," she recalled, her voice steady despite the horror of the memory. "Mr. Itagaki, who was ahead of me, suddenly halted. I handed him the briefcase and called his name again. He turned, his mouth opening as if to speak, but no words came. Instead, a dark stream of blood surged from his forehead, thicker than anything I'd ever seen. And then he collapsed..."

Detective Kenichi, tasked with leading the special investigation into Itagaki's death, found himself ensnared in a web of intrigue and shadowy motives. The relentless investigation spanned a week, a grueling stretch that afforded Kenichi less than 30 hours of sleep. His weary eyes surveyed the calendar on his desk, a bitter smile tugging at his lips.

Amidst the chaos of the case, a call from an old friend in Mumbai had punctuated his exhausting vigil. The phone had roused him from a fleeting sleep, the international call cutting through the midnight stillness.

"This is Kenichi, who is this? What? An international call from Mumbai, India? " he had answered, his voice brisk with curiosity and fatigue.

The caller was none other than me, Ash Morris. While I might not need an extensive introduction, the reasons for my call to Kenichi in Mumbai warrant explanation. It was a call born of urgency and necessity, threads of fate intertwining across continents, drawing me into the enigma of Itagaki's untimely demise.

To truly understand the connection between Kenichi and me, it's essential to recount how we first crossed paths.

It was during a trip to Hokkaido, Japan, several years ago—a time when Kenichi had just graduated from Tokyo University and was yet to begin his career. We met on the slopes, both drawn to the thrill of skiing, and a friendship quickly blossomed.

Kenichi eventually joined the police force, and despite the demands of his new role, we stayed in touch. He visited me twice, and I made it a point to see him whenever I traveled to Japan. Our conversations were always a blend of the ordinary and the extraordinary. I would share my strange and often unbelievable experiences, and Kenichi would listen with an open mind, his imagination boundless and accepting.

One of the reasons our friendship solidified so quickly was Kenichi's unique expertise—his remarkable ability to thrive in the wilderness.

Born in the mountainous regions of central Kyushu, his early life was marked by adversity. Orphaned at a tender age, he claimed to have been raised by the very creatures of the forest—monkeys, wolves, badgers, bears, and even the smallest of insects. When his adoptive father eventually found him, Kenichi was reportedly nestled in the arms of a female monkey, a tale that, while lacking corroborative evidence, speaks volumes of his affinity with nature.

Kenichi's mastery of the natural world was unparalleled. I remember camping with him in the mountains, where he could identify the calls of various insects and knew which ones were the most delectable. His ability to mimic sounds could summon small animals, who seemingly recognized him as one of their own. His repertoire included over 30 bird calls, each so authentic that it could distinguish between genders. His imitation of a male bird call was so convincing that it would often attract flocks of females.

Most astonishing was his claim of fluency in the language of monkeys—a claim he substantiated by demonstrating interactions with them, leaving me convinced of his extraordinary skills.

Kenichi, with his extraordinary affinity for animals, would have seemed destined for a career among them. Yet, he chose the path of law enforcement. When I asked him why, his response was both intriguing and revealing: "I have a very deep understanding of all living things. However, I don't understand people. I think that being a policeman is a job that involves contact with people, so I want to be a policeman and try to understand people further." Kenichi's reasoning was as unique as he was, making him perhaps the only person to join the police force with such a motivation.

The reason for my call from India was rooted in an unusual encounter. While traveling there—on a trip filled with its own adventures, though they lie beyond this tale—I met a zoologist. This zoologist faced a troubling dilemma, and it was Kenichi who immediately came to mind as the potential solution.

The dilemma revolved around a rare pure white tarsier, captured from the forests of southern India. Since its capture, the tarsier had refused to eat and was on the brink of starvation. This particular variant was so rare that it might be the only one of its kind in the world. Losing it would be a tragedy. Given Kenichi's unique rapport with animals, I believed he might be able to coax the tarsier out of its hunger strike.

We secured approval from the "International Wildlife Conservation Association" to bring the tarsier to Japan, and I reached out to Kenichi. On the call, I simply told him I had something extremely important to discuss, without divulging specifics. Unbeknownst to me, Kenichi was deeply embroiled in the Itagaki case, unaware even of the entrepreneur's mysterious assassination. I intended to surprise him, not realizing my visit would complicate his already tumultuous circumstances.

With the tarsier's condition worsening, I quickly departed for Tokyo. Meanwhile, Kenichi remained at his desk, immersed in a sea of reports about the case that seemed to only deepen the mystery. It was evident that Itagaki's death was the handiwork of a professional killer. The killer had stayed in a luxurious hotel suite under a common Japanese name, described by staff as a tall, dark, and handsome man. He had checked in at night, paid upfront for a single day's stay, and left the hotel shortly after the assassination, carrying a fine crocodile leather suitcase.

Despite knowing the killer's profile, identifying him among the hundreds of thousands fitting that description in Tokyo was an insurmountable challenge.

Kenichi turned his focus to Itagaki's life, seeking anyone who might have had the motivation and resources to hire such a lethal professional. The fee for such expertise was staggering, typically over $800,000—a sum no one would spend without grave reason.

Yet, a week of relentless effort yielded little more than a frustrating tangle of dead ends. The only consistent anomaly was the gap in Itagaki's schedule from 8 p.m. to midnight, one to three times weekly—a detail provided by his wife, Sadagumi.

Sadagumi, poised and composed even in grief, sat with an elegance befitting her prestigious Kanto upbringing. "I have the habit of keeping a diary," she told Kenichi when he inquired about her husband's activities. "Of course, my diary only records daily events and trivial matters in the family. Whenever Itagaki had a business appointment, he would tell me, and I would note it down. His social calendar was hectic, sometimes requiring him to attend several meetings in one evening. On occasion, he would return home inebriated, escorted by friends, all of which is recorded in my diary."

Kenichi, attentive and respectful, asked if she would be willing to share her diary with the police to aid in the investigation. Sadagumi hesitated, a slight shift in her elegant posture betraying her internal conflict, yet she remained the epitome of grace and decorum.

Kenichi, aware of her noble lineage and refined demeanor, admired her composure. Her sorrow was measured, her grief contained, as if trained not to let personal tragedy disrupt the carefully curated elegance of her life. The house mirrored her demeanor—immaculately arranged, a testament to her disciplined existence.

To an outsider, Sadagumi's controlled response might seem entirely appropriate, but her internal dialogue told a different story. On the way to the hospital, seated in a car driven by her uniformed chauffeur, her mind clung to one unyielding thought: he's dead.

Seventeen years of marriage had culminated in this moment. Memories of countless mundane grievances, long buried, surged to the forefront of her mind. Yet, amidst the chaos of recollection, a peculiar serenity enveloped her—an unsettling calm that suggested this was a conclusion she had unconsciously anticipated, perhaps even desired.

Sadagumi's reaction to Itagaki's death was complex, a mix of relief and inevitability. While she might not have been able to articulate why she felt this way, the years of subtle pressures and unspoken tensions had taken their toll. The prospect of sharing her diary, a personal chronicle of her life, with the investigator Kenichi brought a momentary tremor to her composed facade.

Kenichi, with his characteristic energy and keen eyes, requested access to the diary. Sadagumi's hesitation was palpable. Yet, her response was measured, her expression apologetic. "Mr. Kenichi, about this matter... because there is still a little bit of my private life in the diary..." she explained.

Kenichi, understanding the delicacy of the situation, responded with tact. "Yes, I understand this. Then, can you please read out the part about Mr. Itagaki's whereabouts in the diary, and I will send someone to record it. Understanding Mr. Itagaki's activities before his death will be very helpful in tracking down the murderer. I think Madam must also hope to catch the murderer as soon as possible!"

Sadagumi, maintaining her composed demeanor, agreed. "Okay, I can agree to this," she said with a hint of sadness that seemed appropriate for the circumstances.

Kenichi arranged for a capable detective to record Sadagumi's readings, using both a pen and a recorder to ensure accuracy. The investigation quickly revealed discrepancies; while seven out of ten of Itagaki's purported appointments were genuine, three were fabrications, cover stories for secret activities.

The question loomed large: What was Itagaki doing during those hours? The answer seemed obvious to me. "Of course he has a mistress, and he uses that time to meet with her," I told Kenichi upon my arrival in Tokyo.

I had just landed at Narita Airport with the frail white tarsier in my care. Two members of the Japan Wildlife Conservation Association met me, their awe at the sight of the rare creature tempered by concern for its deteriorating condition. My thoughts were divided between the urgency of the tarsier's plight and the need to connect with Kenichi swiftly.

As I scanned the bustling airport for Kenichi, I knew that every moment counted—not just for the tarsier, but also in unraveling the enigma surrounding Itagaki's death. The sooner we could merge our efforts, the greater the likelihood of saving the tarsier and solving the case that had entangled Itagaki's last days.

CHAPTER 2

The White Tarsier and the Sealed Door

Kenichi burst through the gate, a blur of motion, deftly vaulting over a luggage cart with remarkable agility. As he reached me, he emitted an uncanny series of sounds, and the previously still tarsier sprang to life, its eyes wide and alert, leaping into Kenichi's waiting arms.

Kenichi's voice sliced through the air, sharp and accusatory. "What happened? Did you mistreat it?" His eyes burned with a reprimand that begged for confrontation.

I quickly raised my hands in defense. "No mistreatment here. It's refused to eat ever since it was captured."

Kenichi stormed off towards the restaurant, muttering curses under his breath. "Every hunter in the world should be ensnared and marched through the Sahara Desert!"

Inside, he seized a bottle of milk with urgency, gently feeding the reluctant tarsier. The creature's large eyes conveyed gratitude as it drank, soon falling asleep in Kenichi's arms, a picture of trust and tranquility.

Kenichi dismissed the Wildlife Conservation Association members and whisked me away to his home. A bachelor, his apartment was a chaotic jungle of plants, an urban rainforest.

Upon arrival, he crafted a cozy nest from a blanket, gently placing the tarsier within. Their exchange of peculiar sounds seemed an unspoken language of kinship.

With a nod, Kenichi tossed me a bottle of wine. We drank, and he regaled me with tales of his recent exploits. I listened intently, offering my insights.

"Yes, mistress! But who is she? Where do they meet?" Kenichi pondered, his fingers tapping a rhythm on his forehead.

I chuckled, "Easy enough to discern. Men sneaking around avoid their own cars and choose secluded meeting spots."

Kenichi interrupted, exasperated, "Tokyo's full of secluded spots!"

I suggested, "Investigate Itagaki's driver. Find out where he dropped Itagaki during his so-called events. That might lead us somewhere."

Kenichi replied, "I did. Each venue was different, high-profile. The driver always watched him enter before leaving."

"I think we can rule out public transportation," I suggested. "These places always have taxis waiting..."

Before I could finish, Kenichi sprang up, slapping his forehead. The sudden movement startled the little white tarsier, which leaped up and wrapped its delicate arms around Kenichi's neck.

Don't underestimate this rare pure white tarsier. It's more than just a bystander in this tale; it holds a crucial role in the unraveling mystery.

How could a tarsier, captured by local natives in the southern Indian jungles, be linked to a top-tier assassin hiding in Tokyo? It seemed impossible, yet the strange tapestry of fate weaves connections between seemingly unrelated entities with invisible threads.

So, don't overlook this rare and charming creature.

I never planned to linger in Tokyo. My mission was simply to deliver the tarsier to Kenichi, and that was accomplished.

I contacted the zoologist in India, reassuring him that the tarsier was thriving — it had not only drunk milk but also devoured a banana, regaining its vigor and already leaping around Kenichi's apartment.

That night, I stayed at a hotel, assured that Kenichi could crack the case. The Itagaki affair, to me, seemed like a straightforward contract killing, hardly intriguing. With Kenichi occupied, I left a message at his office about my return home. Receiving no response, I proceeded to the airport alone.

After checking in, I settled at the terminal. As passengers gathered for my flight, I tried contacting Kenichi again—still no answer. Reluctantly, I headed to board.

Just as I was about to board the shuttle to the plane, an airport staffer rushed toward me, clearly agitated. "Mr. Ash Morris? Who is Mr. Morris?"

"I am," I responded quickly.

"Mr. Morris," he gasped, "there's an urgent call for you from the police station's airport office. You need to take it immediately!"

For a moment, I was taken aback as the staff member caught his breath and said, "It's a call from Officer Kenichi!"

So, it was Kenichi. What could be so urgent? It seemed my flight plans were about to change. Kenichi must have learned about my departure from his office colleagues, as I had left a message there.

I followed the staff member to the airport's police office and picked up the phone, hearing Kenichi's voice, filled with impatience. "Where have you been? I've been waiting forever! I can't stand it anymore!"

His urgency left me momentarily speechless. "Can't stand it anymore"—what could he possibly mean?

Frustrated, I retorted, "If you had called two minutes later, I'd be on the plane already!"

Kenichi, undeterred, responded with determination, "Even if the plane had taken off, I'd have it land again. You're not leaving! No more arguments—get in the police car. They know where to take you. I'll be waiting!"

His insistence was unmistakable, and I realized that whatever awaited me was far more pressing than my original plans.

My curiosity was piqued, especially given Kenichi's uncharacteristically urgent tone. I pressed him for details, "What's going on?"

Kenichi replied, "I don't know yet, which is why I need you here. I need your insight to make sense of this. Please, hurry!"

With that, Kenichi hung up, leaving me with more questions than answers. I turned to the airport staff, "Mr. Kenichi mentioned someone would take me to the location. Who might that be?"

A lively young man stepped forward, "That's me. Ready when you are."

Without wasting time, I nodded, "Let's move quickly. Kenichi's urgency is palpable."

He gestured for me to follow, and we left the airport, jumping into his car. Though the streets of Tokyo were unfamiliar to me, the young man navigated them with ease. After a swift 30-minute drive, we arrived in a quiet, upscale neighborhood and stopped in front of a sleek 12-story building.

As soon as we halted, Kenichi appeared, visibly agitated. He rushed over, pounding the car roof in frustration. "How did you get here? Did you push the car here by your own power?"

I gently nudged him aside, "The car got here as fast as it could. No need for complaints!"

Kenichi cast a glare at the driver but quickly redirected his focus, grabbing my arm and leading me inside. The building exuded luxury, with a marble-paved lobby and opulent decor.

In the lobby, several agents stood alongside a middle-aged man who appeared to be an administrator, his expression oddly inscrutable. Kenichi hurriedly guided me into the elevator, pressing the button for the eleventh floor. His grip on my arm was firm, almost urgent, underscoring his excitement—or perhaps anxiety.

It was clear he needed my support for something significant; otherwise, he wouldn't have summoned me back from the airport with such insistence. Yet, the mystery of what he had uncovered remained.

Stepping out of the elevator, we entered a softly lit hallway adorned with a potted oak and vibrant tiles depicting underwater scenes—a serene setting that belied the tension in the air. On the left was a carved door, guarded by two agents.

Kenichi signaled them to leave, instructing, "Head to the lobby and wait for the draftsman. He'll sketch the woman based on the administrator's description."

As the agents departed, Kenichi grasped the door handle and turned to face me. "This is where Itagaki met a young, beautiful woman."

I felt a surge of frustration. Was discovering a rendezvous location significant enough to warrant my abrupt recall from the airport?

Sensing my irritation, Kenichi preempted my reproach. "We spoke to nearly 20 taxi drivers, four of whom confirmed they had dropped off someone resembling Itagaki here. The administrator verified this was the unit they entered. We used the skeleton key to open it, finding no one inside."

I struggled to hide my annoyance, barely digesting Kenichi's words. "You called me back from the airport for something so mundane and with so little progress?" I asked coldly.

"Just take a look inside first," Kenichi urged, pushing open the door.

His insistence made me uneasy, hinting at something unusual within. As the door swung open, I held my breath, expecting the unexpected.

But what met my eyes was a spacious and elegantly decorated Western-style living room, seamlessly flowing into a dining area. It was tidy, sophisticated—nothing out of the ordinary.

I was about to voice my frustration when Kenichi moved deeper inside, compelling me to follow. He led me to another door, swinging it open. "This is the bedroom," he announced.

The room was undeniably romantic, complete with a large mirror on the ceiling—a quintessential setting for a secret rendezvous. Clearly, Itagaki had invested effort into creating this retreat.

Yet, I still failed to see what warranted my urgent return. Kenichi stood at the bedroom's threshold, gesturing toward a smaller door. "This leads to the kitchen and storage," he explained. Then, pointing to another door, he asked, "Where do you think this door leads?"

His question tested my patience. "Obviously, it leads to another room," I replied curtly.

"And what would that room be for?" he pressed.

Exasperated, I shouted, "A study or another bedroom. If one bedroom suffices for a tryst, it could be an empty room."

Kenichi spread his hands, inviting me to "Please open it and see for yourself."

Were it not for our unique relationship and his enigmatic demeanor, I might have left in frustration. Instead, I paused, scrutinizing him, before approaching the door. I grasped the handle, intending to turn it, only to find it locked.

The locksmith from the Tokyo Metropolitan Police Department was a middle-aged man, seemingly slow in movement but with long, nimble fingers. His practiced hands revealed his expertise at a glance.

He was renowned for unlocking even the most complex and secure locks, a testament to his skill and experience.

"When Officer Kenichi summoned me urgently," the locksmith later recounted, still bristling with indignation, "I anticipated a significant challenge. Yet, upon arrival, he merely tasked me with picking a standard lock. It felt like an affront to my professional dignity!"

Kenichi's explanation was straightforward: "We brought in a locksmith because we couldn't open this door. We used a skeleton key to access the apartment, and according to the administrator, each unit is designed the same way, with two rooms. We opened the bedroom door, but this other door remained stubbornly locked, hence the call for help."

The locksmith recounted his surprise, "I nearly refused when asked to open what seemed like a standard door. But when Officer Kenichi said the skeleton key couldn't unlock it, I was intrigued. This type of lock is quite common, integrated with the door handle—a simple press of a button locks it, and turning the handle unlocks it from inside. Typically, a hairpin or even a toothpick could suffice to open it from outside!"

"So, what happened?" I inquired.

The locksmith's face clouded with frustration and disbelief. "I spent half an hour, starting with simple wire and escalating to complex tools, all to no avail. It's baffling—I pride myself on being able to open any lock!"

Kenichi then turned to me. "That's why I thought of you, Ash. You possess incredible skills, and lock picking is one of your fortes. When I learned you had left the hotel, I called you back from the airport. Can you give it a try?"

And that's how I ended up here.

I gave the door a push, confirming it was indeed locked, the handle immovable. It was perplexing that such a simple lock resisted opening.

Jokingly, I asked, "Where's Mr. Locksmith? Did he consider resigning over this?"

Kenichi, however, remained earnest. "No, he's gone to fetch more advanced tools. If he fails, he might not just resign but take drastic measures like killing himself!"

I bit back the word "hara-kiri," knowing such humor was ill-suited to the gravity of the situation.

"So, you brought me here to tackle this door?" I asked.

Kenichi nodded, "Let the locksmith have another go. If he's unsuccessful, I'll discreetly enlist your help."

I glanced at the door, confident that, with my skills, it would take mere seconds to unlock.

Just then, the locksmith, a determined middle-aged man with a leather tool bag, returned, bypassing us entirely to focus on the door. His bag, worn with age, revealed an impressive array of over a hundred meticulously arranged tools.

As an expert, I recognized many, but there were at least 20 or 30 I couldn't name or fathom their functions. Inscribed inside the bag was a bold declaration: "There is no lock that cannot be opened."

Arrogant as it seemed, the tools suggested it wasn't mere bravado.

The locksmith selected a thin, flexible iron stick, ending in a small hook. To my mind, such a tool should easily suffice for this marble-structured lock, which required merely pressing one or a few pins to unlock. The mystery remained — what made this ordinary lock so extraordinary?

The expert inserted the iron stick into the keyhole with precision, and a soft "click" soon followed. His confidence was palpable, but when he tried to turn the handle, it remained stubbornly immobile. The door was still locked.

His expression faltered slightly, but undeterred, he switched to a small flat tool with sawtooth edges, inserting it into the keyhole. Another "click" echoed, yet the handle refused to budge. The expert's resolve was unwavering as he tried a very thin, rigid wire, skillfully maneuvering it alongside the previous tool.

Despite his efforts with various tools, each more intricate than the last, the lock held fast. Sweat beaded on his forehead, betraying his growing frustration.

Watching the scene unfold, I was taken aback by the lock's resistance. With his expertise, he should have been able to open any lock with ease, even a high-security safe. If he couldn't crack it, what hope did I have?

Nearly thirty minutes had passed, and as the locksmith struggled, I suggested to Kenichi, "Why not just force the door open?"

Before I could finish, Kenichi urgently signaled me to stop, but the words were already out. The locksmith, who had been crouched in concentration, suddenly stood up, glaring at me as if I'd committed a grave offense.

"Who dares to suggest that?" he demanded, his voice laden with indignation.

He waved his hands passionately. "I must open this lock. It's my duty!"

Kenichi's expression turned solemn in response to the locksmith's fervor, but I found the situation rather amusing. With a shrug, I turned to Kenichi and proposed, "Fine, let him keep working on the lock. Meanwhile, I'll just climb in through the window."

The locksmith, blinking in frustration, was clearly affronted by the idea of bypassing his expertise. His pride was on the line, yet he couldn't object to me entering through the window, as it circumvented his task entirely.

Kenichi, suppressing a chuckle, tapped his forehead. "Why didn't I think of that?" he mused.

The locksmith, simmering with irritation, continued tinkering with his array of peculiar tools. Meanwhile, Kenichi and I stepped out onto the terrace through the large glass doors. Just a short distance to our left was the window of the room we aimed to enter.

The window was secured tightly, its view obscured by thick, dark purple velvet curtains. It was only about two meters from the terrace to the window—a simple feat for anyone nimble enough, akin to a task for an amateur thief.

At that moment, one or two agents joined us on the terrace. Observing our plan to access the room via the window, one agent stepped forward eagerly. "I'll do it!" he offered, volunteering for the task.

Kenichi and I exchanged glances and nodded, agreeing. The agent was proficient, and this was a straightforward job for him. He soaked a piece of cloth in water, folded it, and held it between his teeth. Then, he climbed out onto the building's ledge, carefully navigating toward the window. Despite being on the eleventh floor, the building's exterior had plenty of footholds and handholds, making the ascent relatively safe.

In about three minutes, the agent reached the window. Clutching a sturdy water pipe for support, he retrieved the wet cloth from his mouth. Pressing it against the glass, he shattered it with a well-aimed slap, effectively containing the shards. He then tossed the cloth back to the terrace, reached through the newly made hole, and unlatched the window.

Kenichi and I observed from the terrace, just a couple of meters away. We could see every motion distinctly, each detail etched into our memories.

As the agent reached through the glass, he nicked his hand on a shard, a minor injury that bled slightly. He quickly sucked on the wound before trying again, this time successfully unlatching and swinging the window open.

The gentle wind caught the dark purple curtains, causing them to billow outward. With one hand gripping the window's central pillar and one foot on the sill, the agent gave us a confident wave. Displaying a flair for the dramatic, he turned and leaped inside.

His leap, hitting the curtain with a flourish, seemed almost cinematic. Perhaps he was inspired by action films, a nod to youthful exuberance in an otherwise routine task. Such moments often inject a bit of excitement into the mundanity of day-to-day operations.

Yet, whether this playful thought truly crossed his mind—or if it was simply speculation—remains an enigma, forever beyond reach.

CHAPTER 3

The Enigmatic Wall and Doppelgänger

In the courtroom, the investigation into Detective Ishino's mysterious death unfolded with testimonies from seven key witnesses: Ash Morris, Kenichi, passers-by A, B, and C, a housewife drying clothes across the street, and the locksmith.

The locksmith's account was straightforward. "I was focused on unlocking the door when I heard a sudden scream from outside," he stated. "It seemed to come from the terrace. I rushed out to find Officer Kenichi and Mr. Morris frozen in shock, staring at an open window."

When questioned about seeing Agent Ishino, the locksmith replied, "No, I only saw Kenichi and Mr. Morris. It was Mr. Morris who suggested entering through the window."

Kenichi's testimony mirrored Ash Morris's. They had both witnessed the tragic sequence of events unfold in unison. Kenichi recounted, "Agent Ishino executed an exaggerated maneuver, gripping the aluminum support between the windows. It appeared he was showing off his agility. I thought, if he went through the window like that, he'd surely knock down the curtains."

Kenichi paused, visibly distressed by the memory. "His body spun into the curtain—dark purple velvet—when suddenly there was a 'bang.' Something solid behind the curtain stopped him, then bounced him back. His grip on the window support slipped, and Agent Ishino—" Kenichi's voice broke, unable to finish.

The housewife across the street provided a detailed observation from her vantage point fifteen stories high. "I heard a scream and looked down," she described. "I saw a man plummeting from the building. His hands flailed as if to grasp something, but there was nothing. He continued his descent until he hit the ground."

Passers-by A, B, and C corroborated her account. They had been near the impact site, with one narrowly escaping being struck. None heard the scream, only the sudden appearance of a falling figure. Passer-by B, a medical student, checked Ishino immediately, confirming he was already dead.

The court turned to Kenichi and me, probing our actions during the incident. Kenichi, his voice laden with sorrow, confessed, "There was nothing we could do. It all happened so fast. We just stood there, helpless, watching it unfold before us."

His words hung heavy in the air, the courtroom silent except for Kenichi's choked attempt to regain composure. The mystery of what lay behind that velvet curtain and the tragic fate of Detective Ishino remained an enigma that demanded resolution.

Detective Ishino was a rising star, his youth a beacon of promise. Yet, fate had a cruel hand to play. The tragedy unfolded with such swiftness that Kenichi, his mentor, was left adrift in a sea of grief.

"The event was far too abrupt," I added, my voice steady in the courtroom's tense air. "There was no chance to save Detective Ishino. This was an accident, pure and simple. Officer Kenichi bears no guilt."

The presiding judge, youthful and inquisitive, sought clarity: "What caused Detective Ishino to be ejected, rather than leaping through the window?"

Kenichi's response was a single, cryptic word: "A wall."

The moment Ishino plummeted, a stunned silence engulfed us. Kenichi and I stood rooted, paralyzed by shock, as if time itself had frozen, leaving us helpless while Ishino's fate was sealed eleven floors below.

Our eyes remained locked on the open window, the curtain fluttering in the breeze—a silent witness to the chaos, concealing whatever lay in the shadows beyond. We were ensnared by the moment, our senses dulled by disbelief.

It wasn't until the locksmith, his face a mask of confusion, burst into the room that our paralysis broke. Our voices erupted in unison, a cacophony of shock and urgency. I gestured wildly at the window, words failing me, while Kenichi's shout cut through the air like a knife. With a singular purpose, he charged into the house, disappearing down the hallway to reach the street below. I knew instinctively where he was headed—to the spot where Detective Ishino had met his untimely fate.

The locksmith broke my trance, his voice a flurry of confusion. "What happened? What happened?" he demanded, his words echoing the chaos within.

The street below erupted in a cacophony of voices. I peered down, the scene unfolding like a grim tableau. People rushed toward Ishino's crumpled form, a lone bystander kneeling beside him.

Traffic ground to a halt, horns blaring in frustration. Amidst the chaos, Kenichi emerged like a force of nature, pushing through the crowd to reach Ishino. In that moment, clarity cut through my shock. "Oh my God! Call an ambulance!" I shouted, urgency lacing my words.

The passage of time blurred; whether the ambulance arrived swiftly or not seemed inconsequential. The locksmith dashed back inside, while I, driven by instinct, clambered over the balcony railing, my gaze fixed on the open window, the mystery it held beckoning me forward.

As I climbed toward the window, the world around me erupted in screams, a symphony of chaos that I pushed to the periphery of my mind. My focus was singular, unwavering.

I reached the window, gripping the aluminum support with determination. Instead of crashing through, I extended my arm, seizing the billowing curtain with a fierce tug.

The fabric surrendered, cascading down and revealing the unimaginable—a wall.

There it stood, in defiance of logic, a wall where no wall should exist.

The revelation hit like a thunderclap. Behind the seemingly innocuous curtain lay a wall—an impenetrable barrier where open space should have been. The window, a portal to what Ishino believed was a safe entry, was nothing more than a cruel illusion. Trusting the curtain's deceit, he had jumped, only to collide with the unyielding bricks, sealing his tragic fate.

The sight stunned me, akin to the initial shock of witnessing Ishino's fall. Heart pounding, I spun around and bellowed to the street below, "Kenichi, behind the window—it's a wall!" My voice was urgent, desperate to bridge the distance and relay the grim discovery.

Whether my cries reached Kenichi, I couldn't be certain, but I persisted, the words spilling out in a frantic loop, "A wall! A wall!" Each repetition an attempt to comprehend the surreal truth and share its significance with anyone who could hear.

The wall, a perplexing anomaly, was meticulously constructed from brown-yellow heat-resistant bricks, each laid with precision. However, the craftsmanship bore a telltale flaw—irregular cement joints on my side. Clearly built from within the room, there was no space between the wall and the window for the craftsman to stand and polish his work. Its solidity was undeniable, a stoic sentinel where none should exist.

As I examined the full expanse of the wall, which spanned the entire length of one side of the room, questions gnawed at me. Why construct such a barrier? What purpose did it serve, obscuring the window? The logic of it escaped me, yet the reality stood firm.

Driven by an impulsive need for answers, I kicked at the wall, hoping to breach its mystery. My efforts were in vain; the wall remained unyielding, its secret intact.

But where brute force failed, technology offered a solution. As the ambulance whisked Ishino away and the initial shock began to dissipate, Kenichi reappeared with a jackhammer in hand.

Securing myself with a safety belt fastened to the aluminum support of the window, I hefted the jackhammer. Its weight was reassuring, a promise of progress. With a press of the button, the tool roared to life, its "da da" echoing through the room as the tip bit into the brick with relentless efficiency.

The locksmith ceased his work, and a crowd gathered on the terrace, drawn by the spectacle.

As twilight descended, Kenichi's powerful lamp cast a stark beam into the encroaching darkness, illuminating my every move with the jackhammer. The relentless vibration of the tool reverberated through my hands as bricks began to give way, tumbling into the room or slipping into the narrow space between the window and the wall.

In less than ten minutes, a breach appeared—a 60-centimeter square opening that pierced the enigmatic barrier. I motioned to Kenichi, who swiftly directed the lamp's beam into the newly opened cavity. Leaning slightly to the side, I peered into the shadowy recess beyond.

I had steeled myself for the bizarre, prepared for the unfathomable. The locked door and inexplicable wall had primed my mind for the peculiarities that might lurk beyond. Yet, as the intense light flooded the small room, illuminating every corner, my mental fortitude wavered.

What I saw left me paralyzed, my mind grappling with disbelief. I was overwhelmed, consciousness teetering on the brink as a cacophony of blood roared in my ears, drowning out all else. I barely registered Kenichi's voice calling my name, his shouts distorted and distant, as if carried from another realm.

Kenichi later recounted the scene with a mixture of concern and astonishment. "Mr. Morris didn't respond to my shouting," he recalled. "And it wasn't just me on the terrace. Everyone was transfixed by the sheer horror etched on Mr. Morris's face. Knowing him as well as I do, I knew that whatever he had seen must have been beyond imaginable horror."

The lamp in Kenichi's hand continued to illuminate the hole, its beam unwavering. I stood beside it, bathed in light, my expression laid bare for all to see—a mirror of the incomprehensible sight that had left me so stricken.

Kenichi continued to recount the moment. "I've never witnessed such a transformation—a face drained of all color, Mr. Morris's visage turned ghostly white. Despite my shouts, he remained unresponsive, his eyes locked on the scene within the hole. From our vantage point, we couldn't see what held his gaze so completely. When his body began to tremble, I knew I had to intervene. I switched off the high-powered lamp, hoping the darkness would help him regain his composure."

In the absence of the glaring light, Kenichi said I stood immobilized for a full minute before slowly turning my head. The tension in my neck was so pronounced that two of the onlookers swore they heard an audible "click" from my neck bones, a testament to the rigidity that had overtaken me.

Despite their collective shouts—described as loud enough to pierce eardrums—they still felt distant to me, like echoes from another world.

My reply, they claimed, was equally loud, as though I was summoning every ounce of strength to speak. Yet, to my own ears, my voice seemed to drift from far away.

Their unified cry was a mix of curiosity and dread: "Oh my God, what did you see?"

With a voice that felt both foreign and distant, I responded, "I saw myself!"

When one seeks to see oneself, it's typically through reflections or captured images—a mirror's surface, the stillness of water, or the lens of a camera. These mediums offer glimpses of our own visage, familiar and reassuring in their predictability.

Yet, in that moment, as the powerful beam of light penetrated the darkness through the hole in the wall, I was confronted with something beyond these ordinary means. I saw myself—not as a reflection, not as an image, but there, standing alone, unmistakably me.

It was a sight that defied all conventional understanding, a phenomenon that should have been impossible yet undeniably occurred.

The shock of this revelation was profound. I was mentally prepared for the bizarre, ready to face the inexplicable, but nothing could have prepared me for this encounter with the most familiar presence of all— my own. In that instant, the world seemed to tilt, challenging the very foundation of my reality.

The beam of light pierced through the narrow hole in the wall, illuminating the figure before me. At first glance, I was convinced it was him—no, it was me. Standing there, alone, my doppelgänger stared back with a vacant, hollow gaze. The harsh light bathed "my" face, yet my eyes appeared vacant, unblinking, almost oblivious to the blinding illumination.

It was undeniably me. I was staring at myself.

The impossibility of the situation struck me like a thunderclap. I had no identical twin—no brother who mirrored my every feature. Could there truly be another person in the world who mirrored me so precisely? Yet deep down, I didn't perceive him as merely someone who resembled me. I felt, inexplicably, that I was witnessing myself.

This was unlike any reflection from a mirror, where only my outward appearance is visible. In that moment, it was as if I peered directly into the depths of my soul, confronting the hidden aspects of myself—the loneliness, the sadness, the frailty, the helplessness, the emptiness—facets of my being that remained obscured from the world.

I saw myself.

Kenichi and the others, unaware of the nature of my revelation, could only see my reaction—one of utter disbelief and distress. Kenichi, sensing my perilous state, climbed over the edge of the balcony and extended his hand, urging me to grasp it. His voice was a lifeline: "Hold my hand!"

Desperate for an anchor in this surreal experience, I reached out. Kenichi's grip was firm and reassuring as he pulled me back onto the balcony. Once safely by his side, he leaned in, his voice barely above a whisper, "What did you see?"

I gasped, struggling to catch my breath. The shock of seeing myself had left me dizzy, reeling from the impossibility of it all. As my mind steadied, I murmured, "I saw someone exactly like me. I felt that person was me!"

Kenichi, standing beside me, wore a puzzled expression. Clearly, he didn't comprehend the gravity of my words. Without a word, he moved swiftly toward the window, his movements fluid and precise, honed from years spent in the wilderness. In a flash, he was at the wall's opening. Turning back, he shouted, "Highlight!"

An agent stationed on the balcony activated a high-intensity light, directing its beam into the wall's aperture. Kenichi peered into the hole, then quickly turned back.

I braced myself for an expression of shock, but all I saw was confusion. I wanted to demand what he had seen, but before I could, he glanced back into the hole and exclaimed, "I know why the door won't open!"

With astonishing agility, he crawled through the opening.

My heart raced. Despite the room being in an ordinary structure, it exuded an inexplicable eeriness. Its door refused to budge, a wall stood inexplicably beside the window, and I had glimpsed another version of myself. Yet Kenichi entered without hesitation.

I tried to shout a warning, but he was too quick. I moved to follow him, but Kenichi's laughter echoed from the hall. Accompanying his laughter was the locksmith's loud cursing.

I rushed from the balcony back to the hall, astounded to find the door wide open. Kenichi stood there, triumphant, while the locksmith fumed beside him, his face a shade of crimson, muttering curses under his breath.

The locksmith's brow furrowed with irritation as he studied the door. At first glance, it was unremarkable—plain, simple. But beneath its façade, a secret challenge lurked, an intricately hidden twist that defied conventional methods.

Typically, doors swing open in the direction of the handle. But this door defied convention—the handle was merely ornamental. The true mechanism was hidden on the opposite side.

Kenichi's keen eye had noted the door's hinges from the hole in the wall. He realized the trick. Once inside, he simply slid back the bolt, effortlessly opening the door.

Pay attention to this: Kenichi's decisive action revealed the truth—the door was bolted from within.

This meant someone had been inside to lock it. A seemingly obvious deduction.

The room had a window originally, yet a solid brick wall now obscured it. That was a fact.

So, the question remained—how did the person who bolted the door exit the room?

Initially, the situation seemed straightforward. After creating a hole in the wall, I peered inside and saw someone standing there—a person who, in my gut, felt like me. Logically, I could rationalize it as someone who merely bore an uncanny resemblance. Since someone was present, it stood to reason that they were the one who had locked the door.

Yet here lay the conundrum. Kenichi entered through the wall's hole and unlocked the door. I reached the door just as Kenichi emerged. The locksmith stood there, along with other officers stationed in the building. A police draftsman had just walked in through the sole entrance of the residential unit. It was impossible for anyone to have exited through the door. No one could have left via the wall's breach without being spotted by the agent on the balcony.

And yet, the room was empty.

Kenichi stated, "The room was empty. I can't fathom why Mr. Morris was so startled, claiming he saw himself inside. There was no one in there—not a mirror, not a reflective surface of any kind. From the moment I looked, it was clear the room was vacant, and the door mechanism reversed. I crawled through the wall, opened the door, and anyone can attest to its emptiness."

"The room is empty"—those words resonated with a deeper chill. It wasn't just devoid of people; it lacked anything at all. No furniture, no objects, nothing to suggest it had ever been inhabited. A barren space, roughly ten meters square, an ordinary-sized room rendered extraordinary by its utter emptiness.

As I stood at the threshold of the strange, empty room, I replayed the scene in my mind—the moment I'd peered through the wall's hole and seen myself. I was certain it wasn't a trick of the light. I had truly seen... me.

In the ensuing minutes, Kenichi watched me with a mix of sympathy and surprise etched on his face. I offered no explanation, just a shrug of helplessness, suggesting perhaps I was mistaken. Kenichi refrained from pressing further, as there were more pressing mysteries at hand. Why did this ordinary apartment contain such an enigmatic room? What was its purpose? Why was the door installed backward, and why was a wall built beside the window? When had these modifications occurred?

These questions were bizarre, bordering on the incredible. My encounter with my doppelgänger seemed almost trivial in comparison.

Kenichi called out, "Please bring the administrator up here!"

The draftsman, who had recently entered, handed Kenichi a sketch. "This is a portrait of the resident," he explained. "I drew it based on the administrator's description. Please take a look."

Kenichi examined the sketch and frowned. "What does this mean?"

The draftsman sighed, "I've done my best, but the administrator insists that every time he saw the lady, she appeared like this. I had to draw it according to his account."

Curious, I stepped closer to view the drawing in Kenichi's hands. The portrait depicted a woman with trendy, permed hair. The draftsman's skill was evident, yet the woman's identity remained elusive.

The woman wore oversized sunglasses that obscured most of her face. Her collar was turned up, concealing part of her lower face, leaving only a pointed chin visible. It was a face that could belong to any number of women.

Kenichi held up the sketch, a wry smile on his lips. "If this is Itagaki's mistress—"

I interrupted, "Not if. This must be Itagaki's mistress. She likely disguises herself to avoid recognition."

Kenichi's smile turned grim. "No police force in the world could find her with such a vague sketch."

I nodded in agreement. The investigation into Itagaki's mysterious shooting might have made progress with this secret meeting place, yet it only deepened the mystery.

When the administrator arrived, Kenichi showed him the room. The administrator's shock was palpable, his voice a litany of disbelief. "How could this happen? How could this happen?" He was as baffled as the rest of us.

There were layers of puzzles to unravel, each tangled with the last.

Kenichi fixed his gaze on me. "I hope you'll stay and assist me privately."

I needed no invitation. I would stay. After all, I had seen myself in this room. The question lingered: where am *I* now?

Kenichi asked, "How should we begin?"

I pondered for a moment. "If this woman appears in public as described, we might still track her down with the sketch. First, we need to replicate and distribute it. Itagaki, the resident here, is deceased. The woman is the key. We must find her."

Kenichi agreed, handing the sketch to an agent with instructions to circulate it immediately.

"The second step," Kenichi suggested, "is to investigate this peculiar room with the building's owner or the construction company. I'd like you to handle that."

I nodded in agreement. This room, with its oddities, seemed unrelated to the Itagaki case, yet its bizarreness piqued my curiosity. Unraveling such mysteries was my forte.

Kenichi continued, "There's little more we can do tonight. You can start your inquiries tomorrow, or you're welcome to stay with me."

I asked, "Are you packing up for the night?"

Kenichi replied, "There's nothing more to be done here, so yes, I'm packing up."

I gestured toward the enigmatic room. "I want to stay. Here in this room, I need to take a closer look."

Kenichi regarded me with a quizzical expression, clearly puzzled by my desire to remain in an empty space. Yet he didn't object, merely shrugging indifferently. He instructed the police team to withdraw, leaving last himself. Before departing, he asked, "Would you like me to stay with you?"

I shook my head. "No need. It might be better if I'm alone."

Kenichi hesitated, then spoke carefully, "Seeing yourself—it's quite extraordinary."

I didn't disagree. "Even more extraordinary is the existence of such a room."

Kenichi had no rebuttal. He shrugged again and exited. Once he was gone, I closed the door. The neighborhood settled into silence as the police cars departed, leaving me in the stillness of the hall.

My gaze lingered on the open door of the room. It was empty, devoid of any furnishings. The unit comprised two rooms: the bedroom, shared by Itagaki and his mistress, and this strange, inexplicable space.

I recalled once more the moment I'd peered through the wall's hole. I'd done so repeatedly, convinced it was no illusion. I had truly seen myself.

I saw myself standing alone in the room's center, my expression a mix of confusion and helplessness.

I stepped away from the sofa and into the enigmatic room, a space shrouded in an unsettling emptiness. The floor was a sea of checkered teak, each square a silent testament to the room's mystery. I advanced cautiously, my footsteps echoing softly as they landed on the wooden grid. It wasn't long before I had traversed every inch of the floor, feeling the oppressive weight of the void around me. Nothing stirred—not an object, not a whisper of sound—just me and the stale air.

My eyes lifted to the ceiling, only to find it as barren as the rest of the room; not even a light fixture broke its monotony.

What purpose could such a room possibly serve? No theory I conjured seemed to fit. The next morning, curiosity and frustration led me to the office of the building's property company—a major player in leasing operations. The general manager, a slightly rotund man nearing sixty, listened to my account with a bemused expression. His laughter, unexpected and jarring, broke the tense silence.

I bristled, irritation sharpening my words: "I fail to see the humor. Could you explain what's so amusing?"

The general manager, sensing my annoyance, quickly apologized, his mirth subsiding. "I'm truly sorry. We lease residential units—standard two-bedroom, one living room arrangements, complete with furniture. The tenant in question, Mr. Inoue—it might be an alias—has prepaid a year's rent, which complicates our ability to investigate further."

I raised an eyebrow. "Did he arrange the lease personally?"

The manager hesitated, rifling through documents before responding. "One of our salespersons handled it. I'll have her explain the details to you."

I held up a hand, my mind racing. "That can wait. We need to understand why such a peculiar room exists in this residential unit. You must realize, the wall erected next to the window has already claimed an innocent life. I expect a satisfactory explanation."

The manager scratched his thinning hair, genuine confusion creasing his brow. "An unusual room, you say? It's beyond belief. I can hardly fathom it."

I suppressed the urge to retort, "If you doubt it, see for yourself." His bewilderment seemed genuine, so I sighed, relenting. "Very well, please summon the salesperson who arranged the lease. I need to speak with her."

CHAPTER 4

Mystic Indian Rituals and Arcane Symbols

The young salesperson, no older than twenty-five, embodied the quintessential Japanese professional—polite to a fault, her words delivered in the most respectful tones.

"Yes, I remember Mr. Inoue," she began, recalling the enigmatic tenant. "He first contacted us by phone. He never came to our office, instead requesting that we meet him directly at the building."

I produced a photograph of Itagaki, and her recognition was immediate. "Yes, that's Mr. Inoue," she confirmed without hesitation.

It was no shock that Itagaki had chosen a pseudonym for the lease—discretion was paramount when renting a place for clandestine meetings with a mistress.

"Mr. Inoue arrived around five in the afternoon," she continued. "We exchanged pleasantries in the lobby. He expressed a preference for a higher floor, so I showed him the eleventh floor, which he eventually rented."

"Are all the units in the building occupied?" I inquired.

"Yes, every unit is leased. Furnished apartments are quite popular—more expensive than average rentals, but significantly cheaper than hotels." Her response was delivered with unwavering politeness. "He liked the unit immediately and only asked to have the phone removed, preferring to avoid disturbances."

I pressed further, "The unit has two rooms—a bedroom and the other?"

"Each unit mirrors others in layout: a bedroom adjacent to a study. The study is furnished with a desk, bookshelves, a convertible bed, and chairs." Her brow furrowed slightly as she mulled over my earlier account of an empty room with its reversed door and enigmatic wall. "Those peculiarities you mentioned," she began hesitantly, I couldn't quite understand."

"Right now, the 'study' is exactly as I described," I confirmed, feeling the weight of her silent judgment.

Despite her bewilderment, I had no need to elaborate—the facts spoke for themselves.

"When you accompanied Itagaki-Inoue, the room was set up as a study?" I pressed.

"Yes," she replied with conviction. "He signed the contract on the desk in the study, and he paid a year's rent upfront."

"When did he move in?"

"That evening, with a lady and minimal luggage. Such arrangements are common; we don't pry."

I couldn't help but wonder when the ordinary study had morphed into a puzzle. Reversing a door could be done covertly, but erecting a wall? That required manpower and time—an endeavor not easily concealed from building management.

With this thought, I asked, "Has the building manager changed since Mr. Inoue rented the unit?"

The salesperson's eyes widened. "Yes, there was a change. He rented the unit eight months ago. The original manager, Takeo, passed away three months ago."

My heart leaped at the revelation. "How did Takeo die?"

The general manager interjected, "An accident. Takeo had no family. The police informed us it was an accident."

"What kind of accident?"

"He was shot by a bullet in a hunting area. No one knows who fired it."

The pieces clicked into place—an important discovery indeed. I shared my realization with Kenichi, who was already digging into Takeo's "accidental death" file.

"The original manager's death explains the room's transformation five months after Itagaki's lease," I proposed. "Bribing Takeo to smuggle in construction materials under the cover of night would have been easy. Only Takeo would know. I am afraid Takeo's death was no accident."

Kenichi's demeanor turned grave, his usual lightheartedness overshadowed by the weight of our discovery. Even his faithful companion, the little white tarsier, sensed the shift, its playful antics momentarily halted as Kenichi gently nudged it aside.

The tarsier had woven itself into the fabric of Kenichi's life. Returning one evening to an apartment in disarray, Kenichi realized that keeping the wide-eyed, gentle creature by his side was the best way to prevent further havoc. Over time, he found its presence to be a comforting distraction from the chaos.

With the tarsier settled elsewhere, Kenichi turned his attention back to me, a glint of curiosity in his eyes. "You spent the entire night in that room. Didn't anything stand out?"

I sighed, shaking my head. "Nothing."

Undeterred, Kenichi's team had retrieved Takeo's file, and he eagerly leafed through it. The details were sparse and chilling—Takeo's body found in a hunting zone, during peak hunting season. A single bullet to the heart, presumed a stray shot.

After the autopsy, they extracted the bullet—a standard double-barreled shotgun round that had struck Takeo's heart with fatal precision. The forensic doctor noted that the bullet's velocity was weak; had Takeo been carrying something as mundane as a diary in his jacket pocket, it might have deflected the shot, sparing his life. It was this detail that led investigators to conclude that his death was the result of an accidental stray bullet.

As for Takeo's presence in the hunting area? His employer reported that he was on a week-long vacation and had chosen the area as his getaway.

Nothing in the records hinted at foul play. Yet, as Kenichi and I reviewed the case, an unsettling question lingered. Kenichi turned to me, his expression contemplative: "Could a top-tier assassin calculate the perfect distance so that a shotgun's power wanes just enough to lethally strike the heart?"

"Absolutely," I replied.

Kenichi's frown deepened, and he abruptly stood, causing the little tarsier on his shoulder to squeak and scurry to his other shoulder.

"If Takeo was murdered, then Itagaki was the second target. Who do you think might be next?" Kenichi queried.

"Itagaki's mistress," I answered swiftly. "Have we found any trace of her yet?"

Kenichi shook his head, frustration evident. "It's proving difficult with only a sketch."

I took a deep breath, urgency in my tone. "We need to act quickly! If my theory is correct, we should investigate building material suppliers. Whoever constructed that wall would have bought bricks and mortar, likely delivered at night. Skilled labor would be needed, and there's a trail we can follow."

Kenichi nodded, determination in his voice. "My agents will track this down."

He stretched, his demeanor shifting to one of casual camaraderie. "Shall we grab a drink tonight?"

"Yes, let's," I agreed without hesitation.

Kenichi led me to his usual haunt, a dimly lit bar that was sparsely populated. A few waitresses lounged about, fighting off drowsiness. The proprietress, upon seeing us, prodded them awake and approached with a welcoming smile.

She and Kenichi were clearly on familiar terms. "Long time no see! And what's this little creature?" she exclaimed, eyeing the tarsier with delight.

The "little creature" she referred to was indeed Kenichi's tarsier, a charming companion from the dense forests of southern India. With its squirrel-like size, elongated tail, and remarkably expressive eyes, it clung to Kenichi's shoulder, adding an endearing peculiarity to his appearance.

Kenichi offered a brief introduction before ordering, "Another plate of peanuts, unsalted!"

We settled into a secluded corner, clinking our glasses as the ice cubes chimed softly. The tarsier, now perched beside the peanut plate, eagerly sampled its unsalted treat.

Though the Itagaki case loomed over us, we skirted around it, choosing instead to share inconsequential chatter.

The bar's ambiance was understated, the music a gentle hum in the background. A waitress approached, attempting to entice us into more drinks, but Kenichi waved her away. By our third glass, the bar remained quiet, though the atmosphere was at its liveliest, with the lights dimming to set the mood.

Amidst the shadows, a raspy voice pierced the air beside us: "Ah! Chiwodaka!"

To me, the words seemed disjointed—an exclamation followed by a cryptic noun. But for Kenichi, they only brought confusion. Recently returned from India, I understood their significance. This cryptic message could unravel yet another layer of the mystery surrounding us.

In India, I met a zoologist baffled by the tarsier's mysterious hunger strike. He explained that this species was exceedingly rare, teetering on the brink of extinction. The pure white variant, he noted, was even more elusive, unseen for centuries, and revered by local tribes as a supernatural symbol. Known as "Chiwodaka" in their dialect, this name was a closely guarded secret, shared only among the tribe's elite—wise men, elders, and those of significant status.

Now, sitting in a Tokyo bar, I was stunned to hear someone utter this sacred name, "Chiwodaka." It was astonishing that anyone outside the remote jungles of India could be aware of such a term.

I immediately turned toward the voice, my eyes straining to pierce the dim lighting. The source of the voice stood beside our table, but in the low light, his features were obscured. He wore dark brown clothing, his skin blending into the shadows, but his stature was unmistakable—tall and imposing.

Kenichi, oblivious to the significance of the word, seemed irritated by the intrusion and gestured dismissively. "Please go away," he said curtly.

"Wait!" I interjected, urgency in my voice. "This gentleman seems to recognize the white tarsier."

Kenichi's eyes narrowed in confusion, prompting me to explain. "He just used the name 'Chiwodaka,' a name known only to a select few."

Kenichi fell silent, processing this new information. In my eagerness to convey the importance of the encounter, I had overlooked the man's movements. By the time I looked up again, he was already retreating into the shadows.

I jumped to my feet, calling after him. "Sir, please, I need to speak with you!" My voice carried desperation, driven by the sudden realization that this stranger might hold the key to unraveling the web of mysteries we had stumbled into.

The man halted but didn't turn around, his silhouette framed by the dim glow of the bar's exit. I quickly left my seat and moved toward him. He seemed to sense my approach, quickening his pace as I did, maintaining a frustrating distance of just one step ahead. Determined, I pursued him out of the bar and into a shadowy alley.

Once in the alley, he stopped, yet still refused to face me. I approached, his voice emerging in hurried, imperfect Japanese: "Sir, Chiwodaka is a symbol of the supernatural. It should not be kept—it must return to the forest."

"Are you from southern India?" I pressed, sensing his origin from his knowledge of the tarsier's name.

I took a cautious half step closer, straining to see his features in the oppressive darkness. Even facing me, the alley's gloom obscured his face.

His voice remained tense, laden with urgency. "Be careful. Chiwodaka is often not a lucky spirit, but a malevolent one!"

I chuckled inwardly at his warning, dismissing it as another superstition from a remote region.

Before I could respond, his tone grew more insistent. "It has paranormal perception—beyond human—"

But before he could finish, Kenichi's voice echoed down the alley. "Mr. Morris! Ash Morris! Where are you?"

I turned and called back, "In the alley—"

The momentary distraction allowed the man to slip away. By the time I turned back, he was gone, swallowed by the darkness. I considered chasing after him, but Kenichi's hand gripped my arm, pulling me back. "Be cautious. Tokyo nights are unpredictable."

As we stepped into the light, the little tarsier on Kenichi's shoulder caught my eye. Its unusually large eyes glowed with a dark green luminescence, casting an eerie shadow over the alley.

The man's words replayed in my mind, sending a shiver through me. I was momentarily speechless, overwhelmed by a mix of intrigue and apprehension. Kenichi led me back to the bar, his grip firm and reassuring.

Back inside, I inquired with the landlady about the mysterious man. She remembered him well. "He's a first-timer here. Never seen him before. He was alone, drinking quietly, then suddenly approached you. Did he cause any trouble?"

I smiled, shaking my head. "No trouble. He just seemed... not local."

The landlady chuckled, a knowing glint in her eye. "Oh, he's definitely not from around here. He's Indian, isn't he?"

At first, the encounter with the Indian man seemed like a curious, yet benign coincidence—perhaps a sailor or businessman well-versed in local folklore. Nothing extraordinary about an Indian living in Japan with knowledge of the rare white tarsier.

But the following day, when the words "an Indian" resurfaced, Kenichi and I exchanged a look of disbelief. We were speechless, the implications dawning on us with unsettling clarity.

The investigation into the suppliers of bricks and mortar progressed swiftly. By the next day, a middle-aged couple entered Kenichi's office, escorted by two agents. "This couple seems to be who we're looking for," the agent announced.

Kenichi leaned forward, questioning, "Did you sell a batch of bricks sufficient for a three-meter wall?"

The husband, reserved and cautious, nodded. "Yes, about six months ago."

His wife, more forthcoming, added, "It was odd—they insisted on a nighttime delivery to an upscale neighborhood. They also purchased mortar, clearly for building walls."

Kenichi presented Itagaki's photo, inquiring, "Was this the buyer?"

The wife promptly replied, "No, it was an Indian!"

Kenichi and I reacted immediately. He shot up from his chair, forgetting the open drawer before him, which clattered to the floor, its contents scattering. Simultaneously, I knocked a cup off the table, sending it crashing and spilling tea everywhere.

Our reactions startled the couple, leaving them bewildered and unsure of their misstep.

I regained composure first, asking urgently, "What did you say?"

The wife, now subdued, repeated, "An Indian."

Her words echoed ominously. An Indian. Not a common sight in Japan, and eerily coincidental given the strange encounter the previous night.

Kenichi pressed further, "Can you describe him? Please, try to remember."

The couple exchanged glances, the husband hesitantly describing the man, with the wife filling in the gaps. Their combined account painted a picture of an ordinary yet imposing figure—a tall, dark-skinned Indian with deep-set eyes and surprisingly fluent Japanese.

The Indian's peculiar request to deliver bricks at night seemed suspicious initially, but since he was willing to pay an extra transportation fee, the couple complied without further question.

"When we delivered the bricks," the husband recounted, "the building manager helped us load them into the elevator. He was a robust man, but he seemed anxious. It was past midnight, the place deserted, yet he seemed scared of being seen."

This building manager was none other than Takeo, the same man who later "accidentally" died in a hunting area. As suspected, he was entangled in this mystery.

Kenichi probed further, "Did you see the Indian again?"

"No," the wife replied. "He waited in the elevator. Once we loaded the bricks and mortar, he didn't want us to go up and pressed the elevator button himself. The elevator lingered on the eleventh floor for quite some time."

"Another odd thing," the husband added, "was how the manager urged us to leave quickly. Right after, he used a large wet cloth to erase any traces left in the lobby."

"Officer," the wife asked, curiosity piqued, "are we involved in anything illegal? We're just small business owners."

Kenichi reassured her, "It's nothing to do with you, but we need your help. Please provide our sketch artist with a description of the Indian. We're trying to locate him."

The couple agreed, and an agent escorted them out. After their departure, Kenichi and I shared a knowing look. The little white tarsier leaped from its perch on the file rack to Kenichi's head, where he absentmindedly stroked its soft fur.

"Kenichi," I said, "the wall was definitely built by an Indian."

Kenichi rolled his eyes, mulling over the implications. "But where were Itagaki and his mistress while this wall and door were installed? Even if it was done overnight, how could they not notice afterward? What was the secret that kept them silent?"

I paced, contemplating the possibilities. "There's certainly a secret, but we're in the dark. Finding the Indian shouldn't be difficult—there aren't that many in Tokyo, right?"

Kenichi picked up the phone, reaching out to the relevant departments. The answer came swiftly: "There are over 3,400 Indians in the records."

"That's manageable," I said. "We can track them down one by one if needed."

Kenichi petted the tarsier again, perplexed. "But that room was empty, no obvious criminal intent."

He hesitated, choosing his words carefully. "Even though you saw yourself in that room, it's hard to grasp the purpose of this mystery."

I didn't elaborate further on my experience in the room since it was beyond explanation. I simply said, "Only the Indian can provide answers. As for your view that there was no crime, I disagree. Itagaki is dead, and Takeo is dead. If Takeo was involved, he was silenced. Itagaki may have uncovered a secret, leading to his murder."

Kenichi nodded, "If Itagaki's mistress also knew this secret, then she—"

"Her life is in great danger," I finished for him.

Kenichi picked up the phone again, initiating several actions:

First, to check with the accidental death department for any reports of a woman in her twenties who died under mysterious circumstances, as

Itagaki's mistress could have met an untimely end. The results came back: no such discovery.

Second, the couple confirmed the sketch of the Indian, and over twenty skilled agents dedicated themselves to finding him, abandoning all rest. Yet after ten days, they found no leads. No one knew this Indian, nor could they locate him.

The night in the bar and alley had been too dim for Kenichi and me to see the Indian clearly, but the bar owner was adamant. "It's the same Indian man," she confirmed.

And so, the search continued, the pieces of our puzzle still scattered and elusive.

CHAPTER 5

My Tale and the Monkey's Paw Legend

Our investigation led us back to Sadagumi Itagaki, a woman whose grace was overshadowed by subtle sadness. We had pinpointed the exact date when the building materials store sold the bricks and speculated that Itagaki was unaware of this transaction until later. Discovering such a dramatic change in his clandestine meeting place would have surely shocked him—and if anyone could sense that shock, it would be his wife. Thus, we found ourselves once again at Sadagumi's door.

Kenichi, ever the diplomat, offered polite reassurances before posing the question that lingered like an unsolved riddle. "Around six months ago, did Mr. Itagaki behave unusually—perhaps surprised or uneasy?"

Sadagumi paused, her eyes searching the past. "No," she finally said, "I don't remember anything like that."

Her voice carried a casual curiosity as she asked, "Did you find anything else during the investigation?"

Before Kenichi could respond, an unexpected interloper stole the moment. The little white tarsier, snug in his shirt, poked its head out, drawing a startled gasp from Sadagumi. Quickly regaining her composure, she admired the creature's rare beauty.

Kenichi flushed with embarrassment, struggling to contain the playful tarsier, an incongruous companion for a police officer. I intervened, explaining, "This is a very rare monkey from South India, especially the white variant."

I expected the explanation to deflect attention, but instead, Sadagumi's reaction was profound. She let out a soft "Ah," a breach of decorum that hinted at a memory unlocked.

Kenichi and I exchanged glances, the air thick with unspoken questions. What had the tarsier triggered in her mind? The notion that such a creature could connect to Itagaki seemed preposterous, yet her expression suggested otherwise.

We waited, allowing her thoughts to coalesce. Finally, she offered an apologetic smile. "Sorry, I just remembered something."

Her revelation was quietly explosive. "About half a year ago, Itagaki returned home late—almost midnight. He immediately went into his study. I followed him and found him at the bookshelf, searching through the books. He told me, 'Tomorrow, buy me a few books about monkeys, the kind with color pictures!'"

Kenichi and I shared a look of astonishment. Why would a successful entrepreneur suddenly take an interest in monkeys?

Sadagumi's voice remained steady, yet her words brimmed with intrigue. "I agreed to his request," she began, "and he told me, 'Seek out books on monkeys from India. The specifics don't matter—just focus on any you can find, especially those about a monkey known as the tarsier. Buy them tomorrow!'"

Her revelation hung in the air like a puzzle piece snapping into place. Kenichi and I exchanged a look, barely maintaining our composure.

Itagaki's interest wasn't just a passing curiosity; it was an obsession with Indian monkeys—specifically the elusive tarsiers.

Kenichi leaned forward, urgency in his voice. "Did you manage to buy any of those books?"

Sadagumi nodded. "Yes, I bought seven books in total."

"What did he intend to do with them?" I asked, hoping for a glimpse into Itagaki's mind. "Did he ever explain what he wanted to study?"

"He didn't say, and I didn't ask," Sadagumi replied, her gaze dropping momentarily.

Kenichi pressed on, "Where are those books now?"

"They're still in his study. Since he passed, I haven't had the heart to tidy up the room. Please understand—I can't bring myself to open that door," she confessed, her eyes glistening with unshed tears.

We offered quiet words of comfort, aware of the emotional toll. Kenichi gently requested, "Madam, would you allow us to see Mr. Itagaki's study?"

Sadagumi hesitated, her reluctance palpable. "Is it truly necessary?"

"We believe it is," Kenichi insisted softly. "Please, it could be crucial."

With a resigned sigh, Sadagumi rose. "Follow me, then."

We followed her through a short corridor to a hall where a door led to the garden. Opposite stood a mahogany-carved door—the entrance to the study.

The door to Itagaki's study was a masterpiece of craftsmanship, adorned with intricate, age-old carvings. On the right side, a handle and lock appeared standard at first glance. But as Sadagumi approached with the key, she bypassed the obvious handle, reaching instead for a subtle relief on the left. With a deft motion, she removed it, revealing a concealed keyhole.

Inserting the key, she turned it, and the door swung open—not from the handle side, but the opposite. The handle side was fixed with a hinge, cleverly disguised—a mirror image of the peculiar setup we'd found in Itagaki's secret apartment.

Our surprise must have been evident because Sadagumi offered an explanation as she ushered us in. "This door is reversed—an anti-theft measure. A thief would naturally try the handle side and be thwarted."

Kenichi and I nodded, intrigued by the ingenuity. I commented, "That's quite a clever idea. Not something most would think of. May I ask who came up with it?"

With a modest smile, Sadagumi replied, "It was my idea. I'm afraid Itagaki found it more of a nuisance than a deterrent. He often jiggled the handle in frustration, calling it too complicated."

Kenichi chuckled, "Yes, instinct leads us to the handle. How long has it been like this?"

"It's been this way since we moved in—about six years," Sadagumi answered.

Kenichi and I exchanged a glance, recognizing the significance. This wasn't just a quirk; it was a connection, a thread linking the mystery of Itagaki's life with the puzzles we had yet to solve. The reversed door, a metaphor for the hidden truths we were pursuing, hinted that beneath the surface of Itagaki's seemingly ordinary life lay secrets waiting to be unearthed.

The peculiar design of the reversed door, cleverly using a handle to conceal its true mechanism, was indeed a rarity. Yet, here it was, not only in Itagaki's study but also in the strange room where clandestine meetings occurred. This realization struck me with a jolt: Could Itagaki's study and the secret room be one and the same?

If Itagaki was accustomed to this unique door setup in his study, could it have been his idea to replicate it in the secret room? And if so, did he also mastermind the construction of that baffling wall? This challenged my earlier assumption that Itagaki was unaware of these changes.

The question then arose: What was the connection between Itagaki and the enigmatic Indian man?

These thoughts swirled in my mind, momentarily slowing my actions. It wasn't until Sadagumi and Kenichi had entered the study and called for me that I snapped out of my reverie and followed them inside.

The study was spacious and meticulously tidy. If Sadagumi hadn't organized it post-incident, it suggested Itagaki rarely used the room. A frequently used study wouldn't maintain such pristine order.

Sadagumi confirmed my suspicions with a steady voice. "My husband seldom used the study. He was rarely home and had little interest in reading. It was more for decoration than work, so no important documents were kept here."

Kenichi nodded, "We're just here to look at the monkey books."

Sadagumi directed us to a small, wheeled bookshelf near an armchair. "They're all here," she indicated.

This mobile shelf, designed for easy access to favorite reads, held seven or eight books. I approached to examine them first.

As expected, they were all about monkeys, adorned with striking illustrations. Most appeared untouched, their pages crisp and new. However, one book on rare monkeys of southern India showed signs of frequent handling; several pages were missing. The table of contents revealed these pages focused on tarsiers.

Kenichi quickly noted the book's title. I scanned the rest of the study, finding most books untouched and nothing else of immediate interest.

After our investigation, we thanked Sadagumi and took our leave.

As Kenichi and I drove back to the police station, our minds were abuzz with questions. The visit to Sadagumi had left us with more mysteries than answers, and we felt compelled to unravel them. As we passed a bookstore, we decided to stop and investigate further.

"It's really weird!" Kenichi exclaimed, voicing what we both felt. The contents of the torn pages from Itagaki's book had been truly peculiar.

Those missing pages contained detailed, specialized records about the life of small animals like tarsiers, including numerous illustrations. One section focused on the white variant of the tarsier, referred to by local natives as "Chiwodaka," a symbol of the supernatural power. According to legend, the right front paw of this "Chiwodaka" held the power to grant three wishes.

The record described how extremely rare this white tarsier was. Over three centuries ago, one had been discovered and sent to a regional king in southern India. Following tradition, the king severed its right front paw to create a "monkey's paw" with supposed supernatural powers. Yet, there was no record of whether the king ever achieved any magical powers, nor was the "traditional method" detailed. An illustration showed the king's once-grand palace, now a shadow of its former glory.

Kenichi chuckled, holding the tarsier's paw playfully. "I didn't know this monkey's paw could be so powerful! I wish it could solve all the mysteries of the Itagaki case!"

I laughed, reminding him, "Don't be silly. The record mentioned it must be prepared traditionally. A living monkey's paw won't grant wishes!"

Kenichi grinned. "If you had three wishes, what would be your first?"

"I'm not as foolish as you," I replied with a smile. "My first wish would be for endless wishes!"

We both laughed heartily. As I leafed through the book, my eyes widened in surprise. "The author of this book is—" I began, but my words were cut off by my own gasp. "It's him!"

Kenichi leaned in, curious. "Him? Who is he?"

"This little monkey," I pointed to the tarsier, "was given to me by a zoologist I met in India. He wrote this book!"

Kenichi pondered this revelation. "So, the zoologist doesn't believe in what he wrote. If the 'Chiwodaka' paw really granted wishes, why give it to you?"

"Of course, it's just a legend," I replied. "Who would truly believe such a thing?"

Kenichi frowned, considering another angle. "But why did Itagaki tear out those records?"

Pacing back and forth, a sudden clarity struck me. Waving my hand, I exclaimed, "Listen, I think I can piece together a story from the fragments we have!"

Kenichi settled back in his chair, intrigued. "Alright, let's hear how the master of deduction spins a plausible tale."

I began to weave together the narrative I had constructed from the scattered clues, hoping it would illuminate the shadowy connections in the Itagaki mystery.

As we reviewed the details, a story began to form in my mind—a tale of intrigue that linked an Indian man, familiar with the "Chiwodaka" legend, to the Japanese entrepreneur, Itagaki.

The Indian, perhaps a persuasive storyteller, had spun a web of legends about the mystical monkey's paw, claiming it could grant three wishes. Such tales, ancient and modern alike, have always held an irresistible allure.

Caught in the spell of possibility, Itagaki might have believed that this Indian could grant him supernatural power. The Indian would have set conditions, requiring a secluded location, which led Itagaki to offer the room he used for clandestine meetings with his mistress. To ensure privacy, they constructed a wall and reversed the door, adding layers of secrecy to the rituals that were supposedly to endow the monkey's paw with its power.

But reality fell short of expectations. The "Monkey's Paw" legend was just that—a legend. Disappointment followed, and the Indian's true intentions were eventually revealed, leaving Itagaki disillusioned.

As I concluded my theory, Kenichi shook his head, clearly unimpressed. "That's it? What kind of reasoning is this?" he critiqued.

Annoyed, I defended my logic. "It explains the origin of the strange room!"

Kenichi sighed, pointing out the flaw. "Itagaki was killed by a professional gunman. You really think the Indian would spend so much to hire a hitman after his deception was uncovered?"

I paused, realizing the inconsistency. Of course, no con artist would invest heavily in a losing scheme.

Kenichi continued, "And what about the death of the administrator, Takeo? How does that fit in?"

Again, I was at a loss for words.

"Plus," Kenichi added, "the room was locked from the inside. Who could have left after locking it? And what about the strange phenomena you witnessed? They don't fit your narrative."

I conceded defeat, waving off my failed theory. "Fine, let's drop it. But one thing is clear—Itagaki was definitely fascinated by the 'Monkey's Paw' legend."

Kenichi remained skeptical, his mind elsewhere. Just then, a young agent peeked through the door, reporting, "The Missing Department has news—"

Kenichi cut him off, his patience wearing thin. "I'm dealing with enough already. No more from the Missing Department!"

The agent hesitated, unsure, until I gestured for him to continue. "Come in, tell us what you know."

With a salute, the agent entered, explaining, "A singer named Yunko has been missing for over ten days. From her photo, she resembles Itagaki Ichiro's mistress."

Kenichi's demeanor shifted immediately. "Why didn't you mention this sooner?"

The young agent, unfazed by Kenichi's outburst, simply nodded. "Yes, sir!"

"Where's the photo of the missing Yunko? I need to see it now!" Kenichi demanded, urgency in his voice.

Kenichi eagerly took the large envelope from the young agent and extracted a photograph. The woman in the image was strikingly beautiful, with a sharp jaw and eyes full of life. Kenichi placed the photo beside a sketch of Itagaki's mistress, then quickly used a pen to draw large black glasses on the photo. He looked at me expectantly.

I nodded in agreement, "Yes, it's the same person!"

Kenichi's excitement was palpable. "What's the exact date of her disappearance?"

The young agent promptly responded with a date—the very day Itagaki had died.

Kenichi's interest piqued further. "Bring me all the information on Yunko! Quickly!"

The agent acknowledged with enthusiasm and rushed off. Kenichi rubbed his hands together, anticipation fueling his actions. I cautioned, "Don't get too excited. Remember that she's been missing for a while."

Kenichi was undeterred, brimming with confidence. "Once we know who she is, we can find her!"

I considered voicing my concern—that Yunko could be dead—but held back, not wanting to dampen Kenichi's spirits.

We received Yunko's information in record time and found ourselves at her residence. It was a modest apartment in a typical Tokyo neighborhood, barely 15 square meters. The space was divided by screens into a sitting area and a sleeping area, with a small kitchen and bathroom.

The apartment was in disarray. The closet doors stood ajar, off-season clothes strewn on the floor. Drawers were left open, suggesting a hasty departure. Any seasoned detective could deduce that the occupant left in a rush.

An agent from the Missing Investigation Division accompanied us and remarked, "It's been like this since we first arrived."

Kenichi surveyed the scene, flipping through items casually. "She left in a hurry. Who reported her missing?"

The agent replied, "Her manager, that guy named Naka."

The agent's tone suggested a lack of respect for Naka, hinting that he wasn't held in high regard.

As if on cue, a commotion erupted in the corridor. A voice shouted, "What are you doing? It's not my fault. Can you police be a little nicer? I'm a taxpayer, a good citizen!"

The agent grimaced. "That's Naka."

The door swung open to reveal a man in his thirties, clad in a flamboyant top with sausage-tight pants. His long hair swayed as he chewed gum nonchalantly, swaggering into the room with an air of indifference. He casually placed one foot on a round stool, casting a dismissive glance around the room.

Instantly, I understood why the agent had referred to him as "that guy." He exuded the type of persona often associated with dubious nightclub or bar managers—men whose livelihoods remained in the shadows. I observed him silently, but Kenichi lacked my patience.

With swift determination, Kenichi approached Naka, catching him off guard. In one fluid motion, he kicked the stool from under Naka's foot, causing him to teeter precariously. Before Naka could hit the ground, Kenichi grabbed his shirt, yanking him upright. His gaze bore into Naka's eyes. "Listen," Kenichi said, his voice low and fierce, "what I need from you is vital to solving the deaths of three people, including a detective. If you want to avoid trouble, answer my questions honestly."

Naka's bravado faltered, his face paling. Though he seemed ready to argue, his eyes darted around, chewing his gum with newfound vigor.

Kenichi, however, wasn't about to let him off the hook. He swiftly pinched Naka's throat and delivered a firm slap to his cheek. The suddenness of it startled Naka, causing him to gulp down his gum audibly. I hadn't expected such a rough approach from a Japanese detective, but Kenichi's seamless execution suggested he was no stranger to this tactic.

I couldn't suppress a chuckle at Naka's helpless expression, now gumless and chastened.

Kenichi, having made his point, patted Naka on the shoulder. "Now, tell me—how did you discover Yunko was missing?"

CHAPTER 6

The Singer, Her Manager, and the Scream

Before delving into how Naka discovered Yunko's disappearance, it's crucial to understand the context of Yunko's life—a life that plays a pivotal role in this complex and unexpected mystery. The officially documented information on Yunko is straightforward and lacks depth, but it hints at a much more intricate and poignant story that we learned from various sources.

Yunko, full name Suzuki Yunko, was a 24-year-old woman from Shizuoka Prefecture. Her parents divorced when she was young, and she was raised by her mother. At 15, she won a singing competition, which set her on a path to pursue a career in music. She moved to Tokyo at 18, hoping to make her mark in the music industry.

In Tokyo, Yunko navigated the challenging music scene and became a minor professional singer. Her career plateaued at 23 when she abruptly stopped performing. Managed by Naka, a nightclub manager, she once sang on television but failed to capture any significant attention.

In a city like Tokyo, stories like Yunko's are far from rare. Thousands of aspiring "female singers" exist, but only a minuscule fraction rise to fame. Yunko's life, as summarized in official records, might seem unremarkable, yet it reflects the struggles of a young woman from a small town trying to find her place in a bustling metropolis.

The venues where Yunko performed were lowbrow entertainment spots, places where a young woman might face exploitation and disrespect.

Kenichi and I, upon reading Yunko's background, exchanged a knowing look but kept silent. We both felt the weight of her story—one of many urban tragedies that occur daily but never cease to unsettle us.

Having subdued Naka with practiced ease, Kenichi began his interrogation once Naka was seated, his demeanor shifting from defiant to pleading.

Kenichi asked, "How did you realize Yunko was missing?"

Naka swallowed, his voice strained. "Yunko... she always contacted me every few days—"

Kenichi cut him off. "You're her so-called manager? She stopped singing, so why were you still in touch with her?"

Naka looked pained. "We were good friends. Yunko had no family in Tokyo. I believed in her talent. She had a unique voice, not like Yamaguchi Baihui, but her classical Japanese songs—"

Kenichi interrupted again, his patience waning. "Stick to what's important."

Naka nodded, hurriedly continuing, "I was trying to find her a place to sing again. She had talent. She saw me as a friend."

Kenichi's voice turned sharp. "Friend? Or did she just lend you money?"

Naka's face flushed as he stood abruptly, ready to defend himself, but words failed him. Defeated, he sank back into his seat, unable to refute Kenichi's implication.

After Naka sat back down, he admitted with a resigned sigh, "Yes, she often lent me money, and I never repaid her. But we truly were friends."

His candid admission made Kenichi and I reassess him. Kenichi's demeanor softened, and he gently patted Naka's shoulder. "Alright, go on. How did you find out she was missing?"

Naka continued, "Yunko and I were like siblings. Whenever she was unhappy or troubled, she would confide in me. The last time I saw her was over two weeks ago. That night, she suddenly stormed into the bar and ordered a large glass of strong liquor. By the time I found her, she had already downed it."

Naka's eyes met ours, confusion written across his features. Despite his rough exterior and shady affiliations, Naka seemed to genuinely care for Yunko, revealing a softer side beneath his tough facade.

He paused, recounting the night he last saw Yunko at the bar—a place not known for attracting single female patrons, given its low-brow atmosphere and clientele. The waitresses, clad in scanty outfits, endured lewd comments and groping from inebriated patrons, playing along with well-rehearsed flirtations to keep the rowdy crowd entertained.

Yunko's presence was an anomaly, but the doorman, recognizing her as Naka's friend, allowed her entry. According to the doorman, Yunko had "rushed in with her face covered," a telling sign of distress.

The bartender recounted, "When Miss Yunko entered, she had her hands over her face and demanded, 'Give me a strong drink, a double— no, a triple!' Her voice was hoarse."

Though surprised—Yunko wasn't known for drinking hard liquor— the bartender obliged, serving her a triple shot of American whiskey. "She downed it almost in one go," the bartender continued. "A drink like that is tough for anyone to handle, yet she did it. She choked and coughed, tears streaming down her face. But it seemed she had already been crying before she even entered."

As the bartender moved to assist her, Naka, who worked there as a so-called "manager," arrived. Yunko, tears streaking her face and trembling, recognized him immediately. She rushed into his arms, seeking comfort.

Naka, concerned, asked urgently, "Yunko, what's wrong? What's happened?"

Yunko was too overwhelmed to speak, making only a series of sobbing sounds as Naka helped her to a secluded corner of the chaotic bar. The place was a cacophony of drunken revelry, with music blaring and patrons in various states of inebriation, ensuring that Yunko's distress went largely unnoticed.

It's important to note that Naka's account has been corroborated by multiple witnesses, making it a reliable narrative.

Once seated, Yunko clung to Naka, who, despite his rough exterior, shared a genuine, brotherly bond with her. He gently patted her back, urging her to share her troubles. "Don't cry. Whatever it is, you can tell me," he reassured her.

Yunko lifted her tear-streaked face, her makeup a blurred mess of blue and gold from her tears. Her lips quivered as she struggled to speak, and finally, she let out a piercing scream: "It's terrible!"

Kenichi, myself, and other detectives conducted thorough interviews with everyone present that night—customers, staff, and even a patron who had briefly stepped outside. This man's account provided a vivid picture of the impact of Yunko's scream.

"I had just stepped out, letting the door close behind me. The bar was its usual lively self," recounted the patron, a sober and composed company employee. "But suddenly, I heard a woman scream, 'It's terrible!' even through the closed door."

The patron paused, recalling the moment. "I turned back and opened the door again. I frequent this bar, but I'd never seen anything like it. The place was packed, yet eerily silent. It was like stepping into a silent movie."

"Everyone was turned toward a corner of the bar. The room was smoky, the lighting dim, and from where I stood, I couldn't see much. But it was clear the scream had come from that direction."

"Though I couldn't understand why she screamed 'It's so scary,' her voice sent chills down my spine. I think everyone felt the same, which is why the bar fell into that strange silence."

The patron's account, along with others, painted a picture of an unsettling, pivotal moment. Yunko's scream was more than an expression of fear; it was a catalyst that shifted the atmosphere and hinted at the gravity of her distress. This incident was a crucial piece of the puzzle, suggesting deeper layers of fear and mystery surrounding Yunko's disappearance.

Naka's account of the events that night closely mirrored the other witness statements. The guest who had just exited the bar was the farthest from Yunko when she screamed, while Naka, standing right by her side, was the closest.

"I was really scared by her scream!" Naka admitted, a lingering fear evident in his voice. Trying to reclaim his bravado, he puffed out his chest and added, "You know, I'm definitely not a timid person!"

Kenichi cut him off sharply, "Enough with the nonsense. Continue!"

Naka, visibly flustered, quickly complied. "Her scream was so piercing. I never knew Yunko had such a high and sharp scream in her. Sure, she could hit high notes while singing, but this was something else entirely. It felt as if my eardrums had burst—everything went silent. Then I realized it wasn't just my hearing; the entire bar had fallen into silence."

Kenichi, his impatience boiling over, pressed on. "We know all this. Why did Yunko scream like that? What horrible thing happened to her?"

Naka, visibly frustrated, struggled to keep his temper in check. The veins on his forehead revealed his mounting stress. Sensing the tension, I stepped in. "Let Mr. Naka speak at his own pace," I urged gently.

Grateful for my support, Naka nodded vigorously. "Thank you, sir. You're a true gentleman!" His words were a subtle jab at Kenichi, but Kenichi let it slide, more interested in uncovering the mystery behind Yunko's scream.

Naka continued, "I was shocked by her scream and immediately asked, 'What did you do?'"

His tone had been slightly reproachful, as such an outburst was quite inappropriate in public. Yunko's body trembled violently, and Naka had to hold her arms tightly.

As the bar patrons slowly recovered from the shock, Yunko regained her composure, freeing herself from Naka's grip. With a voice almost back to normal, she apologized to the room, "I'm sorry, everyone. I lost my composure for a moment. I'm sorry for disturbing you."

With that, she turned to leave. Amidst the murmurs in the bar, Naka realized he needed to follow her, but by the time he reacted, she was already near the door. He called out to her, and she briefly looked back but kept walking. Naka sensed something was off, so he pushed through the crowd to follow her. But by the time he reached the street, Yunko had vanished, likely having jumped into a taxi and disappeared into the night.

"I haven't seen her since that night," Naka concluded, his voice tinged with regret.

Kenichi's frustration boiled over. "You idiot! You saw she was acting strangely and didn't follow her home? You've been to her place before!"

Naka, visibly crestfallen, didn't fight back. "You're right. I should have followed her. But later, about half an hour after she left, I assumed she had gone home. I called her place, but the line was busy. I thought it meant she had returned safely."

After Naka reported Yunko's disappearance, the investigation officer who entered her residence noted that the phone receiver was resting on its stand, undisturbed.

"I thought she might have been dealing with something upsetting, which is why she seemed so emotional that night," Naka explained. "So, I didn't think much of it initially. But when I called her every day afterward and couldn't get through, by the third day, I started to worry. I went to her place, knocked on the door, but no one answered. That's when I got anxious and contacted the police. At that time, I thought—"

Naka hesitated, and Kenichi prompted him, "Did you think she might have committed suicide?"

Naka nodded, his expression somber. "Yes, I feared she might have, and it scared me."

The fact that the phone went unanswered for three days was alarming. If Yunko had returned home after that night at the bar, even briefly, and made a phone call, this call could be crucial. It raised questions about her hurried departure and her alarming scream.

Kenichi pressed on, "Why did you suspect she might commit suicide? Did she tell you she was feeling unstable? What was causing her distress?"

Kenichi's questions were pointed, and Naka seemed caught off guard. "I think it was a relationship issue," he replied. "She hadn't performed in nearly six months but was still living comfortably. Recently, she even upgraded to a larger infrared remote-controlled color TV."

The tension in the room was palpable as I frowned at Naka. "You didn't ask Yunko about her source of income?" I inquired, my voice a blend of curiosity and disbelief.

Kenichi's response was as cold as the steel-gray sky outside. "A man like him doesn't need to ask," he retorted, his words as sharp as a blade. "He knows it clearly. If a woman like Yunko can sustain herself without the mundane drudgery of work, aside from being a mistress, what else could it be? A miraculous lottery win from gambling, perhaps? No, a man like him turns a blind eye. If Yunko has someone supporting her, it means he can keep borrowing money from her with less guilt."

His disdain sliced through the air, turning Naka's face a furious shade of crimson. His fists clenched tightly, a visible testament to his simmering anger.

But Kenichi was relentless, his eyes narrowing as he bore into Naka. "Am I right, Mr. Naka?" he taunted, stretching out the title in a long, mocking drawl devoid of any respect.

Naka, pushed to the brink of his patience, erupted. With a roar, he lunged forward, his fist flying towards Kenichi. Instinctively, I intercepted the punch mid-air. "Mr. Naka," I warned, my voice steady despite the chaos, "assaulting a police officer is a serious crime!"

Breathless with rage, Naka struggled to regain his composure. I turned to Kenichi, imploring, "What do you gain from this, Kenichi? Mr. Naka is aiding us, providing vital information about Yunko."

For a moment, Kenichi stood frozen, his expression unreadable. Then, almost reluctantly, he muttered, "I'm sorry." His apology hung in the air, directionless, as if he himself was unsure who it was meant for.

As Naka's anger subsided, I pressed on. "You had no idea about Yunko being kept as a mistress?"

Naka's bitter smile spoke volumes. "Oh, I knew," he confessed, his voice tinged with the weariness of experience. "It was always a suspicion, as Mr. Kenichi so astutely pointed out. A girl like Yunko lives comfortably without working. If not supported by the wealthy, then what? I've seen it too often in this city's nightlife."

Her words resonated with a familiar melancholy, a bitter sigh escaping my lips. The city teemed with such stories, each more heartbreaking than the last.

"I once confronted Yunko," Naka continued, his voice tinged with frustration. "She was evasive, never revealing the truth. I even tried to investigate, but hit nothing but dead ends."

Suddenly, Naka's gaze met mine, a question burning in his eyes. "Who supports Yunko?"

Kenichi's answer was swift, "An entrepreneur named Itagaki Ichiro."

Naka's reaction was immediate; he slapped his thigh with the force of realization. "Then it's simple. Of course! It must be Itagaki! He must have whisked Yunko away on a secret trip!"

Kenichi's gaze was as sharp as a blade as he glared at Naka. "Itagaki Ichiro has been shot dead!" he announced, his voice devoid of any emotion.

Naka's face turned ashen, his mouth agape in shock. It took him a moment to find his voice. "When did this happen?" he finally asked, his words barely a whisper.

"It was the day after Yunko screamed in the bar," Kenichi replied, his tone grave.

Naka's eyes widened even further. "Then, is it Yunko—"

Kenichi cut him off with a dismissive wave. "Yunko isn't the murderer. The one who took out Itagaki is a first-class professional killer. Yunko couldn't possibly afford someone like that."

Naka, no fool, quickly connected the dots. "Regardless, Itagaki's death must be tied to Yunko. Her blood-curdling scream that night surely has something to do with it!"

Kenichi and I exchanged a knowing glance. Naka voiced exactly what we had been thinking all along.

But the question lingered like a shadow: what horrific event had Yunko encountered to provoke such a scream? Only Yunko could provide the answer, yet she had vanished without a trace.

I broke the silence, reminding Kenichi, "Did Yunko and Itagaki have a tryst that night?"

Flipping through his small notebook, Kenichi shook his head. "No, Itagaki was with his wife at a party that evening. The party was held at— wait, wait—" He paused, a flicker of realization crossing his face, but then dismissed it with a wave. "It's probably insignificant. The party was far from Itagaki's home, and they had to pass by the tryst location."

I shrugged, skepticism lacing my words. "No matter how daring, Itagaki wouldn't dare stop there with his wife in tow."

Kenichi chuckled, a humorless sound. "Of course not, but as they drove past, a glance at the tryst spot would have been hard to resist."

I remarked offhandedly, "So what? It doesn't explain what happened afterward."

Kenichi nodded in agreement, though the puzzle remained unsolved.

* * *

Itagaki Ichiro's mood was foul as he exited his office that night. His displeasure stemmed from Yunko and their clandestine meeting spot.

The previous night, at around 11 o'clock, he'd driven past and noticed light seeping through the curtains.

No one should have been there. He and Yunko hadn't planned to meet. Yet, the light was undeniable, a beacon of mystery that now cast long shadows over Itagaki's fate.

Itagaki's clandestine glance at the rendezvous point as he passed by seemed innocuous at first, just a fleeting moment of nostalgia or curiosity. Kenichi and I had speculated about this, but initially dismissed it as irrelevant to the events that followed.

Every man might indulge such a secretive glance. Yet, as time peeled back the layers of mystery, we realized its significance. That glance held a hidden weight we hadn't appreciated at first.

"Yunko was home alone that night, wasn't she? She entered the bar around 11:30?" Kenichi queried, piecing together the timeline.

Naka confirmed, "Yes."

"Then perhaps she experienced something dreadful at home, prompting her to flee to the bar," Kenichi suggested.

Naka shook his head firmly. "No, that doesn't add up."

Kenichi's irritation was palpable. "Why not?"

"If something terrifying had occurred, she'd have sought help at the police station just down the street," Naka reasoned, gesturing towards the window. I followed his gaze and indeed, there was the police station, a beacon of safety Yunko bypassed. Naka's logic was undeniable. Why would she run to a bar and scream instead of seeking the immediate refuge of the police?

Kenichi, though reluctant, seemed to accept this reasoning.

"Where is your bar located?" Kenichi asked, his curiosity piqued.

Naka mentioned the location. Despite my unfamiliarity with Tokyo, the name struck me. "Ah," I exclaimed. It was near the spot where Yunko and Itagaki had their trysts.

Kenichi and I shared a moment of realization, pointing at each other. "Yunko is in—"

But Kenichi interrupted, dismissing the thought. "No, Itagaki wasn't there that night. Why would Yunko go alone?"

"Maybe she was seeking solace and ended up encountering something horrifying," I suggested.

Kenichi shook his head. "She's been there many times for their meetings. What could be so terrifying?"

"Don't forget about the strange room," I reminded him.

Naka, oblivious to our cryptic exchange, watched us with puzzled eyes.

Kenichi mumbled, "Yes, the strange room."

"We must find Yunko," I urged. "Only she can unravel what happened."

Kenichi's expression turned inscrutable, as if wrestling with an unsettling thought. "Did Yunko... did she see herself in that strange room too?"

The question hit me like a jolt. The memory of seeing "myself" in that room was one I avoided discussing. It defied explanation, and Kenichi's previous skepticism had often bordered on mockery. Yet now, his demeanor was serious, devoid of any jest.

I hesitated before replying, "Maybe."

Kenichi rubbed his face, weariness etched in his features. "But after leaving the bar, where did she vanish to?"

The question lingered, heavy with uncertainty, as we grappled with the enigmatic pieces of Yunko's disappearance, each clue leading deeper into a labyrinthine mystery.

CHAPTER 7

Tears in the Study and a Mysterious Call

After leaving the bar, Yunko climbed into a taxi and instructed the driver to take her home.

As the car sped through the city streets, her heart pounded violently, each beat echoing the turmoil of her thoughts. That night played out like a relentless nightmare, one she couldn't seem to wake from.

It had all begun so innocuously. At three in the afternoon, she was at home, as she often was, attempting to find solace in the mundane. The television droned on with uninspiring programs, so she turned it off, opting instead for the comfort of a record. But even that was short-lived; halfway through, she silenced the music.

The singer's voice resonated with an elegance that deepened her sadness. Yunko had once possessed such a voice, a gift now lost to her. No one knew the truth behind her sudden withdrawal from singing—only she understood the devastating secret: she had lost her voice.

A tiny tear in her vocal cords had rendered her incapable of reaching the soaring high notes that had defined her career. Her dreams of singing had been cruelly extinguished.

It was during this bleak period that she crossed paths with Itagaki. A man of success and sophistication, he pursued her with relentless charm and generosity. Yet Yunko felt nothing but emptiness towards him. With her singing career in ruins, she found herself trapped in the sprawling city with limited options. Becoming Itagaki's mistress seemed the only viable path for survival.

The nights spent with Itagaki were the lowest points of her existence. His laughter, filled with self-satisfaction, grated on her nerves, feeling like a devil's beckoning call. Yet, she forced herself to smile, to play the part he expected, ensuring he felt his investment was worthwhile, securing her place under his financial wing.

Each return from their encounters left her desperate to cleanse herself of the lingering shame. An hour-long shower became her ritual, a futile attempt to wash away the humiliation of selling herself, a reality she faced with grim resignation.

After silencing the record player, the phone rang. Itagaki's calls were always curt, dictating her life with few words: "Meet me at seven," or "I'm busy, we'll speak tomorrow."

That afternoon, his message was the latter. "I'm not free tonight. I'll call you tomorrow," he said before hanging up.

Yunko sat motionless, the phone still in her hand, before finally rousing herself. She poured half a glass of whiskey and downed it in one go. Alcohol had become her refuge since her voice abandoned her, its fiery embrace offering a fleeting sense of security, a temporary balm for her fractured soul.

She contemplated a second glass but hesitated, setting it aside. What was there to do now? Perhaps she could indulge in a good meal, though the thought of food seemed unappetizing. Yet, it was a distraction, a small comfort in a life that had gone so astray.

That afternoon drifted by in a haze for Yunko, each moment blurring seamlessly into the next. Her life, a monotonous cycle of routine, seemed to dull her memory, leaving only vague recollections of tidying an already pristine room and meticulously chopping vegetables in the kitchen. As dusk settled, the sudden ring of the phone shattered the quietude.

Emerging from the kitchen, Yunko wiped her hands on her apron before answering the call. A familiar thought crossed her mind—perhaps Itagaki had changed his plans, as he occasionally did. If so, she would need to prepare herself quickly. With this in mind, she glanced at the mirror while picking up the receiver.

Instead of Itagaki's voice, however, a stranger's voice filled the line. It was deep, magnetic, and carried an alluring quality that could easily captivate, yet it was unfamiliar to her.

"Miss Suzuki Yunko, please" the voice intoned.

Startled, Yunko replied, "Speaking."

The stranger continued, "Will everything go according to plan tomorrow? I usually offer a final opportunity for reconsideration. If there are changes, inform me now."

The voice exuded confidence, the words flying out with precision and clarity. Yet Yunko was bewildered. "What did you say? I don't understand!" she protested.

The stranger chuckled softly. "I see, everything proceeds as originally planned."

Trying to interject, Yunko began, "What—"

But she was cut off. "Don't worry, I won't fail. Expect results by noon tomorrow. If you remain at home, watch the news on TV or listen to the radio."

Yunko, still perplexed, attempted to clarify. "I'm sorry, sir, do you have the wrong number?"

A mocking laugh followed. "Understood. No more words, I apologize for disturbing you."

Before Yunko could respond, the line went dead. She stood there, phone in hand, momentarily paralyzed by the abruptness of the exchange. It was a natural reaction, a brief suspension in time as she replayed the conversation in her mind.

Despite her efforts, the stranger's words eluded her grasp, like a dream fading upon waking. She assumed it was a case of mistaken identity, yet the caller had unmistakably addressed her as "Suzuki Yunko."

Yunko finally set the phone back in its cradle and returned to the kitchen, her mind still clouded by the unsettling call. Distracted, she nicked her finger with the knife, a sharp pain snapping her back to reality. Instinctively, she put her finger in her mouth, tasting the metallic tang of blood.

The call lingered in her thoughts, and a sudden urge to see Itagaki overtook her. Though love had never been part of their arrangement, and despite Itagaki's professions of affection which she met with feigned tenderness, Yunko had always regarded their relationship as purely transactional. Itagaki paid for the pleasure of her company, while she received financial security in return.

Yet, over time, Itagaki had inadvertently become a pillar in her life. Without this arrangement, perhaps affection might have blossomed. Now, she felt an inexplicable need to confide in him about the call. Was their secret known to others?

She ate her dinner absentmindedly, her thoughts racing. Several times, she reached for the phone to call Itagaki, only to remember his strict prohibition against contacting him at home or work. It was a rule she dared not break.

By nearly ten o'clock, loneliness gnawed at her resolve, driving her to leave the house. With no particular destination, she wandered the streets, hoping to escape her solitude. Time blurred, and soon she found herself at the familiar location of their rendezvous.

"Since I'm here, I might as well go up and sit for a while," Yunko mused, her thoughts tinged with a hint of irony. "Perhaps Itagaki will be there. But that would be a miracle," she acknowledged, clutching the key that was always with her like a talisman of access to this secluded part of her life.

Approaching the building, she instinctively adjusted her hair, donned her sunglasses, and turned up her collar—a practiced disguise to ensure she remained unnoticed and unrecognized. It was a ritual she performed every time, a cloak of anonymity she wore like armor.

Inside the lobby, the administrator greeted her with a nod, a routine exchange that barely registered in her distracted mind. Yunko returned the gesture with a stiff nod of her own, slipping into the elevator as though fleeing from an unseen chaser. Only as the elevator ascended did she allow herself to exhale, a breath she hadn't realized she'd been holding, the sense of security returning as she rose.

When the elevator doors parted, Yunko stepped out, her movements automatic. She unlocked the door to the apartment, the click echoing in the silence, and flipped on the lights. The opulence of the room unfolded before her, its elegance as expected, yet devoid of life.

Sinking into the plush sofa, she cradled her head in her hands, the weight of confusion pressing down on her. The room, despite its splendor, felt like a mirage—its beauty superficial, a mere stage for Itagaki's pleasures. Here, in this luxurious cocoon, everything seemed both real and unreal, a paradox she struggled to reconcile.

As the thought crossed her mind, Yunko stood, intent on leaving the suffocating illusion behind. But just as she was about to depart, a strange sound reached her ears—a haunting cry emanating from the study. It was a sound like no other, a sorrowful lament that seemed to seep into her very bones, chilling her to the core. The crying started as a faint murmur but soon crescendoed into a clear, heart-wrenching wail, unmistakably that of a woman in deep distress.

Yunko froze, her heart pounding with a mix of fear and disbelief. How could there be someone in the study? Her thoughts tangled in confusion, and her instincts screamed at her to flee, yet curiosity rooted her in place.

As she swallowed hard, her mind drifted back to the first time Itagaki had brought her to this place. She had been awestruck by the grandeur, a country girl dazzled by the splendor of Tokyo. "It's so gorgeous!" she had exclaimed, genuinely impressed.

Itagaki had beamed at her reaction. "Do you like it? This will belong to us from now on. It's our world," he had declared, his satisfaction evident.

Yunko had kissed Itagaki on the cheek, noting the two distinct rooms. Itagaki, ever the charmer, pulled her into his arms, their connection sealed with a long, lingering kiss. He lifted her effortlessly, carrying her into the bedroom—a space designed for comfort and indulgence. There, he placed her on the bed, and she acquiesced to his desires, as she always did.

Afterward, as they prepared to leave, her curiosity got the better of her. "That room is?" she asked, gesturing towards the other door.

"It's the study," Itagaki replied, adjusting his tie with casual ease. He opened the door, revealing a simply furnished space—a desk, a bookshelf, a long sofa. As Yunko took in the room, Itagaki wrapped an arm around her waist, whispering suggestively, "Next time, maybe we can try on the sofa—"

Before he could finish, Yunko gently pushed him away with a smile, stepping back as she watched him close the study door.

It was the first and only time she'd glimpsed the study.

Their meetings followed a well-worn pattern. Time was always scarce, and Itagaki would whisk her into the bedroom immediately, ensuring she left first, maintaining discretion. She never had the opportunity—or the need—to explore the study further. It was clear that for Itagaki, the bedroom was the main attraction.

Yet, there was a moment, a memory slightly hazy with time, when Yunko had casually suggested, "The study should also be tidied up!" It had seemed a simple enough remark.

She recalled standing in the living room, Itagaki still in the bedroom. As she walked towards the study door, hand reaching for the handle, Itagaki's reaction was startling. He burst from the bedroom with an uncharacteristic urgency, his expression tinged with panic, stopping Yunko in her tracks.

His haste was so great that he nearly stumbled, yet he quickly found his footing and barked, "Leave it alone!"

Surprised, Yunko withdrew her hand immediately. She was accustomed to following Itagaki's directives without question. He steadied himself, his voice now calmer yet still firm. "The study is empty. It's best left that way."

Yunko nodded, acquiescing as always, but the incident lingered in her mind. Itagaki's uncharacteristic panic hinted at something more within those walls, a mystery she had yet to uncover.

Itagaki had looked like he wanted to explain something that day, but the words never left his lips. Their routine unfolded as usual, the familiar pattern unbroken.

But there was another time, a moment lost in the haze of memory, when something slightly different occurred. They had agreed to meet, and Itagaki, as was his habit, usually arrived first. This time, however, Yunko unlocked the door and found herself alone. Itagaki was running late, by a mere three minutes.

As she waited, curiosity tugged at her, a lingering echo of Itagaki's previous panic. She found herself drawn to the study door, her hand resting on the handle. It wouldn't budge; it was locked. She paused, contemplating the significance of the locked door, when Itagaki burst in, apologizing for his tardiness.

"The traffic was terrible, I'm sorry for being late!" he exclaimed, moving towards her with his usual charm.

Yunko slipped into her role with practiced ease, her voice tinged with feigned longing. "I thought you wouldn't come and I'd never see you again," she replied, playing her part perfectly.

Itagaki embraced her, his voice filled with reassurance. "How could it be? How could it be?"

Despite these reassurances, the study remained an enigma, its door a barrier to secrets untold. Yunko had only interacted with the study three times, yet each encounter deepened its mystery.

Now, in the night's unsettling silence, the sound of a woman's sorrowful cries emanated from behind its locked door.

Swallowing nervously, Yunko's mind raced with possibilities. Could Itagaki have another mistress ensconced here? The idea seemed implausible—Itagaki's life was too regimented for such complications.

So who was the woman crying within the study's confines?

After standing frozen in shock for what felt like an eternity, Yunko summoned her courage and called out, "Excuse me, who is in here?"

Her voice echoed through the apartment, but only the haunting cries answered her. Gathering her resolve, she approached the door, knocking lightly. "Who is in there?" she asked again.

The cries diminished to soft sobs, and a tremulous voice finally responded, "It's me!"

The cryptic reply only fueled Yunko's curiosity. "Who are you? Why are you here? Why are you crying?" she pressed, her questions met with silence.

"Please open the door," she implored, but the silence stretched on, the mystery deepening around her like the shadows of the night.

She gripped the handle, trying to turn it, but it wouldn't budge. Then, as if in response to her request, the door slowly swung open—though in a direction she hadn't anticipated. The unexpected movement caught her off guard, and as the door revealed its secrets, Yunko was met with a sight that left her speechless.

Standing in the doorway was the woman from the study—the same woman whose cries had filled the apartment with an eerie sorrow.

But this woman wasn't a stranger; she was Yunko herself.

It was as if she was gazing into a living mirror, one reflecting not just her physical features but the emotional depth she rarely allowed herself to acknowledge. The woman was strikingly beautiful, even through her tears, with expressive eyes and a delicate chin. Her sorrow and helplessness were palpable, yet her appearance was undeniably captivating.

Yunko found herself staring into her own eyes, eyes that were hauntingly familiar yet filled with an unfathomable sadness. The sight of herself in such a state was something she could never have anticipated. A shiver ran through her as she recognized the profound despair in those eyes—her despair, laid bare in a way she had never confronted.

The shock was so overwhelming that Yunko didn't remember fleeing. But flee she did, driven by an instinctual need to escape the haunting reflection. Her mind blanked as she turned and ran, colliding with the door in her haste before wrenching it open and sprinting down the stairs. She avoided the lobby, bypassing any chance of encountering the administrator, and burst into the night, making a beeline for the bar.

Once there, she gulped down a large glass of whiskey, her hands trembling. Naka helped her to a secluded corner where, safe at last, she released a cry—a piercing scream that seemed to cut through the air. It was the sound of sheer terror and disbelief, a cry that echoed the turmoil roiling within her.

The scream surprised even her with its intensity. It was as if all the emotions she had suppressed erupted in that single, raw outburst. The image of her own face, etched with sorrow, grief, and despair, was seared into her consciousness. It was undeniably her, a manifestation of all the fears and doubts she kept buried beneath her glamorous exterior.

As a third-rate singer turned businessman's mistress, Yunko had always avoided pondering her future. She pushed away thoughts of what lay ahead, choosing instead to focus on the present, on maintaining the facade of youth and allure. But the woman in the study had been thinking those very thoughts, her expression a reflection of the inner turmoil Yunko had long ignored.

In a man's arms, she was the epitome of beauty and charm, a figure of desire. Yet deep down, she knew that sadness and desperation lay beneath the surface. That night, she had seen it all—seen it in her own eyes, heard it in her own cries. And now, it was something she could no longer deny or ignore.

Yunko screamed, feeling an overwhelming need to release the pent-up terror and confusion inside her. The scream cut through the bar, drawing startled glances from the patrons. As the echoes died down, a wave of calm washed over her, as though the act had purged her of some of the fear. Embarrassed by the attention, she quickly apologized to those around her and hurried out, her cheeks flushed with a mix of shame and urgency.

She hailed a taxi and directed it home, her mind racing with thoughts of the strange encounter. Once she arrived, she wasted no time, her first instinct to grab the phone and call Itagaki. He needed to know about the bizarre and unsettling experience she'd had at their secret meeting place.

With the phone to her ear, she lowered her voice, mindful of discretion. "Please, Mr. Itagaki," she requested.

The voice on the other end replied politely, "I'm sorry, Mr. Itagaki and his wife are out at a party and haven't returned yet."

Disappointment and frustration gnawed at Yunko. She hung up, her mind whirling with unanswered questions. As she set the receiver down, the phone rang unexpectedly, the shrill tone startling her anew. Heart pounding, she picked it up again.

Meanwhile, elsewhere in the city, Itagaki had passed by the rendezvous spot. Noticing the lights on, he felt a moment of unease. It wasn't typical for the lights to be left on, and he made a mental note to check in later.

Back at the bar, Naka, concerned for Yunko, tried to reach her by phone. But the line was busy, tied up by the conversation Yunko was having and then the sudden incoming call.

The strange voice came through the phone once more, asking urgently, "What's going on? Is there any accident? Do you want to change your plan?"

Yunko's hands trembled violently, the voice sending a chill down her spine. It was the same mysterious caller who had disrupted her life, setting off a chain of events that led her to the rendezvous and the shocking encounter with herself.

Overwhelmed, she slammed the phone down, her breath coming in ragged gasps. Her eyes flickered to a mirror behind her, but she turned away quickly, terrified of seeing the reflection of despair and helplessness she now associated with her own image.

Confusion and fear coursed through her as she considered her next move. The only thought that crystallized was the need to leave—leave this place, leave Tokyo. Frantically, she packed a suitcase, her hands moving with urgency and desperation. Without a backward glance, she left her home behind.

Meanwhile, Itagaki had returned to his home. Seizing a moment when his wife was distracted, he attempted to call Yunko. But by then, she was already gone, her path leading her far from the city.

Yunko boarded a night train, curling into herself, hiding behind dark glasses, her gaze avoiding the passengers around her. The fear of seeing herself again, of confronting that haunting reflection, kept her in a state of anxiety.

Her journey took her to Shizuoka, yet she hesitated to leave the station. Instead, she purchased another ticket, moving forward without destination, driven by an indescribable urge to flee. She found refuge in a small, unfamiliar hotel, a place where she could pause and catch her breath.

In the solitude of her room, Yunko felt a semblance of relief. The past hours had been a blur of flight, her mind unable to articulate what exactly she was escaping from. Was it herself? Since witnessing her own reflection, a deep-seated fear had taken root, one that threatened her sanity if she stayed in one place too long.

Settling in, she sipped hot tea, seeking comfort in its warmth, and turned on the TV. What she saw next froze her world: the news report announcing that Itagaki, a prominent businessman from Tokyo, had been mysteriously shot dead.

Shock immobilized her as she stared at the screen, her mind reeling. Itagaki was dead, and she was adrift in a sea of uncertainty. How had it come to this? Had his wife discovered their affair, leading to this tragedy? With Itagaki gone, what path lay before her?

As the news broadcast continued, Yunko remained rooted in place, the images on the screen fading as her thoughts spiraled. The small room felt like a cocoon, isolating her from reality.

"I should go back to Tokyo," she thought eventually. Itagaki's death would undoubtedly trigger an investigation, and the police would seek her out. Did others know of their relationship?

Dawn broke, and Yunko left the hotel, resuming her aimless journey. She moved from town to town, her identity concealed until the police released a sketch on television. Startled, she changed her appearance, but the inevitable happened: her true photo was broadcasted, forcing her to make a decision.

Resolved, Yunko prepared to return to Tokyo, facing whatever awaited her there. The journey she'd begun in fear would end with a confrontation with reality, and she knew it was time to stop running.

Yunko stepped off the train at Tokyo Station, her suitcase clutched in her hand, weariness etched into her features. As she moved to leave the platform, she sensed a presence approaching—a tall man with an air of quiet authority.

Instinctively, she halted, turning to face him. He was striking, with dark hair and a charismatic presence, his attire suggesting sophistication and confidence. His gaze was fixed on her, and she couldn't shake the feeling that he might be a police officer—an embodiment of the detectives she had seen on TV.

"I'm back," she said, a hint of resignation in her voice. "I don't know. I don't know at all."

The man raised an eyebrow, his voice smooth and calm. "Miss Yunko, I shouldn't be meddling."

Before he could finish, Yunko's body stiffened, and her suitcase slipped from her grasp, thudding to the ground. Recognition dawned on her. His voice—it was the same as the stranger who had called her twice before.

Her mouth fell open, words eluding her as the man stooped to retrieve her suitcase. "I think we should talk," he suggested, his tone polite yet firm. "Every officer in Tokyo is looking for you."

"Are you not a police officer?" Yunko managed to ask, her mind racing.

He chuckled softly, his demeanor surprisingly relaxed. "I didn't expect you to be in the mood for jokes. For both our sakes, we need to have a good conversation."

Confusion clouded her thoughts. "You—sir, what connection do you have with me?"

The man frowned slightly, as if amused by a private jest, then reached out, taking hold of her arm with gentle insistence. Without further explanation, he guided her out of the station and into a waiting taxi. Yunko's attempts to speak were gently but firmly silenced by his presence.

Despite the strangeness of the situation, Yunko felt no fear. The man's calm demeanor and the intriguing air about him kept her curiosity piqued instead.

The taxi journey was silent, and soon they arrived at an alley. The man led her through it, casting her suitcase aside with little ceremony.

"My clothes!" Yunko protested, surprised by the casual dismissal.

He ignored her concern, continuing to lead her through the narrow passageway and into another waiting taxi. Again, he offered no opportunity for conversation, leaving Yunko to grapple with her thoughts.

Who was this enigmatic man, and where was he taking her? The questions swirled in her mind, but the answers remained elusive. Each turn of the taxi brought her further from the life she had known, toward a destination she could not yet fathom.

CHAPTER 8

An Indian Legend

The discovery of Yunko's suitcase in the alley triggered a flurry of activity. Once it was delivered to Kenichi's office, Naka was called in to identify it. With a quick glance, he confirmed, "It's Yunko's. The suitcase and the clothes are all hers."

Kenichi and I exchanged a knowing look. Naka's certainty left no room for doubt.

Naka chimed in, her voice ringing with confidence, "So Yunko has been in Tokyo all this time!"

Kenichi scoffed, shaking his head. "Don't jump to conclusions. Yunko must have been moving around the country and only just returned to Tokyo."

I nodded in agreement with Kenichi's assessment. "Exactly. Look at the clothes. The thicker ones are on top, suggesting she's been to colder places up north recently."

As I spoke, Kenichi meticulously examined each item in the suitcase, pulling out seemingly inconsequential things—receipts, ticket stubs, and the like. The dates on these items painted a picture of Yunko's recent travels, tracing her path across the country.

Yet, despite her wanderings, she had returned to Tokyo. She had to have heard about Itagaki's death and known that the police were searching for her. So why leave her suitcase abandoned in an alley?

The question gnawed at me, and I voiced my concern. "Yunko might have run into trouble."

Kenichi's brow furrowed in thought, and just then, the little white tarsier perched on his shoulder leapt into the suitcase. It burrowed into the clothes, making a cozy nest in the corner, its eyes gleaming with satisfaction.

"Get out of there!" Kenichi commanded, gesturing emphatically. I had spent enough time with Kenichi to know that the tarsier usually obeyed him without fuss.

But this time, the tarsier remained stubbornly nestled among the clothes. Kenichi's frustration mounted, and he raised his voice, but the tarsier responded with a defiant squeak, baring its teeth in a show of rebellion.

The sudden change in the little tarsier's demeanor was both unexpected and alarming. Its transformation from a gentle companion to a fierce little creature caught us off guard.

Kenichi, usually patient and kind, let his irritation get the best of him, resulting in a more aggressive approach. As he reached out to the tarsier, I could see the animal's defensive instincts kick in.

"Kenichi, be careful!" I warned, but it was too late. The tarsier bared its sharp teeth and snapped at Kenichi's hand, leaving a painful bite on the edge of his palm.

Anger flared in Kenichi's eyes as he reacted instinctively, but the nimble tarsier was already on the move, leaping from the suitcase to the table and then out the window.

Despite the pain and bleeding from his hand, Kenichi raced to the window, calling out in a series of strange, urgent noises. It was a language only the tarsier could understand, perhaps an attempt to coax it back or to express regret.

The tarsier paused on the windowsill, torn between the familiar and the unknown, its eyes reflecting a moment of indecision.

Then, piercing through the air came an unfamiliar sound from outside—a sharp, haunting noise that wasn't quite a whistle but carried the same compelling urgency. The tarsier's hesitation vanished, replaced by a clear decision as it leapt out into the alley below.

The window of Kenichi's office offered a view into a narrow, shadowy alley. As I edged closer, my instincts sharpened by an innate curiosity, I noticed a flicker of movement—a small tarsier leaping into the open. Swiftly, I pressed a hand against the table, vaulted over, and arrived at the window just in time to witness the scene unfolding below.

There, in the dim recesses of the alley, stood a tall, dark-skinned Indian man. His eyes were fixed upward, filled with anticipation. In his hand, he clutched an object of peculiar design, almost ritualistic in appearance, as if it held secrets of ancient worlds. The tarsier, with an agile grace, descended toward him. The man's face broke into a quiet cheer, his hands raised in a welcoming gesture.

Kenichi's office was perched on the third floor, heightening the drama below. Perhaps overwhelmed by the impending moment or the fear of dropping the tiny creature, the Indian let the strange object slip from his grasp. Everything transpired in a blur—the object clattered to the ground just as the tarsier nestled safely into his hands.

In one swift motion, the Indian pivoted and sprinted toward the alley's exit. "Stop him! Stop the Indian!" I shouted, my voice echoing through the narrow passageway.

Several passers-by were caught in the fray of my cry. Among them, a robust young man attempted to block the Indian's escape. But like an unstoppable force meeting an immovable object, the Indian's momentum sent the young man sprawling to the side.

Kenichi, having rushed to the window beside me, surveyed the scene. Perhaps he hadn't seen as much, but he discerned enough—the Indian was escaping with the tarsier.

With a shout, Kenichi dashed out, and I followed in pursuit, bursting from the office, racing down the stairs, and skirting the building to reach the alley.

Despite our haste, precious minutes slipped away, granting the Indian ample time to vanish into the city's labyrinthine corridors.

As we reached the alley, Kenichi sprinted toward its exit, driven by determination, while I paused to retrieve the fallen object.

From the vantage of the third floor, the object had been inscrutable— a mystery defying identification. Now, even in my hands, it remained enigmatic, a relic from an unfathomable tale. It was a riddle wrapped in an enigma, beckoning for its secrets to be unraveled.

The object, an intricate weave of leaves, lay in my hands—a curious artifact shaped like a crescent, about the size of a comb. Its design was rough, yet meticulously tight, with protrusions that resembled the petioles of leaves. Its purpose remained as elusive as its construction, a puzzle waiting to be solved.

A memory flickered in my mind: the Indian had brought this peculiar object close to his lips. It was not food—certainly not something to be consumed. Yet, it had produced a sound, a haunting call that had compelled the little tarsier to leap into the Indian's embrace, ignoring the familiar coaxing from Kenichi.

Intrigued, I attempted to replicate the sound by blowing through the leaves, but silence greeted my efforts. Just as I was about to try with more force, Kenichi stormed back, his face a mask of frustration. "What are you doing?" he demanded.

I extended the artifact toward Kenichi, my words deliberate and clear. "This is what the Indian left behind. It was the sound from this thing that made the little tarsier defy you and leap into his arms."

The transformation in Kenichi was instant and dramatic. His expression twisted with a mix of disbelief and indignation, as if I had spoken of a personal betrayal. His face flushed with a deep crimson, veins pronounced against his temples. "I don't understand what nonsense you're talking about!" he retorted, his voice sharp with anger.

I shrugged, maintaining my composure. "Face it, Kenichi. The Indian clearly knows how to charm the tarsier better than you do."

In hindsight, perhaps I shouldn't have said it, though every word was true. The truth often stings sharper than a lie.

Before I could even finish, Kenichi's frustration erupted. With a cry that echoed the tarsier's own, he swung his fist, a blur of motion I hadn't anticipated. The punch landed squarely on my left cheek with a resounding "bang," the force of it sending a jolt through me.

Shocked, I retaliated instinctively, landing a blow on his chest with more force than intended. He fell back, his cry this time unmistakably human.

Spectators gathered at the alley's ends, drawn by the commotion.

Nursing our respective bruises, Kenichi and I exchanged sheepish smiles. "I'm sorry," he muttered, his voice tinged with regret. "I was too impulsive."

I nodded, understanding all too well the pride and passion that drove him. "Let's move on. The Indian is the key to unraveling this mystery."

Yet, Kenichi's gaze remained distant. "Yunko is more important," he insisted.

"She is," I agreed, "but we need to find the Indian too. We must divide our efforts."

Reluctantly, Kenichi nodded."Fine. Leave the search for the Indian to me," I offered.

This time,his agreement was quick. "We'll meet daily. If there's news about Yunko, you'll know immediately."

With a firm handshake, we sealed our truce, acknowledging the misunderstanding that had flared between us. As Kenichi set off, I turned my attention back to the object. Solving its mystery was the first step, a thread that might lead us deeper into the enigma that had entwined our fates.

The artifact was an intricate weave of leaves, and upon closer inspection, I counted seven petioles. The leaves were intricately cut during the weaving, each roughly 15 cm long and 10 cm wide, with an oval shape. The edges bore fine serrations, and a layer of fine white hairs covered the surface. The front was a dark, waxy green, while the back was a paler shade, with a grayish-white hue along the veins.

Despite my detailed examination, I couldn't identify the leaves. My botanical knowledge was decent, but these leaves eluded me.

I turned to books, hoping for a match, but found none. It was time to consult an expert.

The head of the university's botany department, a man of considerable repute, was my next stop. His office was a testament to his expertise, lined with cabinets of reference books and specimens. Surrounded by young assistants, he exuded the air of authority.

When I presented my query about the leaves, he responded with a dismissive glance, his eyes barely acknowledging my presence.

"Leaves? What tree do they belong to? Bring it here," he said, with an air of indifference.

I handed him the artifact, and he examined it with a casual flick of the wrist. "This is the leaf of the quinine tree!" he declared confidently.

Politely, I challenged his assessment. "Please, examine it again. The quinine tree's leaves aren't this large, nor do they have such dense white hairs."

Surprised, he reconsidered, listing another tree. Again, I corrected him. This back-and-forth continued until he had exhausted five possibilities, each one incorrect. Finally, he met my gaze, his previous dismissiveness replaced by genuine curiosity.

I suggested, "Perhaps we should consult the reference books."

With renewed focus, the expert and his assistants dove into research. I joined them, leafing through thick volumes and comparing specimens. After three hours, the expert sighed, his confidence waning. "I'm sorry," he admitted, his eyes downcast. "There are too many plant species, and new ones are discovered regularly. This leaf—"

He trailed off, unable to complete the thought. As I prepared to leave, he escorted me to the door, offering a parting insight. "While I can't identify the exact tree, I'm certain it grows in a dense, tropical rainforest—likely with high rainfall."

His words sparked a thought. "Like the jungles of southern India?" I asked.

He pondered for a moment before nodding. "It's possible."

This revelation added a new layer to the mystery, hinting at origins far removed from the urban landscape we inhabited. The trail was leading us deeper into uncharted territory, where both history and nature intertwined in secrets waiting to be uncovered.

Taking a deep breath, I carefully tucked the enigmatic artifact away and left the expert's office. My mind buzzed with connections, each one leading me back to the jungles of southern India.

The leaves, the sound, the Indian—it all began to form a picture. The artifact had fallen from the hands of an Indian who used it to produce a sound that seemed ordinary to us but irresistible to the tarsier, a creature of the southern Indian jungles. Despite its bond with Kenichi, the tarsier couldn't resist the call, leaping into the Indian's arms.

Kenichi had a rare gift for befriending monkeys, yet the sound had a pull that transcended friendship. It was a sound from the tarsier's homeland, a call it couldn't ignore.

The logical conclusion? The leaves, too, likely hailed from the same jungled origins. The Indian, possessing them, must have ties to southern India. But why would he want the tarsier? It wasn't simply for profit. Zoos would pay handsomely for such a rare creature, yet this felt personal, shrouded in mystery rather than commerce.

My first task was clear: find this Indian.

Kenichi and his colleagues had scoured the city with no result. But now, armed with the knowledge of the tarsier, the search felt more focused. An Indian with a white tarsier would be easier to spot.

I began my hunt in the bars of Tokyo, tracing the Indian's last known haunts. Bar after bar, I inquired, my questions met with blank stares and shaking heads. As midnight approached, my hopes dimmed. Until the 151st bar.

The proprietress, kind and perceptive, offered a clue. "Indians rarely visit regular bars. They have their own spot, a small, secluded place. Try there."

Her directions were vague, but I followed them into the city's quieter corners. There, a tipsy Indian revealed the truth: not a bar, but a gathering place for Indians in Japan, more akin to a private club.

Stepping inside, I found myself in a spacious living room. The air was thick with the scent of spices and incense. Indians sat cross-legged on the floor, a serene scene centered around an elder with white hair and beard. He played a multi-stringed instrument, each note weaving an intricate tapestry of sound.

The sound of the polychord was mesmerizing, casting a spell of silence over the room. When I entered, curious eyes turned toward me, but no one spoke. As I settled into a cross-legged position, mirroring the others, the initial surprise faded, replaced by acceptance.

An Indian woman approached, offering me a cup filled with a drink of an unusual flavor. Observing the others sipping it without hesitation, I followed suit, trusting in their silent assurance that it was safe.

The haunting melody of the polychord continued, and soon, the room was bathed in the soft glow of candlelight as four Indian women lit numerous candles, extinguishing the electric lights. The atmosphere transformed, thick with mystery and a touch of the surreal.

The music halted abruptly. The elderly Indian, with his white hair and beard, gently laid down the instrument. "In ancient lands, there are tales as old as time itself," he began, his voice low and compelling, more entrancing than the music had been. The room grew even quieter, drawn into the gravity of his words.

His gaze fell upon me, piercing through the candlelit gloom, compelling me to sit straighter. "A stranger has joined us," he intoned. "I wonder what story the stranger seeks. Here, all we offer are stories."

Caught off guard, I hadn't considered what tale I wanted. Yet, his question provoked an immediate response from me: "I wish to hear the story of the little white tarsier."

The room shifted subtly, the eyes of the attendees now appraising me with a new intensity. Even the old man paused, his fingers idly strumming a discordant note on the strings.

In the lingering silence, he sighed, "I did not expect a stranger to seek such a tale." His gaze deepened, probing. "This story is one of disappointment."

"Please," I urged, "tell it."

He sighed again, his tone flattening into that of a seasoned storyteller distanced from his tale. "White tarsiers are mystical creatures, emissaries of the monkey god from ancient lore. Legends say that anyone who captures a white tarsier will be granted three wishes."

My heart raced; the tale mirrored whispers I had heard before. Yet, the astonishment in the eyes of the gathered Indians suggested this legend was not common knowledge.

I steadied my breath as he continued, "Throughout history, many have sought the white tarsier, lured by the promise of wishes. But only one succeeded—a prince. Granted his wishes, the monkey god first instructed him to 'look at yourself.'"

My curiosity surged, and I interrupted, unable to contain myself. "What does 'look at yourself' mean?"

Though my interruption drew disapproving glances, the old man remained unperturbed. "An excellent question. I tell the stories, but the meaning behind the monkey god's words is beyond me. I only know how the story unfolds."

He paused, awaiting my signal to proceed. With a resigned smile and a gesture, I urged him on.

"The prince agreed to the divine challenge," the old man resumed. "He looked at himself..."

The old man's words landed like a bolt from the blue. He recounted how the supernatural monkey god had commanded the prince to "look at himself," and then revealed that the prince had indeed "seen himself." The gravity of this statement struck me deeply, demanding my full attention.

When I first inquired about the tale of the white tarsier, I sought nothing more than an ancient legend. I hadn't anticipated the depth and richness of the narrative the Indian elder would unveil, nor the profound phrase "saw himself."

To many, such a phrase might seem opaque, a puzzle whose solution eludes even the most diligent seeker. But I understood it perfectly.

Because I had seen myself.

The old man continued, "After the prince saw himself, the supernatural monkey god asked, 'What are your three wishes now?'"

Without a moment's hesitation, the prince responded, "My first wish is to be happy. My second wish is to be happy. My third wish remains—to be happy."

I swallowed hard, my mind reeling. The old man pressed on, "The Monkey God, bound by his promise to grant three wishes, found himself unable to fulfill these simple desires. He sighed and said, 'I'm sorry, I cannot grant any of your wishes.' The prince, desperate, implored, 'Why, Great God? My wishes are simple—just to be happy!' The Monkey God replied, 'Simple? This is the hardest wish of all. Journey the world, find a truly happy person, and I will grant your wishes.'"

The old man's fingers danced over the strings, the room steeped in an almost sacred silence. The challenge was laid bare, the ultimate quest for happiness—a quest that transcended myth and reality, echoing through the ages.

The old man's voice softened, almost as if he were recounting a personal memory. "So the prince traveled, day after day, year after year, his journey spanning the globe. Decades passed, and the young prince became an old man. When he returned to the Monkey God, he was asked, 'Have you found a happy person?' The prince replied, 'No.' The Monkey God sighed, 'There are no happy people in the world. I cannot grant your wish. But now, you may make three new wishes.' Without hesitation, the prince declared, 'I need only one wish!'"

The old man paused, letting the weight of the story settle in the air. His gaze swept across the room, finally landing on me. "Stranger, the story is over."

Stunned, I protested, "It's over? No! What was the prince's final wish?"

The old man sighed, "Stranger, the story ends here. What is the prince's final wish? The storyteller does not reveal it. But if you must know, consider this: If you were the prince, after decades of wandering without meeting a happy person, what would your wish be?"

I was left speechless, the question hanging in the air like a riddle. The answer seemed so obvious, yet so profound.

The prince, and indeed anyone in his position, would have only one wish left to make. But no one dared to speak it aloud.

The old man resumed his instrument, its notes plain yet powerful, resonating with an understated poignancy that was more unsettling than sadness.

Just as the melody began to weave its spell, I interrupted, my voice urgent, "Now, another white tarsier has appeared!"

The room erupted in a mix of anger and intrigue. My words had stirred something in them, shifting their ire to curiosity.

The old man's expression remained unchanged, his tone calm, "Really? Whoever possesses it can have three wishes."

Determined, I pressed on, "Do we make a wish to it?"

The old man shook his head slowly, "The story doesn't mention that. It only says that after the prince found the white tarsier, he sought the magical monkey god."

"Are you suggesting the tarsier leads people to the monkey god?" I probed further.

"I don't know," the old man replied, a storyteller bound by the limits of his tale.

Realizing I would glean no more from him, I took a deep breath and addressed the gathering. "There was indeed such a white tarsier. I brought it to Tokyo and entrusted it to a friend skilled with monkeys, but it was lured away by an Indian using a strange sound."

I retrieved the curious artifact from my pocket and extended it towards the old man. His eyes widened slightly, and he requested, "Let me see it."

I handed it over, and he lifted it to his lips. The sound that emerged was like a harmonica, strange yet not unpleasant. Finished, he returned it to me with a nod. "This is a leaf flute, crafted from leaves. People in southern India can make these simple instruments."

"Does it hold any special significance?" I asked.

The old man examined the leaves with a curious eye, finally shaking his head. "I've never encountered leaves like these before. Beyond that, there's nothing particularly special about them."

I leaned in, lowering my voice. "I'm looking for an Indian gentleman. He looks like—"

My words faltered as I glanced around the room. The realization struck me hard: nearly every Indian man here bore a resemblance to the one I sought. I had never truly seen his face clearly enough to describe him. Tracking him down seemed an insurmountable challenge.

I hesitated, then continued, "This gentleman has a white tarsier. If anyone happens to see him, could you let me know?"

A man of evident status stepped forward, his voice calm yet commanding. "If the white tarsier possesses such supernatural power, whoever holds it will surely seek out the supernatural monkey god as quickly as possible."

His words struck a chord, a revelation dawning. "Where is the supernatural monkey god?" I blurted out.

The gentleman chuckled, a knowing smile on his lips. "Why, in India, of course!"

Laughter rippled through the room, but I was not amused. Instead, frustration gnawed at me. Of course! How had I missed the obvious? The Indian, with his mysterious leaf flute and the white tarsier, would surely have returned to India. Yet here I was, scouring Tokyo's bars. Foolishness.

Despite my misstep, the evening had not been wasted. The old man's tale of the white tarsier—or "Chiwodaka"—had enriched my understanding. Discrepancies existed between the legend he shared and the one documented in books. The old man spoke of the tarsier guiding its possessor to the monkey god, while the texts hinted at crafting a "monkey paw" from its forelimbs.

But one element remained consistent: the white tarsier could grant three wishes, as the legend foretold.

I bowed deeply to the old storyteller, gratitude in my eyes. "Thank you for sharing such an evocative story." With determination rekindled, I left, calling Kenichi to arrange for some assistance, then headed directly to the airport.

At the immigration office, I clung to a sliver of hope. If the Indian had indeed left for India with the tarsier, it would have been documented. This was a crucial lead, one that could unravel the mystery.

I approached the officer managing immigration records, requesting a list of Indians who had departed Japan following the tarsier's disappearance. To my surprise, the list was brief—only nine individuals.

The officer in charge gathered customs officials, guards, and related staff to help piece together the mystery. As I described the Indian man's appearance and mentioned he might have smuggled a small monkey out of the country, a middle-aged customs officer suddenly exclaimed, "Ah!"

"Yes, there was such an Indian man," he recalled, nodding with certainty. "He left on a night flight. There weren't many passengers then, and he didn't have much luggage—just a handbag."

I leaned in, urgency in my voice. "Could the little monkey have been hidden in the handbag?"

The officer looked slightly sheepish. "Well, we focus mainly on metal detection. Plus, drugs and marijuana are costly here in Japan, so no one usually takes them out. So, we didn't notice—"

His hesitation was palpable. I couldn't help but smile ruefully. "Without seeing the monkey, how can you be sure this is the Indian I'm looking for?"

The officer's confidence grew as he recalled the encounter. "I did reach into his bag and felt a ball of fur. When I looked at him, before I could even question it, he said, 'It's a toy, for the child back home. A Japanese toy, so cute!'"

The senior official frowned, a note of reprimand in his voice. "You didn't even take a closer look?"

The customs officer wiped his brow, clearly flustered. "I peeked inside and saw a ball of white fur, looked just like a toy. So I let it go."

My mind raced. The Indian could have anesthetized the white tarsier, passing it off as a toy to smuggle it out.

While I didn't know this Indian's name, it seemed all flights were bound for New Delhi. A bitter smile played on my lips. Finding an Indian in Japan was challenging enough; locating him among 30 million people in New Delhi was near impossible.

However, I had gleaned a critical piece of information: the Indian had indeed returned to India with the white tarsier. The chase wasn't over—it was merely shifting to a new and daunting arena.

CHAPTER 9

Yunko's Hunt for a Hitman

The Indian man was a pivotal figure in this tangled web of mysteries.

First, he had "kidnapped" the elusive white tarsier.

Second, the strange room we had discovered was linked to him, as he had been seen purchasing building materials for it.

Third, he might also be connected to the deaths of Itagaki and the administrator, Takeo. Given these ties, finding him was crucial.

I spoke with conviction, driven by the urgency of my mission.

"Kenichi," I addressed him directly, "I need to go to India to find this Indian man!"

Kenichi's eyes widened in disbelief, mirroring the tarsier's own innocent gaze. He regarded me as if I'd just proposed the most ludicrous idea imaginable, remaining silent.

Admittedly, my plan did sound outrageous: travel to India to locate a single Indian man. With only the vaguest of clues—his gender—I was essentially searching for one man among 800 million.

After a tense pause, Kenichi finally spoke, his voice tinged with skepticism. "How exactly do you plan to find this Indian in India? Aren't you abandoning me with this task?"

I offered a rueful smile. "I believe the root of all these mysteries lies with him. I'm not entirely without leads. I suspect he would first seek out the mythical supernatural monkey god. Someone must know where this legendary figure resides, narrowing down my search considerably."

Kenichi mirrored my grim expression. "I think finding Yunko here might solve our problems."

I couldn't even muster a bitter laugh. "It seems we share the same plight. You seek a Japanese woman in Japan, and I seek an Indian man in India. Our chances are equally bleak."

Kenichi retorted, "At least I know her appearance, name, and details!"

I spread my hands in concession. "True, you have information, but you still haven't found her."

My words struck a nerve, leaving Kenichi visibly frustrated. He glared, swallowing his frustration. Failing to find Yunko had been a significant blow to him.

Despite having all her details and using every available resource, Yunko remained elusive. All he had managed to locate was her suitcase—a tantalizing clue, yet utterly confounding.

Kenichi, consumed by frustration, slammed his fist onto the table, causing everything on it to rattle violently. His voice, raw and primal, echoed through the room. "Where on earth did this woman go?"

The only clue we had was Yunko's suitcase, discovered in a narrow alley—a silent testament to her presence in Tokyo. Yet, her whereabouts remained a mystery.

In that alley, Yunko had been whisked away by a tall, enigmatic man, her suitcase discarded as he ushered her into a taxi. Normally, a woman in such a predicament might scream or struggle, but Yunko had done neither. Her initial resistance had waned, leaving her in silence, her lips pressed tightly together in defiance.

Her sharp jawline accentuated her allure, and even as the man hurriedly focused on their destination, he couldn't resist stealing glances at her. Yunko felt a flicker of worry, marveling at her own calmness in the face of uncertainty. She couldn't explain it, but she felt a strange sense of safety with him.

Yunko's life had been a tumultuous journey, marked by unsatisfying relationships and secret entanglements. She yearned for security, a feeling she inexplicably found with this stranger. Was it his height, his confident demeanor, or the firm grip on her arm that soothed her fears? Whatever it was, her anxiety faded, replaced by a daring curiosity. "Where are you taking me?" she asked, a hint of mischief in her voice.

The man's composure faltered momentarily, embarrassment clouding his features. He hesitated before responding, "A place suitable for conversation."

His words were vague, leaving much to interpretation. Yunko knew such a place could mean many things, yet she remained silent, pondering the possibilities. After a pause, the man instructed the driver to head to an unfamiliar address, distant from their current location.

The silence in the taxi was almost tangible, the man releasing her arm as they drove on. Oddly, Yunko found herself wishing he hadn't. The sense of security she derived from his touch lingered in the air.

As the taxi wove through increasingly desolate streets, Yunko peered out at the shadowy landscape, her thoughts racing. Who was this mysterious figure? He was the one who had phoned her, asking cryptically, "Has the plan changed?" What plan was he referring to?

Yunko shook her head, trying to clear the fog of confusion. Since Itagaki's sudden death, her life had spiraled into chaos. She had been running, unsure of her next move. And now, this stranger—was he a detective, suspecting her involvement in Itagaki's demise? Should she reveal her connection to Itagaki to the authorities?

Her mind swirled with questions, each more pressing than the last, as the car carried her further into the unknown.

In the depths of her mind, Yunko grappled with an unsettling realization. How could there be another woman, a perfect replica of herself, in that study? The woman's face mirrored her own, etched with misery and helplessness. The pain was too profound to dwell upon, yet it was unmistakably etched in her expression.

As these chaotic thoughts swirled, Yunko barely registered the car coming to a stop. Pain flared in her arm as the strange man seized it once more, guiding her out of the vehicle.

They stood at the entrance of another alley, lined with quaint bungalows that seemed relics of a bygone era, so out of place amidst the city's rapid development.

The man led Yunko through the alley, halting before one of the bungalows. Its traditional architecture was matched by the old-fashioned door, which bore a wooden sign displaying the owner's name.

Yunko's eyes fell on the sign: "Iron Smith."

The man produced a key, sliding it into the lock. Despite the door's antiquity, the lock was modern, a stark contrast to its surroundings.

The door swung open, and the man gestured for Yunko to enter. She hesitated on the threshold. Though he had shown no aggression, the seclusion of this place made her wary of what might unfold.

"Is this your house?" she asked, her voice tinged with uncertainty.

The man frowned, nodding in affirmation.

She glanced again at the sign. "Mr.Smith? Why did you bring me here?"

He accepted the name without dispute but bristled at her next words. His glare was fierce, his voice dripping with impatience. "You've been here before. Let's talk inside."

Yunko's heart skipped a beat. His words confused her. She wanted to protest, but his commanding presence silenced her objections. Reluctantly, she stepped inside, and Iron Smith followed, closing the door behind them.

Inside the gate lay a traditional garden, its serene gravel path leading across a wooden bridge over a koi-filled pond, guiding them toward a modest building.

The setting was quintessentially Japanese, reminiscent of gardens Yunko had visited before. Yet, if she had been here previously, surely she would remember Mr.Smith. But meeting him at the station felt like their initial encounter.

Was it truly their first meeting? Doubt crept into Yunko's mind. Why had she followed this stranger so willingly, without any fear, despite his peculiar behavior?

Uncertainty gnawed at her, leaving her unable to trust her own instincts.

As they approached the building, Iron strode ahead, his pace quickening. The structure appeared unremarkable at first glance, but Yunko noted an unusual feature: a small iron box affixed to the closed sliding door. Iron unlocked it with a key, revealing an array of buttons inside. Some bore numbers, while others were distinguished by color.

Puzzled, Yunko watched as Iron deftly pressed a sequence of buttons with practiced ease. She had no idea what they controlled.

After pressing the buttons about ten times, Iron closed the box. Moments later, the sliding door glided open on its own. He entered first, and Yunko's curiosity propelled her to follow. Iron flicked on the lights, revealing a comfortably furnished interior. Yet, Yunko's unease grew as the sliding door shut automatically behind them.

Iron seemed to be making a conscious effort to maintain his composure. With a courteous gesture, he invited her to sit. "Please, make yourself comfortable."

Yunko obliged, settling into a traditional seated position by the low table, feeling slightly vulnerable with Iron towering above her. She looked up, meeting his intense gaze.

"Alright," Iron began, his voice steady but with an undercurrent of tension. "Now that it's just us, we can speak freely just like last time."

Yunko was taken aback, momentarily at a loss for words. "Just like last time"? Had she crossed paths with Iron here before?

The notion seemed absurd. Her mind raced, scrutinizing her surroundings. Nothing felt familiar.

But when Yunko met Iron's piercing eyes again, her confidence wavered. "Have I met you before? Here?" she inquired, her voice tinged with uncertainty.

Her question hung in the air, and Iron's demeanor shifted from controlled to agitated. He lowered himself onto the cushion across from her, pointing a finger accusingly before withdrawing it, realizing the rudeness of the gesture. His voice, however, was laced with frustration. "What are you planning? To betray me? Report to the police?"

A wave of confusion washed over Yunko, but Iron's words sparked a moment of clarity. She chuckled softly, grasping at a plausible explanation: Iron had mistaken her for someone else.

"Mr. Smith, you must have me confused with another person," she suggested, leaning forward slightly.

For a moment, Iron's resolve faltered, but his gaze grew even more scrutinizing. "Miss Suzuki Yunko," he said, his tone icy.

Instinctively, Yunko replied, "Yes."

Iron leaned in, his words cutting. "A singer who never quite made it, and the secret mistress of Itagaki Ichiro?"

Yunko's lips parted, yet no words came. Iron continued, reciting her address and phone number with precision. Yunko's eyes widened in shock.

"Am I mistaken?" Iron pressed, his expression unyielding.

Yunko struggled to respond. "I—I am indeed Suzuki Yunko, but perhaps—perhaps there's someone similar to me—"

She hesitated, unable to voice the implausible idea of an exact double. It defied logic.

Iron scoffed, leaning back. "And you don't remember who I am, do you?"

His words hung heavy in the room, leaving Yunko grappling with the surreal situation unraveling before her.

Iron's words dripped with irony, yet Yunko clung to them as if they were a lifeline. "Yes! Yes! I've truly never seen you before!" she insisted, her voice trembling with desperation.

Her declaration seemed to ignite a fuse within Iron. With an explosive "bang," his fist collided with the low table, sending a shockwave of fear through Yunko, who instinctively retreated.

"Shall I introduce myself, then?" Iron's voice was a cold, cutting whisper.

Yunko swallowed hard, nodding. "Okay! Okay!"

Lowering his voice to a conspiratorial murmur, Iron said, "I am a first-class professional killer."

Yunko's heart raced, fear clawing at her chest. But Iron's next revelation was a dagger to her soul, nearly halting her heart.

"One month ago, one night," he continued, his voice steady and low, "you came to me and asked me to kill a man named Itagaki Ichiro."

For a full minute, Yunko stood frozen, her mind struggling to process his words. Then she erupted, waving her hands frantically, her voice pleading. "Sir, don't talk nonsense! There is no such thing!"

Her denials came in a torrent, but Iron's gaze remained icy. He waited patiently, like a predator stalking its prey, until her frantic movements slowed. "It doesn't matter," he said calmly. "I executed it cleanly; no one knows it was me. However, you're different. Normally, clients never meet me, nor do they know where I live. But you, we've met, and you know too much. In my line of work, I must be cautious."

As Iron spoke, Yunko's anxiety mounted, her voice breaking into sobs. "Sir, I don't understand what you're talking about!"

Iron inhaled deeply, his gaze never wavering. "There's something I don't understand either. How do you know so much about me?"

Now Yunko was truly crying. "I don't know anything! You're a stranger to me—I know nothing about you!"

Anger and a mocking tone tinged Iron's voice. "If, when you left Shizuoka for Tokyo, you had chosen acting over singing, you'd be an international star by now!"

Tears streamed down Yunko's face as terror gripped her, like a dark abyss swallowing her whole. Between sobs, she repeated the same words, "I really don't know what you're talking about!"

Suddenly, Iron shouted, halting her cries. With a rough grip, he seized her arm and yanked her off her seat. "You may not have expected it, but last time, because you appeared so abruptly, I had to protect myself and record all your actions!"

Yunko, still bewildered, saw only Iron's fierce visage through her tear-filled eyes.

Then, the chilling reality of "recorded everything" dawned on her. It meant every moment was captured on videotape.

Iron dragged her into a dimly lit basement, where she confronted the truth—everything was recorded, every moment laid bare before her eyes.

After Yunko finished watching the "recorded" footage, she sank into a chair, feeling both weightless and disoriented, as if she were floating on clouds. Her hands clutched the armrests tightly, her expression one of fear, as if she might tumble from her precarious perch at any moment.

Iron's piercing gaze bore into her, silently demanding an explanation.

For a long time, Yunko could only repeat the same phrase, her voice a whisper filled with disbelief: "That's not me, that's her! I've seen her too, alone and crying in an empty room!"

But what did Yunko truly witness in those recordings?

The tape whirred to life, feeding images to the television projector until a series of distorted lines on the screen resolved into a coherent picture. It was the entrance to Iron's residence. Yunko recognized the wooden sign beside the door, the same one that revealed the tall, enigmatic man's identity as "Iron Smith." Yet, there she was on screen, standing at that very door, pressing the doorbell repeatedly.

(This couldn't be—she hadn't rung the doorbell earlier. Iron himself had approached, opening the iron box to unlock the door! The realization hit Yunko like a shockwave.)

On the screen, the version of Yunko ringing the bell looked anxious, her features etched with profound sadness, though hatred simmered beneath the surface.

The door swung open, and Yunko hurried inside. (Her shock deepened. She had been here before. Wasn't it the gravel path beyond that door?)

The gravel path didn't appear in the recording. Instead, after a flurry of static, the scene cut to the interior hall. Yunko sat across from Iron.

Iron looked wary and skeptical, yet Yunko's gaze was unwavering, intense. He spoke first, his voice cautious: "Excuse me, young lady, who are you—"

"My name is Suzuki Yunko!" the recorded Yunko declared. (The shock reverberated through her once more. Typically, when one hears a recording of their own voice, it sounds foreign because the sound waves bypass the inner ear's vibrations, unlike when you hear the external world. Yet, as a professional singer accustomed to recording and replaying her own voice, Yunko knew this voice intimately.)

(It was unmistakably her own voice. Yunko's body trembled with the revelation, unable to comprehend the unfolding enigma.)

The recording continued to play, unraveling a scene that seemed beyond belief. Iron, eyebrows slightly raised, asked, "May I inquire what business you have with me? I don't believe we've met—"

But Yunko on the screen cut him off sharply. "I know you. You operate under dozens of aliases. Here in Tokyo, you go by Iron Smith ."

A flicker of discomfort passed over Iron's features, his face twitching with tension. Yet Yunko pressed on, her voice steady and unyielding. "You have a lucrative income, untaxed. You're a first-class professional killer."

Iron's discomfort deepened, his expression darkening. Despite his imposing stature, he seemed cornered, while Yunko, though small and seemingly fragile, held the upper hand.

Struggling to regain his footing, Iron forced a smile, though it failed to mask his unease. "Miss, I have no idea what you're talking about."

In a surprising twist, Yunko laughed softly, motioning for him to come closer. Reluctantly, Iron leaned forward. Yunko mirrored his movement, whispering something in his ear.

Whatever she said sent a visible tremor through Iron. He clutched the corner of the low table, as if the words had knocked him off balance.

Watching the scene unfold, the real Yunko couldn't suppress a bitter smile. What could she have possibly said to rattle him so profoundly? The whispered words were too quiet to be captured on tape. Yet she was certain she had never spoken to him, and the woman confronting Iron was not her.

The enigma deepened, leaving Yunko to grapple with the surreal mystery of her doppelgänger and the chilling encounter captured on film.

(That woman is not me, it's her! The memory of the woman hiding in the empty room suddenly flooded back to Yunko. It's her, it must be her! Yunko's mind screamed in silent insistence: It's her!)

On the screen, the events continued to unfold with relentless momentum. Iron, visibly shaken, sprang to his feet, his face twitching with agitation as he paced back and forth. Yunko regarded him with a mixture of pity and disdain. After a few tense moments, Iron finally demanded, "How did you come to know these things?"

"Someone told me," Yunko replied, her voice steady.

Iron reacted as if scalded by a hot iron, his voice rising in a sudden shout: "Who? Who told you?"

"Of course someone," Yunko retorted with a cryptic smile.

Iron's expression shifted from anger to a volatile mix of emotions, as he pointed at Yunko, his words stumbling over themselves. "You—what do you want—what?"

Yunko's face twisted with hatred as she spat out her demand. "It's simple. I want you to kill someone."

Iron fixed his gaze on her, his eyes narrowing.

"The man is Itagaki Ichiro," Yunko continued, her voice dripping with venom. "I'm his mistress. He professes love, but only spends a few hours with me before returning to his wife. I want him dead. He toys with me, flaunting his wealth. I want him dead!"

Iron's demeanor shifted to icy calm as he scrutinized Yunko with cold detachment.

(Yunko, watching this, felt a jolt of shock.)

(I really hate him so much! Yunko thought, but quickly rejected the idea. She dared not harbor such hatred openly, because Itagaki supported her financially. Even if she loathed him, she would bury that hatred deep within, never to speak of it. So why did she voice it here? The one who wanted Itagaki dead wasn't her—it was the woman crying in the empty room!)

"If I kill this man named Itagaki—" Iron began, letting the implication hang in the air.

"Then your secret will remain safe," Yunko interjected, her tone hard as steel.

Iron's voice dropped to a frigid whisper. "In fact, I don't need to kill anyone, as long as—"

With a deliberate motion, Iron mimicked pulling a trigger, aiming an imaginary gun at Yunko.

His meaning was unmistakable. The simplest way to ensure his secret stayed hidden was to eliminate Yunko herself.

(Yunko, witnessing this revelation, felt a chill of fear. What should she do? He was right. Threatening a professional killer was not just foolish—it was a death sentence.)

However, the Yunko on the screen remained composed, her lips curling into a confident sneer. "You must know," she said calmly, "that since I dared to approach you, I've entrusted everything I know to someone reliable. If anything happens to me, these secrets will be exposed."

Iron's expression grew darker, his face taut with frustration. Yunko pressed on, "How about it? It's a fair deal, isn't it?"

Running a hand over his chin, Iron tried a different angle. "I think you might just be acting on impulse. The man you want to kill is your lover. Sure, he used his wealth to control you, but that's a common transaction in big cities. No one forced you into it. Why do you want him dead?"

(I don't want to kill him—Yunko's mind screamed in protest. The desire to kill Itagaki wasn't hers; it belonged to another woman, the one hidden away in that study, the one who cried alone!)

But the narrative unfolding on the screen diverged sharply from Yunko's internal turmoil.

The screen's Yunko wore a sinister expression. "Of course, I have another reason to want him dead."

Iron rubbed his hands together, intrigued. "Alright, tell me. Before I take someone's life, I like to know the reasons behind their death."

Fixing Iron with a steady gaze, Yunko opened her handbag, retrieving a pistol and placing it on the low table between them. "Take a look at this gun," she said.

(The real Yunko, watching this, felt a shock of disbelief. A pistol? She had never owned one, never even touched such a deadly object. It wasn't her—it was that other woman!)

The tape continued its relentless spin, the events of that day playing out on the screen for her to see.

Iron paused, then picked up the pistol with a practiced ease, as if it were as familiar to him as dough to a baker.

CHAPTER 10

A Custom Pistol's Deadly Secret

Iron deftly unloaded the magazine, revealing two bullets nestled inside. His eyes narrowed as he scrutinized the gun more closely, his expression suddenly shifting to one of incredulity. With swift precision, he dismantled the firearm into three parts, then leveled a bewildered gaze at Yunko. "This gun—where did you get it?"

Ignoring his question, Yunko pressed on. "As a professional killer, you must have an intimate understanding of various weapons. So, what is this pistol, and what makes it special?"

Iron inhaled sharply, his mind racing. "I've only encountered a gun like this once before. This is the second time—" He paused, locking eyes with Yunko. "You shouldn't have a gun like this."

Yunko met his gaze unflinchingly. "No matter how I acquired it, tell me what's unique about it."

Iron sighed, lifting the magazine in his hand. "Alright. There are two bullets in the magazine, and this gun can only fire two at once. It looks ordinary, indistinguishable to an untrained eye. But it's crafted with advanced technology. When you pull the trigger, both bullets fire simultaneously—one forward, one backward from the handle."

Yunko remained composed, gesturing for Iron to reassemble the gun. In a mere three seconds, he complied. Yunko took the pistol, pressing it to her forehead, mimicking the act of firing. "Mr. Iron, if I pull the trigger like this, intending to shoot someone else in the head, what happens?"

Iron chuckled dryly. "As I've explained, two bullets discharge simultaneously in opposite directions. You'd hit your target, but you'd also shoot yourself in the head."

Yunko placed the gun back on the table, her demeanor serene.

"Why ask?" Iron probed. "No one would use it that way; they'd surely die."

Yunko lowered her head, her lashes fluttering with the quick blinks of her eyes. Her voice was steady. "Someone gave me this gun, instructing me to kill with it, insisting I hold it just so, to ensure a swift, painless death for the target."

Iron uttered an incredulous "oh," confusion deepening. "This person?"

Before he could finish, Yunko continued. "This person promised that once I killed, he would be free to marry me, and we could live openly and happily together."

Iron's astonishment grew. "This person—"

Yunko's eyes hardened. "This person is Itagaki Ichiro. And he wants me to kill his wife, Sadagumi."

Iron swallowed hard, even his seasoned composure rattled by the revelation. "So Itagaki's plan was not just to eliminate his wife, but also you!"

Yunko lifted her head, her expression wooden and sorrowful. "I think so. He gave me the gun and taught me how to shoot. He also told me that his wife, Sadagumi, would be attending a women's gathering in two days. There would be a large crowd outside an auditorium. If I approached her, shot her, and fled immediately, no one would catch me. Moreover, there was no connection between Sadagumi and me. No one would suspect I was the murderer."

Iron groaned, "And he promised you that after Sadagumi's death, you'd take her place?"

Yunko bit her lower lip and nodded.

Iron pressed further, "That's the position any mistress would desire. Why didn't you go through with it?"

(Yunko watched in silence, surprisingly detached, as if engrossed in a captivating TV drama. The unfolding events felt distant, disconnected from her reality.)

(Deep down, she was convinced that the woman on the screen wasn't her, but someone else entirely. Perhaps Itagaki had enlisted that woman for such a twisted task. Who could say what their relationship entailed?)

(A strange sensation washed over Yunko as she pondered this. If the woman wasn't her, then who was she? Why did she feel an unsettling sense of recognition when she first saw her?)

On screen, Yunko's lips twitched slightly. "I was shocked, too terrified to even pick up the gun. But Itagaki kept persuading me. Once Sadagumi was gone, I could have everything. From a struggling singer from a poor background, I could become the wife of a prosperous businessman. He kept professing his love, lamenting the pain of our clandestine affair. It was unbearable for both of us, he claimed. There was no other solution; he couldn't divorce Sadagumi. He assured me that if I followed his plan, Sadagumi would die painlessly."

Iron murmured, "And you too, I suppose, would feel no pain."

Yunko's smile was bitter. "I was swayed by his words, believing that erasing Sadagumi would grant me everything. So I took the gun and promised to follow his plan. Itagaki assured me that the police would see it as the act of a deranged woman, killing without reason. With a slight change in appearance, no one would ever find me."

Iron merely grunted in acknowledgment. Yunko continued, "The moment I took the pistol, I resolved to act—"

"But you didn't," Iron interrupted. "Sadagumi is still alive, and so are you."

"Yes," Yunko admitted, "because an Indian man visited me an hour before the planned act and told me something."

(Yunko, watching this, blurted out in frustration, "Damn it!")

(An Indian!)

(As far as Yunko could recall, she had encountered Indians no more than three times in her life, and each instance was marked by nothing more than a passing curiosity. She had never engaged in any meaningful interaction with them. Indians!)

On the screen, Iron echoed her surprise: "Indians? What do they have to do with this?"

Yunko replied, "I don't know. That day, I was preparing for the event an hour before Sadagumi was to attend. I donned a wig, changed my makeup, wore sunglasses, and a collared shirt. I placed the pistol in my handbag. As I stepped out, there he was—the Indian, standing right at my door, poised to knock."

Iron asked, "Had you seen him before?"

"No!" Yunko exclaimed. "When he saw me, he asked, 'Miss Suzuki Yunko?' I nodded, shocked. Then he said, 'Take out the pistol from your handbag. I'll tell you what's special about it.' My strength evaporated at that moment. I could barely stand. I collapsed to the side, and the Indian caught me. I was drenched in sweat, paralyzed by fear. He helped me sit, then went to close the door. All I could do was stare at him, wide-eyed."

Iron snorted, "Naturally, any criminal reacts this way when caught."

Ignoring Iron's comment, Yunko continued, almost as if speaking to herself.

"After closing the door, he reached out to me. I had no will to resist, so I handed him the gun wrapped in a handkerchief. He took it apart with the same ease you did," she said, gesturing toward Iron. "He explained its features, saying, 'Pull the trigger and both Sadagumi and you will die.' I was beyond shocked, repeating, 'Why would Itagaki want to kill me? Why?'"

Iron raised an eyebrow. "This Itagaki must have another mistress, perhaps more appealing than you. He wants you to eliminate his wife, thus ridding himself of both complications."

Yunko screamed, "Impossible! Itagaki only has me as his mistress. He's no longer young. Even if his health is decent, he struggles to keep up with me, let alone manage a second mistress. He simply wants Sadagumi gone but fears I would cling to him, preventing him from finding someone better. So he plans to eliminate me, too!"

Iron shook his head, unconvinced. "Seems my hypothesis stands."

"No, it's different!" Yunko's voice was sharp, almost shrill. "At least I know there is no second woman!"

Iron's voice dropped, yet its clarity pierced the tension. "Is that so? Is this all about self-esteem?"

(Yunko stared at the screen, her eyes wide with disbelief. The events unfolding were too absurd to be true. How could she be involved in such madness? What was the woman on the screen trying to achieve?)

On the screen, Yunko bore a sad expression, her eyes distant as if lost in thought. She seemed unaffected by Iron's words, murmuring softly, "Perhaps it's self-esteem. Even if I'm being used, I must hold onto some sense of dignity, right?"

Iron sighed, a flicker of sympathy passing over his face. "And the Indian?"

Yunko took a deep breath. "The Indian seemed to understand my plight. He asked me, 'Miss Yunko, if Itagaki wants to kill you, what will you do?' Anger boiled over, and I blurted out, 'I'll kill him first!'"

She continued, "The Indian shrugged, saying, 'You don't have the means to kill anyone yourself, but I know a professional killer. He operates mainly in Tokyo, and he goes by the name Iron.'"

As she spoke, she glanced at Iron, whose complexion darkened at the mention of his name. Yunko pressed on, "I asked how I could find this killer. The Indian gave me your address, along with some of your secrets—the ones I whispered to you earlier. They are indeed your secrets, aren't they?"

Iron's expression grew more severe. Yunko recounted, "After divulging that information, the Indian simply left through the door. That's how I knew where to find you."

Her narrative concluded, she met Iron's gaze. Silence stretched between them until Iron finally spoke. "Alright, I'll kill Itagaki Ichiro for you."

His acceptance was delivered with a chilling calmness, as if it were a mundane task. Yunko rose and bowed deeply, expressing her gratitude. "Thank you! You've helped me so much."

Iron's face twisted with a bitter expression, as though words failed him. Yunko added, "Since you've agreed, Mr. Smith, I should take my leave."

With that, she turned and exited. Iron did not escort her out; instead, he watched her retreating figure.

The tape ended there. Iron moved to switch off the projector, then turned his attention to the real Yunko. Her voice broke the silence, urgent and insistent: "That's not me, it's her! I've seen her too, crying alone in an empty room!"

Iron's gaze hardened, and he strode over, seizing Yunko's arm with a grip that made her wince. He shook her slightly, his voice a command. "Say it again!"

Yunko repeated her claim, "That's not me, it's her, I've seen her too, alone in an empty room crying!"

For the next thirty minutes, Iron employed both threats and persuasion, trying to extract the truth. Yunko recounted the situation when she encountered "that woman," yet she maintained, "That's not me."

Eventually, Iron, exasperated, resorted to drinking heavily from a bottle of wine. The liquid dribbled down his chin, but he paid it no mind. He approached Yunko, who sat meekly on the sofa, and leaned over her, his arms bracing the armrests. His physical presence was imposing, and Yunko, feeling dwarfed, could only meet his gaze with a mix of fear and defiance.

Iron gave a weary smile, his voice low. "Ms. Yunko, as a professional killer, I live with constant vigilance. I can't afford for anyone to know my secrets."

Yunko replied with a sense of helplessness, "I don't know any of your secrets. That woman isn't me; it's her!"

Iron, having listened to Yunko's account of her encounter with "that woman," managed a strained smile. "I hope you can tell that to everyone, but the Indian—he knew my secret. I need to find him. I can't have anyone knowing my secrets, and I need to understand how he discovered them."

Yunko was on the verge of tears. "I haven't seen any Indian at all!"

Iron's thick eyebrows furrowed, but Yunko sighed in frustration. "You don't believe a word I say, do you?"

Iron groaned, straightening his posture. "Alright, you claim to have seen a woman who looks exactly like you. Take me to her, then!"

Yunko hesitated, swallowing nervously. "The police in Tokyo are searching for me. That place... it's where I dated with Itagaki. If you go—"

Iron interrupted, "Don't worry about me. I've gone through great lengths to find you. Even if the police see me, they won't recognize who I am. I must meet this woman you mentioned!"

With a resigned sigh, Yunko agreed. "Fine, I'll take you there. But when I saw her that night, I was terrified and fled. I can't be sure she's still there."

Iron paced, silent and contemplative.

"The police have known about that place for a while," Yunko added, "Maybe, maybe—"

Iron's tone turned sharp and commanding. "Unless you've been lying this whole time, take me there immediately!"

Yunko stood up, her compliance evident. Iron seized her arm again, guiding her back to the hall. Yunko picked up her handbag and followed Iron outside. They got into his car, heading towards the location where Yunko had once seen the mysterious woman and had her secret rendezvous with Itagaki.

Meanwhile, I had informed Kenichi about my decision to go to India to track down the Indian, but Kenichi was against me pursuing such a seemingly hopeless endeavor.

However, I believed the Indian held the key to unraveling all these strange occurrences. Without finding him, none of the mysteries could be solved.

This led to a minor disagreement between Kenichi and me.

Around 7 PM that evening, I boarded an Indian Airlines flight bound for India.

I never anticipated that two hours into the flight, soaring at nearly 10,000 meters, I would hear Kenichi's voice again.

At that moment, I was reclining comfortably in my seat, eyes closed, seeking rest. A stewardess with a scarlet mark on her forehead approached me, her voice gentle. "Sorry to disturb you."

Opening my eyes, I was uncertain of the situation. Beside her stood an experienced-looking crew member in uniform.

The stewardess inquired, "Mr. Ash Morris?"

I nodded, acknowledging the situation. The man in uniform gestured for the stewardess to leave and introduced himself as the co-pilot. Realizing something significant was happening, I stood up, and he motioned for me to follow him towards the cockpit.

"I'm the co-pilot," he explained.

"Oh," I replied, "What's the issue?"

"It's not an accident," the co-pilot assured me. "A police officer from the Tokyo police, Mr. Kenichi, wants to have an emergency call with you. We are obliged to let you talk to him, but we hope to keep the call brief."

Surprise and a tinge of irritation coursed through me. Kenichi had a knack for pulling me back at critical moments, and now, it seemed urgent enough to warrant using the plane's radio system. What could possibly have happened this time?

I agreed, following the co-pilot into the cockpit. A communicator handed me a headset, and I immediately inquired, "Kenichi, what's going on?"

Kenichi's voice crackled through, brimming with excitement. "The murderer of Itagaki Ichiro has been found!"

I was taken aback. "Really? Who is it? Why did he kill Itagaki?"

Kenichi's tone shifted to one of frustration. "Unfortunately, he's dead. Can you come back as soon as possible? There are some strange elements, and I'm at a loss."

My curiosity piqued, I retorted, "How can I come back? The plane's already out of Japanese airspace. You can't just turn it around. Unless I have a grenade, which I don't!"

Speaking in Japanese, I hadn't anticipated the radio communicator understanding, but his nervous expression prompted me to lighten the mood with a playful face.

Kenichi continued, "The plane will stop in Hong Kong. You can disembark there and catch a flight back to Tokyo immediately."

I couldn't help but smile wryly at the thought of my constant back-and-forth, like a soldier exiled to the front lines.

"Is it worth it?" I asked.

"It must be," Kenichi insisted. "Otherwise, you can ignore me forever. Also, Yunko has been found!"

I swallowed hard. "Is she dead too?"

"No," Kenichi replied, "but she's told a story no one would believe. She's currently detained by the police and undergoing psychiatric evaluation."

"Maybe she was overstimulated," I suggested, pondering the bizarre twists of the case.

Kenichi's voice charged with an urgency that demanded attention. "Perhaps, but there are two aspects of her strange tale that will undoubtedly captivate you. First, she spoke of an Indian. Second, within that peculiar room, she claimed to have seen a woman—a mirror image of herself—sobbing with heart-wrenching despair."

I felt my breath catch. "She saw herself?"

Kenichi's eyes gleamed with a knowing mirth. "Indeed. Now, tell me, would such a revelation prompt you to leap onto the next flight?"

I cursed him, "You're a scoundrel. You know I'll definitely come!"

His laughter rang out, a sound both infectious and unsettling. As it echoed in the small space, I returned the phone to its cradle and gave communicator a firm pat on the shoulder, a silent gesture of thanks. The operator watched me with wide eyes, still shaken, as I stifled the urge to lighten the moment with humor. Instead, I opted for a quiet exit from the cockpit.

The ensuing hours blurred into a repetitive cycle of landings, takeoffs, and endless waiting. By the time I touched down in Tokyo, the city was still cloaked in night.

Kenichi awaited my arrival at the airport. Without delay, I slipped into his car, and we sped toward our destination. Yet, nothing could have prepared me for where Kenichi would lead me.

Our journey ended at a place I had never imagined—a morgue.

The mortuary, a repository for the silent, exuded an eerie chill, a tangible reminder of humanity's eternal quest to unravel the enigma of life and death.

Kenichi, clearly no stranger to these somber halls, exchanged a few words with the staff before guiding me to the cold storage room. With practiced ease, he opened a long iron drawer and drew back the white shroud.

Beneath the cloth lay a man—striking in his handsomeness, with features that spoke of a vibrant individuality—perhaps thirty-five or thirty-six years old.

The lifeless eyes of the man stared blankly into the void, his skin darkened by death and touched by a layer of ice. With a deliberate motion, Kenichi wiped the frost from his face. "The hotel staff identified him as the man who rented the room on the day Itagaki met his end."

I furrowed my brow, considering. "A professional killer, perhaps?"

Kenichi nodded. "Indeed, a consummate professional, skilled in the art of concealment. We've got his body, but his past remains an enigma. All we have is a name—Iron Smith."

Pulling back the cloth a bit more, I glimpsed the bullet-riddled chest, the wounds dark and ominous against his skin. Hastily, I covered him up again. "How did Iron meet his fate? It seems he faced a barrage of bullets."

Kenichi confirmed, "Yes, four officers fired upon him, striking him eight times."

"A shootout? Where did it occur?" I pressed.

"It happened at the rendezvous where Itagaki and Yunko met clandestinely," Kenichi explained.

He outlined three critical locations in this tangled web: Yunko's residence, Itagaki's abode, and, most pivotally, the trysting place.

Kenichi deployed a team of skilled operatives to surveil these sites. Undercover agents, working in shifts, maintained a round-the-clock vigil. At the trysting place, one posed as a lobby administrator, two as cleaners stationed at the stairwell, while another, disguised as an elevator repairman, monitored the building's movements.

Kenichi elaborated on this strategy, suggesting that the architect of the peculiar room—the Indian—might return. He believed that lying in wait might prove more fruitful than pursuing this shadowy figure to India. Kenichi withheld further details. Instead, he suggested, "You'll gain more insight from the firsthand accounts of my four agents. They're waiting at my office."

With no alternative, I joined him for the drive back to his office.

The four agents awaited us there. Rather than delve into their individual appearances, I'll refer to them simply as Agents A, B, C, and D. Together, they recounted the events that had unfolded, weaving a narrative as compelling as any tale of intrigue and danger.

CHAPTER 11

The Demise and Secrets of a Hitman

Agent A, stationed in the lobby under the guise of a building manager, recounted his long, uneventful nights from 7 PM to 7 AM, accompanied only by an elderly and dull night shift manager. Kenichi teased him about his boredom, suggesting he might prefer the company of Kurihara Komaki. Embarrassed, Agent A stumbled over his words, but I interjected, injecting some humor, "The wait must have been tedious, but it finally bore fruit, didn't it?"

Revitalized by this, Agent A nodded eagerly, "Yes, it did. That night—"

With a cautious glance towards Kenichi, he continued, "I was starting to drift off when the glass doors swung open, and in walked a man and a woman. Despite her disguise of dark glasses and an upturned collar, I recognized her instantly as Suzuki Yunko, the one we've been searching for!"

Agent A's excitement was palpable. "I nearly sprang up, but caught myself just in time to avoid alerting them. As soon as they entered the elevator, I radioed my colleagues upstairs."

He gestured to Agents B and C, who rose and saluted. Agent B admitted, "At first, we thought it was a prank to break the monotony. But seeing the elevator ascend, we sprung into action, taking a strategic position on the stairwell to observe who emerged."

Agent C picked up the tale, "Our nerves were taut. We dared not act immediately, fearing they'd escape. Yunko used a key to open a door, while the man, vigilant and wary, scanned their surroundings. We held our breath, lest he detect us."

Kenichi interjected with impatience, "Enough with the embellishments. Just stick to the facts!"

Agent C grimaced but complied. "When Yunko entered, the man followed. I alerted my colleagues, and we converged on their location."

Agent D continued, "Responding to the call, I arrived as they disappeared inside. We quickly decided to act. I rang the doorbell, and a tense voice asked, 'Who is it?'"

(To streamline the narrative and enhance clarity, the agents' accounts will be synthesized and recorded here.)

Agent D's quick thinking led him to respond to Iron's suspicious inquiry with, "It's the building manager. I noticed you just arrived and need to inform you of something important."

Iron's voice, tense and dismissive, echoed from within. "I'm busy now. Come back tomorrow!"

The four agents exchanged knowing glances. "Come back tomorrow" was not an option. With Yunko cornered in the apartment, they couldn't let this opportunity slip away. Their eyes communicated a unanimous decision: it was time for action.

Agents A and B took a step back as Agents C and D prepared to force entry. Just as they were about to shoulder the door, a piercing scream erupted from inside. It was Yunko, her voice carrying a chilling note of desperation. "Look, it's her, not me!"

Despite the unsettling cry, C and D charged the door, their shoulders crashing against it with a thunderous boom. The door quivered but held firm. From inside, Iron's voice rose again, this time laced with palpable fear. "Who are you? Who are you?"

Unfazed, Agents C and D regrouped for a second attempt. This time, their combined force was enough to burst the door wide open, sending them stumbling into the room. As they regained their footing, Agents A and B readied themselves to follow.

But before they could move, the sharp crack of gunfire split the air. Two shots rang out in quick succession, and both A and B dropped to the ground, their mission abruptly halted by the deadly sound.

The scene unfolded with a harrowing intensity as Agents A and B hit the floor, their eyes locking onto Iron, who stood like a man possessed, gripping a powerful military pistol. His wild demeanor and the tight grip on the bolt signaled an unwavering intent to continue his assault.

In the chaos, there was no time to assess the immediate aftermath of the initial gunshots. Instincts kicked in, and both agents, while rolling to evade further fire, drew their weapons. Shots were exchanged in a flurry of smoke and sound, the echo of gunfire ricocheting off the walls.

Agent A felt the cold bite of a bullet graze his shoulder, quickly followed by a searing heat. His strength waned, but not before he managed to squeeze off four successive shots, emptying his pistol into the fray.

Agent B, more fortunate in his positioning, found cover behind a sofa. From this vantage point, he returned fire with precision, aiming to subdue the threat.

Agents C and D, having anticipated the imminent danger, had already hit the ground as they breached the door. Their quick reflexes spared them from Iron's first volley, his bullets barely missing their mark. The near miss left their skin tingling with the heat of close proximity, a stark reminder of the deadly stakes at play.

Amidst the chaos, the agents' coordinated response was both instinctive and calculated. Their collective barrage of 21 bullets found their mark, riddling Iron with a barrage that left him staggering.

Described with striking consistency by all four agents, the aftermath was undeniable.

Iron, now mortally wounded, turned—whether by choice or the sheer force of impact was unclear—and faced the open door of the study.

There stood Suzuki Yunko, miraculously untouched in the crossfire. The storm of over 20 bullets had somehow spared her, a fact that defied the odds and seemed almost providential. Yet, in the heat of the moment, the agents' focus remained solely on Iron.

As the echoes of gunfire faded, Iron's body betrayed him. Blood flowed freely from his wounds, the steady drip onto the floor a grim metronome in the sudden silence. The agents watched, transfixed, as life ebbed from the man who had been the center of their deadly encounter.

Iron's final moments were as enigmatic as they were haunting. After taking a faltering step towards the study, his body succumbed to its mortal wounds, yet not before he uttered a question that perplexed everyone present: "Who are you?" His voice, barely more than a whisper, carried a weight of bewilderment as his life flickered out.

The four agents recounted these tense moments with a clarity that painted a vivid picture of chaos and confusion. They had expected resistance from a cornered killer like Iron, but his dying words hinted at a mystery deeper than they had anticipated.

As I absorbed their accounts, the question loomed large: Why had Iron asked "Who are you?" not once, but twice? It was a question that suggested the presence of an unknown figure, someone unseen by the agents or anyone else in the room.

I directed my inquiry towards the agents, "Who was in the study?"

Their responses were tinged with uncertainty and shared glances. Agent A stated, "No one, there was no one in the study. Just us, the deceased, and Yunko."

"Then who was Iron addressing?" I pressed, a frown creasing my brow.

Agent B admitted, "We don't know. There was no one else."

I reiterated the oddity, "Before you entered, you heard Iron ask, 'Who are you?'"

In unison, they confirmed, "Yes!"

Turning to Kenichi, I voiced the crux of the puzzle, "This doesn't add up. Iron wouldn't have asked that unless he encountered someone unfamiliar."

Kenichi's expression mirrored my frustration, "You're right. It's logical if only logic applied here. But from the strange room design to Itagaki's death, logic seems elusive."

Realizing the futility in further questioning a dead man, I shifted focus to the living. "Where is Miss Yunko? She holds the answers to many of our questions. Where is she?"

Kenichi's expression was a blend of resignation and concern as he assured me, "She's unharmed. I can take you to see her." With a gesture, he dismissed the agents.

"Wait a minute!" I called out, halting their retreat.

Turning back, I asked, "What steps did you take with Yunko after Iron's death?"

Agent A recounted, "I approached Miss Yunko and said, 'Miss Yunko, you are under arrest!' Then, pointing at the deceased, I asked, 'Who is this? What are you doing here?'"

"And how did she respond?" I pressed.

Agent A shrugged, his expression perplexed. "Her response was baffling."

Impatience crept into my voice. "How so?"

"She insisted, 'It's not me, it's her! It's another woman!'" Agent A relayed slowly, as if to emphasize the oddity of her words.

Despite his deliberate pace, the meaning eluded me. The words were clear, but their implication was a mystery. I glanced at Kenichi, whose bitter smile suggested he was as puzzled as I was.

"Let me see Yunko," I requested.

Kenichi nodded, and we proceeded down a stark, narrow corridor. The corridor was a study in white—walls, doors, ceiling, and floor—all bathed in dim lighting, creating an oppressive atmosphere. The unsettling sounds emanating from rooms on either side—murmurs, laughter, cries— only deepened the discomfort. This was no ordinary place; it was a mental hospital.

As we walked, the realization of our location was unsettling. I repeatedly asked Kenichi about Yunko's condition, but received no answer. The truth became clearer as we reached the end of the corridor, where a psychiatrist in a white robe opened a small, barred window in a door.

Kenichi gestured for me to look. Peering inside, I finally laid eyes on Suzuki Yunko.

Meeting Daliang Yunko for the first time was an unsettling experience. Her beauty was undeniable, even though her pallor suggested distress. The room was stark, and she sat on the bed's edge, her face expressionless, muttering to herself. Her words were a soft chant: "That's not me, it's another woman."

I turned to Kenichi, who offered a resigned smile. "She keeps repeating that."

When I looked back at Yunko, she met my gaze with a sudden look of terror, which quickly morphed into an innocent smile. She pointed at me, her laughter light and carefree, like a child's delight at seeing candy.

Puzzled by her reaction, I heard Kenichi behind me, "She's about to say the next line."

As if on cue, Yunko declared joyfully, "You are not her! You are not her! You are not her!" Her laughter was infectious, but soon her demeanor shifted, her eyes darting around as if wary of invisible threats. Her head dropped again as she resumed her mantra, "It's not me, it's another woman."

I stepped back, seeking insight from the doctor, who only offered a helpless shrug. Kenichi explained, "I was on the scene shortly after the incident. She's been like this since. The doctor says her mind's overwhelmed and can't process anything."

I asked, "Didn't you try questioning her?"

Kenichi's frustration was evident. "I had a million questions, but she just repeats the same thing. What can I do?"

Turning to the doctor, I asked if there was hope for her recovery. His response was cautious, "Theoretically, sudden shock-induced mental conditions can improve, but it takes time."

I paced the floor, considering my approach. "Please open the door. I'll try speaking with her," I requested.

Kenichi's expression was skeptical, clearly reflecting past attempts that bore no fruit. Nonetheless, the doctor silently acquiesced, retrieving the key to unlock the door. I motioned for Kenichi to remain outside, wanting to minimize any potential distress for Yunko. Just as I was about to enter, a thought struck me. I turned back and whispered to Kenichi, "What about Naka?"

Kenichi let out a groan, "That guy!"

Despite his reluctance, I believed Naka might be the key to breaking through to Yunko. "Bring Naka here. He's her only family. Seeing him might help her recall something important."

Kenichi nodded, understanding the potential significance. "Alright, I'll call Naka and continue to work on identifying the deceased."

With a deep breath, I stepped into the room. Yunko's reaction to my entrance was calm, almost detached. She rose to her feet, her gaze meeting mine without alarm. I gestured for her to sit, and she complied, her actions steeped in the ingrained politeness typical of Japanese women. Despite her mental turmoil, these small gestures gave me hope that a connection could be made.

With no other options for seating, I joined her on the bed, positioning myself beside her. Her ability to adhere to basic etiquette suggested that somewhere beneath the surface, the real Yunko was still present. This gave me a sense of cautious optimism that perhaps, with the right approach, we could begin to unravel the mystery surrounding her cryptic words and the events that had spiraled into chaos.

Yunko looked at me with an innocent curiosity, her head slightly tilted. I softened my voice, hoping to reach through the fog clouding her mind. "Miss Yunko, I already know a lot about you."

To my surprise, she responded immediately, though predictably, with her familiar refrain: "It's not me, it's another woman."

I nodded and smiled gently. "Of course, it's not you."

Her eyes widened with a sudden, childlike joy. "OK!" she exclaimed, a typical expression of happiness. "It's not me!"

Encouraged by this reaction, I continued with sincerity, "It's not you, but who is the other woman?"

I wasn't sure what to expect. Her repeated assertion seemed a desperate attempt to deny something, perhaps something she felt no one believed. My question was more appeasement than inquiry, yet it provoked an unexpected response.

Yunko paused, her expression shifting to one of deep confusion. Her voice was tinged with bitterness as she replied, "Another woman? It's me!"

Her words were a paradox, a contradiction that defied logic. If not for her evident mental distress, I might have ended our conversation right there. Yet, her statement, though nonsensical, hinted at a complex inner turmoil.

I pressed on, asking gently, "Do you remember Itagaki Ichiro ?"

Her response was a blank stare, her head tilted in puzzlement.

I tried again, "Do you remember who you are? You're a singer, a beautiful girl from Shizuoka, living alone in Tokyo..."

I listed the details of her life, hoping to spark recognition, but she simply shook her head, her eyes devoid of comprehension.

Forty minutes later, Naka arrived.

By then, I had abandoned my attempts to communicate with Yunko, resigned to sitting in silence beside her. When Naka entered, he gasped softly, rushing to Yunko's side.

Yunko reacted with a burst of emotion, leaping up to embrace Naka. "It's not me! It's another woman!" she cried.

Naka comforted her, stroking her hair and patting her back. "What other woman? Did that Itagaki have someone else?"

But Yunko was lost in her mantra, "The other woman is me!"

Naka turned to me, bewildered. "What's wrong with Yunko? What is she talking about?"

I offered a bitter smile. "She's mentally ill," I explained, recounting briefly to Naka how Yunko had been found by the police.

As Yunko clung to Naka, he gently moved her back to sit and lifted her chin with genuine care. Despite his tough exterior, his concern for her was palpable, almost familial. "Yunko, don't worry. Take your time. Things won't get worse; they'll surely get better," he reassured her.

His sincerity struck a chord with me, revealing a depth of feeling that was both comforting and admirable. It seemed Naka's bond with Yunko was authentic, akin to that of siblings, which only increased my respect for him.

Yunko seemed to take in Naka's words slowly, as if she hadn't heard such kindness in a long time. Her sigh was long and deep.

Naka turned to me, questioning, "Who was the person with Yunko that the police murdered?"

Given Naka's background, his disdain for the police was apparent in his choice of words. I clarified, "The identity is still unknown. Kenichi is investigating. The deceased shot first."

Naka scoffed, "Whenever the police kill someone, they always claim it was self-defense. What can I say? The law's on their side, after all."

Ignoring his criticism, I was about to suggest that Naka try asking Yunko some questions to see if she would respond to him when an agent burst in. "Mr. Morris, we've identified the deceased. Kenichi wants you to come immediately!"

With Yunko unable to provide answers and the deceased's identity now known, it was crucial to investigate further. I told Naka, "Stay with Yunko. I'll keep you updated."

I hurried out with the agent, who drove swiftly through the city, sirens blaring as we sped through red lights toward a quiet, upscale neighborhood.

On the way, the agent filled me in on how they identified the deceased. "We distributed his photos widely, even on TV. A neighbor recognized him and called in, identifying him as Iron Smith, residing in a Japanese-style house here. Kenichi and others went to investigate and found significant secrets of Iron Smith."

"What kind of secrets?" I asked, eager for details.

"This Iron Smith was a notorious professional killer," the agent revealed.

Frustrated, I replied, "We already knew he was a killer. What did you find at his home?"

The agent quickly clarified, "No, it's more than that. He's linked to several major unsolved murders worldwide. It's shocking to discover such a killer living quietly in Tokyo!"

I chuckled, "In a city like Tokyo, nothing should surprise us. There are plenty of criminals who could rival a hitman."

The agent nodded in agreement as we arrived at a congested alley, packed with police vehicles and a few RVs displaying secret emblems of senior international law enforcement—a testament to Iron Smith's notoriety.

Unable to drive further, I exited the vehicle and navigated through the crowd.

The garden was ablaze with searchlights, illuminating a flurry of activity. Inside the house was a bustling scene, a stark contrast to the usual tranquility of such a neighborhood.

As I entered, I heard Kenichi's voice, raised and fervent. "I don't agree, absolutely not!" he declared passionately.

The scene was chaotic. In a crowded traditional Japanese hall, the atmosphere was anything but respectful. I immediately spotted Kenichi, visibly agitated, confronting an older man who retorted, "Kenichi, you lost your control!"

The tension was palpable, underscoring the gravity of the revelations surrounding Iron Smith's dark past.

Kenichi, still catching his breath, lowered his fist but stood firm. "I'm sorry, but I still don't agree!" he repeated, his resolve unwavering.

When he noticed me entering the room, he seemed relieved, as if seeing an ally. "Mr.Morris will definitely support me!" he exclaimed, his voice carrying over the tense crowd.

I surveyed the scene: a charged gathering of high-ranking officials, including a senior member of the Tokyo Metropolitan Police Department and several Westerners, all senior figures in international policing. Among them, two generals in military attire stood out. The room buzzed with heated exchanges, a fraught assembly of military and police leaders trying to find common ground amidst discord.

Stepping into the fray, I raised my hands and called for calm, "Everyone, please be quiet!"

The command worked; the room hushed. A few Japanese officials eyed me with suspicion, their expressions questioning my authority. However, recognition from several senior international officers helped quell their skepticism, establishing my presence as significant.

Kenichi, seeing me as a potential mediator, hurriedly explained the crux of the matter. "Ash, just in time. I need your guidance. I've been leading the Itagaki case, and now we've found the murderer. His identity is complex, tied to numerous major crimes. Both the military and international police want to take charge. How do we proceed?"

A senior international police officer interjected, "This murderer is crucial to resolving over ten unsolved international cases!"

A general in military regalia added, "No, the military must take responsibility!"

Kenichi gestured emphatically, "No! That cannot happen!"

Understanding the stakes, I spoke up, "I understand the contention here. While this murderer's identity is indeed critical, his exposure was through the Itagaki case. Kenichi should continue his investigation."

Just as I finished, dissent rose, but I gestured for patience. Addressing the international police leaders, I assured them, "I promise Kenichi will share all findings from his investigation with the international police."

The leaders conferred briefly, their consensus apparent as they nodded in agreement with my approach. I turned to the senior Japanese military officer, "The military will also receive the same information, facilitating a collaborative and comprehensive investigation."

Despite initial resistance from the assembly, my assurances to the international police and the military about information sharing seemed to have quelled the tension. As the senior officers began to discuss amongst themselves, I seized the opportunity to suggest, "Then please, let's clear the area to ensure the investigation proceeds unhindered."

A younger Japanese police officer, likely Kenichi's superior, fixed me with a skeptical stare. "Excuse me, in what capacity are you making these requests?"

With a confident smile, I replied, "In my personal capacity. My position allows me to ensure the international police cooperate fully, and without my involvement, the Japanese police might find their leads severely limited."

Before the officer could respond, Kenichi interjected, "Exactly. Without Mr. Morris, we may find ourselves at a dead end." His tone was resolute, and he added, "And if forced otherwise, I would resign immediately."

Kenichi's firm stance effectively silenced further objections. Together, we politely but assertively persuaded everyone to leave, which was no small feat and took a good half-hour. Eventually, only Kenichi, myself, and a few of his agents remained in the room.

After the chaos subsided and the room cleared, Kenichi approached me with a sense of urgency and gravity, holding the notebook that had sparked such a commotion. In it, Iron Smith had recorded six years' worth of his activities as a professional killer, each entry succinct yet chilling in its implications.

Kenichi handed me the notebook, and I began to leaf through its pages. The entries were methodical, listing payments received, dates, locations, and the identities of those who had been killed. Each line painted a stark picture of Iron Smith's ruthless efficiency and the breadth of his operations.

The cases were indeed shocking, involving high-profile figures and mysterious circumstances that had puzzled investigators for years. Yet, despite the wealth of information about the victims and logistics, there was a glaring omission: the identities of those who had hired Iron Smith. His discretion in omitting his clients' names spoke volumes about his "professional ethics" and the dangerous circles in which he moved.

Kenichi watched me as I reviewed the entries, his expression a mix of concern and determination. "What do you think?" he asked, eager for insights.

I pondered over the notes, then replied, "Itagaki Ichiro is not noted here. But this confirms Iron Smith's role in several major cases. Hiring him wasn't cheap. Each hit cost at least $900,000. We need to consider who had the motive and means to employ him, especially for someone like Itagaki Ichiro, who appears minor compared to other targets."

Kenichi nodded, recognizing the anomaly. "Exactly. Itagaki's name stands out. But now that we have access to Iron Smith's lair, I'm optimistic we can find more answers here," he said, gesturing for his team to begin their thorough search of the premises.

CHAPTER 12

The Split Duo and the Monkey God

The search team was an elite group of seasoned experts, among them Kenichi and myself, each of us equipped with a keen eye for detail and a knack for uncovering hidden truths.

Iron Smith's residence was nothing short of astonishing—a fortress of secrets cloaked within ordinary walls. His bedroom defied expectations, boasting three separate doors and windows armed with cutting-edge microwave anti-theft systems. The security rivaled that of a royal palace, evoking the grandeur of the King of Iran's fabled defenses.

As we delved deeper, we unearthed a labyrinth of secret compartments, hidden in the most unexpected places. Behind the imposing refrigerator in the kitchen, a cleverly concealed compartment within the heating unit held a king's ransom in cash—a testament to Iron's clandestine operations.

The search spanned a relentless day and night, with each revelation pushing fatigue to the periphery of our consciousness. The trove of information we amassed was staggering, particularly the array of strange and lethal weapons—enough to render even the most sophisticated intelligence agencies awestruck.

Amidst this arsenal, only two items truly piqued our interest: a pair of videotapes tied to the enigmatic Itagaki case. The rest merely confirmed Iron Smith's notoriety as a prolific assassin, a fact that captivated the international police and Japanese military far more than it did us.

Kenichi and I were driven by a singular quest: to uncover the identity of the mysterious benefactor who had commissioned Iron to eliminate Itagaki, and to unravel the motive behind this deadly contract.

Thus, in the labyrinthine depths of Iron's stronghold, those two videotapes became our most valuable find—keys to solving the puzzle that lay at the heart of this intricate web of intrigue.

Using the projection equipment in Iron Smith's basement, we watched the first tape. To our shock, it revealed Yunko visiting Iron Smith, demanding that he kill Itagaki. The scene was unfathomable and raised more questions than it answered.

Yunko's involvement seemed illogical. Her livelihood and future were tied to Itagaki. Without him, her prospects were bleak, forcing her into difficult choices in a city as unforgiving as Tokyo. If she harbored resentment towards Itagaki for exploiting her, it still didn't explain why she would go to such lengths.

As we processed the footage, the mention of an "Indian" caught our attention. Kenichi's bitter smile mirrored my own astonishment. The reference to this enigmatic figure hinted at a deeper, more complex web of intrigue.

The Indian seemed to be a ubiquitous presence, a shadowy figure pulling strings from afar. His connection to Yunko and Iron Smith suggested he was pivotal to the entire series of events. Identifying and understanding this Indian became paramount, as he appeared to be the key to deciphering the mystery that enveloped the Itagaki case and beyond.

After viewing the first videotape, this conclusion crystallized in my mind. Kenichi, however, arrived at a different understanding. With a sigh, he remarked, "So it was Yunko all along."

Puzzled, I probed further, "What do you mean by that?"

Kenichi replied, "Yunko hired someone to commit murder. It's as clear as day!"

I shot Kenichi a piercing look, my gaze sharp enough to unsettle him. "You're oversimplifying the situation," I retorted. "You're ignoring the role of the Indian!"

Kenichi exclaimed, "That Indian again!"

"Yes," I echoed, "that Indian! He's the one who guided Yunko to Iron, who instructed her on how to coerce him."

Kenichi dismissed my theory with a wave of his hand. "The Indian has nothing to do with it! Itagaki planned to eliminate both his wife and mistress in one move. Yunko discovered his malicious scheme and hired a professional killer to stop Itagaki. That's the story!"

I couldn't help but sneer at his conclusion. "How convenient," I remarked.

Kenichi's irritation was palpable. "What are you implying?"

"Isn't it obvious?" I continued. "The murderer is dead, Itagaki is dead, and the supposed mastermind is now insane. The case is neatly wrapped up, the 'truth' is revealed, ready to be filed away."

I emphasized "the truth is revealed" with a hint of sarcasm, ensuring Kenichi understood my skepticism. He caught my meaning and sneered back,

"Then what do you propose we do?"

"I don't know yet, but I'm going to find that Indian," I declared.

Kenichi didn't argue. Instead, he offered, "There is still another videotape. Do you want to watch it?"

I had no idea what awaited us on the second videotape, and frankly, I was weary of debating with Kenichi. The complexity of the situation left me grasping for clarity, with the elusive Indian figure seeming to hold the key to the mystery.

As Kenichi inserted the second tape, we watched intently. It captured the entire sequence of events: Yunko's return to Tokyo and her subsequent journey with Iron.

Once the tape concluded, Kenichi and I were left speechless, our minds swirling with confusion. We exchanged silent glances, each of us grappling with a torrent of new questions that only compounded our existing doubts.

Finally, Kenichi broke the silence. "What are we to make of this? Yunko denied ever meeting Iron Smith."

"Exactly," I concurred. "Yunko claims it wasn't her who first approached Iron, but another woman—"

At that, we both sprang to our feet, as if struck by a revelation.

Kenichi exclaimed, "What did you just say?"

I echoed, "That's precisely what Yunko kept insisting. It's not her, but another woman!"

The phrase Yunko repeated—"It's not me, it's another woman!"—suddenly took on a new significance.

Kenichi took a deep breath, "So there's another woman who looks exactly like Yunko, and she's the one who orchestrated the murder."

I challenged him, "And she shares Yunko's name too?"

Kenichi hesitated, struggling to reconcile this. But he quickly offered, "Perhaps this woman used Yunko's name because they're identical in appearance."

I countered his theory sharply, "Did she also steal Yunko's lover and meeting spots?"

Kenichi had no retort, frustration etching his features. "Then what's your theory?" he demanded.

I could only manage a wry smile, admitting, "I don't know. But I sense there aren't two separate women. Both women on the tape are Yunko. There's no other person involved."

Kenichi paused, considering this. "So, you're suggesting Yunko might be suffering from severe schizophrenia? That she's mentally split into two personas, A and B, without A knowing what B is doing?"

I rubbed my face thoughtfully. Kenichi had latched onto a part of what I was trying to convey, but there was more to it than just severe schizophrenia. Human language often falls short when trying to articulate concepts that have never been part of our shared reality. It's like trying to describe a color that doesn't exist in our spectrum.

Kenichi's use of "severe schizophrenia" was insightful. Schizophrenia can indeed lead to a dual personality, where one part of a person might be completely unaware of what the other part is doing, much like Yunko might have been with Iron. This is something documented in psychiatric files.

But my thoughts drifted beyond this. I was considering a scenario far stranger: what if a person's split wasn't just mental, but physical? Imagine someone becoming two distinct entities, identical in appearance, yet different in thoughts or actions. Perhaps one part is cautious, while the other is bold enough to act.

Everyone harbors another side, a hidden facet that rarely surfaces. But what if something triggered these hidden aspects to manifest tangibly? If these dual aspects became independent in both mind and body, encountering each other would be like looking into a mirror—a profound and unsettling experience.

I had entertained this notion because I had once experienced "seeing myself" in a way that defied explanation. It was a bizarre encounter, and language failed to fully capture it. This idea, while hard to grasp, lingered in my mind as a possibility.

Kenichi had suggested Yunko's actions were the result of severe schizophrenia—her visit to Iron a forgotten episode. But what if, during this time, another Yunko existed elsewhere? Two Yunkos, both facets of a single being, operating independently.

I wasn't sure if this was a clearer explanation or if it muddied the waters further.

I chose not to delve too deeply into this with Kenichi, as he hadn't experienced "seeing himself." Without such an experience, the concept seemed implausible. Instead, I simply said, "It might be severe schizophrenia, but we can't dismiss the idea of 'another person.'"

Kenichi looked at me intently. I gestured in resignation. "Remember when Iron Smith entered the meeting place? He cried out twice, 'Who are you?'"

Kenichi replied, "But there was no one else there!"

I sighed, grappling with the complexity of the situation. "It's hard to convey this to others. From a straightforward investigative standpoint, the Itagaki case could be considered closed. But my perspective differs from yours."

Kenichi listened silently, his expression unreadable. I continued, "I want to resolve every lingering question until we have a concrete answer. Only then will it be truly over, so I—"

Before I could finish, Kenichi interjected, completing my thought, " have to find that Indian man!"

We shared a moment of understanding. Rising from our seats, I said, "The videotapes should remain confidential, except for the first one, which can serve as evidence that Yunko hired the killer."

Kenichi nodded his agreement. "We also need to ensure Yunko sees Naka frequently. She might reveal the truth to him."

Kenichi frowned, showing his disdain for Naka, but he agreed nonetheless.

I added, "If Yunko recovers, please get in touch. I'll give you my contact information."

Kenichi promptly pulled out a small notebook to jot down the address I provided—an address in India, belonging to a zoologist who had once tasked me with bringing a rare white tarsier to Japan. He was also the author of a book on monkeys, which included the mystical legend of "Chiwodaka."

Once I was in India, I knew that this contact would be my first stop. The Indian zoologist, renowned for his deep research into tropical primates, was named Nadsim.

After parting ways with Kenichi, things finally proceeded smoothly. I wasn't summoned back at the airport, nor did I receive urgent calls during my flight. Two hours after landing in India, I found myself comfortably ensconced in a rattan chair in Nadsim's living room.

Nadsim greeted me warmly. His living room, while not opulently furnished, exuded comfort, with furniture crafted from aged tropical rattan, its soft sheen lending a quaint charm. He smiled, "So, where have you hidden it?"

I was taken aback. "Hidden what?"

Nadsim laughed, "The white tarsier! I've heard from Japan that it's thriving under your friend's care. Surely you were asked to bring it back. Did you hide it in your clothes? Be careful not to smother it!"

I smiled wryly, gently extricating myself from his enthusiastic grasp. "Things didn't go as planned."

Concern flashed across Nadsim's face, his voice quivering slightly, "The little tarsier—"

Understanding his worry for the rare creature, I hastened to reassure him, "Don't worry. I believe it's in good health."

Nadsim's eyes widened, "You 'believe' it? What do you mean?"

"The tarsier was kidnapped by an Indian," I explained to Nadsim, recounting the bizarre incident where an Indian man played a peculiar "flute" that emitted a strange sound. When the tarsier heard it, it leaped eagerly into the man's arms.

As I narrated the tale, Nadsim's expression turned increasingly peculiar, and he began pacing the room. When I finished, he just stared at me in disbelief.

"Why? Don't you believe it?" I asked.

"It's not that I don't believe you," Nadsim replied. "But this method of catching tarsiers is known only to the locals living deep in those forests!"

I produced the flute, a simple instrument fashioned from leaves. "The Indian left in such a hurry that he forgot this. A Japanese botanist couldn't identify the leaves."

Nadsim examined the flute, nodding. "Yes, this tree grows only in southern India. It's crucial for tarsiers."

I was puzzled, so he elaborated, "Tarsiers groom themselves constantly, and over time, hair accumulates in their stomachs. They need to eat these leaves to eliminate the hair build-up. These trees are their preferred habitat."

"The flute made of these leaves—" I began, but Nadsim anticipated my question.

"The leaves have serrated edges that vibrate in the wind, producing a unique sound," he explained. "Tarsiers are comforted by it, which is why locals use it to capture them."

I nodded, absorbing the information. "The Indian clearly knows a lot about tarsiers. He even referred to the white variant as 'Chiwodaka.'"

Nadsim frowned, contemplating the Indian's motive. "Why would he kidnap the tarsier? He can't sell it to a zoo without revealing his theft."

I shrugged, speculating, "Maybe he intends to cut off its right front paw to create a 'monkey's paw,' granting him three wishes."

Nadsim gave me an amused look.

"Or perhaps he believes the tarsier can lead him to a supernatural monkey god, who will fulfill his wishes."

Nadsim waved his hand dismissively, "Where did you hear these fantastical tales?"

I chuckled, "Some are from your own work, and some from an old Indian storyteller. Though the stories vary, they share a common theme: the rare white tarsier appears every few centuries and is linked to granting three wishes."

Despite the whimsical nature of my words, my demeanor was serious. Nadsim, however, laughed heartily.

"I can't believe you're taking these legends seriously!" he exclaimed between chuckles.

I spoke earnestly, "Don't laugh. We both come from ancient civilizations rich in mythology. These legends may be imbued with mysticism, but they're not necessarily baseless."

Nadsim was taken aback by my seriousness, observing me intently. "What do you want?"

"I need your help," I replied straightforwardly.

He spread his hands in acquiescence. "As long as it's within my power. But remember, I'm no supernatural monkey god. I can't grant you three wishes!"

I waved off his jest. "I'm serious. I want to learn everything I can about the legend of the supernatural monkey god."

Nadsim sighed, showing a hint of reluctance. "My field is primatology, not mythology. However, I have a friend who is an expert in ancient Indian myths. He might be able to assist you."

"Please introduce me to him!" I urged.

Nadsim scrutinized me for a moment, ensuring I was sincere. Once convinced, he made a phone call, speaking animatedly with the person on the other end.

After a five-minute conversation, he hung up and said, "You can see him now."

"I still need your guidance," I added. "There are many questions I have for you."

Nadsim raised his hands in mock surrender. "Only if they're about monkeys. I'm not interested in mythological gods!"

I chuckled, patting his shoulder. "Deal."

Nadsim graciously provided a car and driver, and I set off to meet the mythologist without delay.

Upon arrival, I found the expert amidst a sea of ancient tomes, pacing thoughtfully. Despite the books scattered about, he moved with precision, avoiding stepping on their fragile pages.

Many of the texts were in Sanskrit, their age evident from their worn covers. The expert eventually paused at a bookcase, extracting a manuscript. He opened it and gestured for me to join him, pointing to an illustration. "This is the legendary supernatural monkey god said to grant three wishes."

"Are there many such monkey gods?" I inquired.

"Indeed, there are numerous legends," he replied. "But only this one is associated with granting wishes."

I reached to take the book for a closer look, but he pulled it back gently, allowing me only a glimpse over his hand. The manuscript, with its ochre-yellow sheepskin pages, was evidently precious, and he was wary of any damage.

Peering at the illustration, I saw the "supernatural monkey god." The artistry was rudimentary, reminiscent of a child's drawing.

The most prominent feature was the monkey head. Though the figure resembled a monkey, it was clearly a person with a monkey's visage. A tall "crown" adorned its head—more like an elaborate headdress than a typical crown. The body was unmistakably human, clad in garments of a peculiar style, unlike the conventional depictions of deities I had seen before.

I examined the illustration for a moment before turning to the myth expert. "This monkey god—"

The expert interjected, "This was drawn by an artist based on descriptions from someone who claimed to have seen the monkey god."

I was puzzled. "If that's the case, why are there so many unclear details?"

The expert looked a bit embarrassed. "The person who described it to the painter never actually saw the monkey god. It was his ancestor who supposedly had the encounter. It's a family legend, passed down through the generations."

I had to suppress a smile. The idea of a "family legend" being passed down for hundreds of years made me skeptical. Who knows how accurate the painting is to the real "supernatural monkey god"?

My amusement must have been apparent because the expert quickly added, "This is the only visual depiction of the supernatural monkey god we have."

I composed myself and replied, "So, this monkey god is essentially a human with a monkey head?"

"Correct," the expert nodded.

"Does this monkey god truly grant three wishes?"I asked.

The expert paced to a desk, carefully turned the pages of an ancient book, and read for a while. Then he looked up, saying, "According to these records, the supernatural monkey god sends a messenger every few centuries. This messenger, called 'Chiwodaka,' is an extremely rare pure white tarsier that guides people to the monkey god."

I had heard similar stories, but hearing it from the expert, grounded in such ancient texts, gave it weight.

I ventured another theory, "There's also a story about cutting off a monkey's paw and—"

The expert waved dismissively. "That's a Western tale. It's often confused with these legends because it involves monkeys. Folklore can be quite muddled."

His explanation made sense, and I agreed. "About the 'Chiwodaka' legend, I once heard an old man in Tokyo mention that the supernatural monkey god makes people 'see themselves.' What could that mean?"

The expert scrutinized me before consulting the old book. After twenty minutes, he frowned. "There's no mention of such a phrase here. It seems meaningless."

I understood his skepticism. The phrase "see themselves" would sound cryptic to most. I pressed on, "I'm curious how the white tarsier guides people to the monkey god. Does it know the location?"

The expert chuckled, "You're rushing things."

I was taken aback. "What do you mean?"

The expert suggested, "When you find the little white tarsier, you'll understand naturally. Why the rush?"

I hesitated, not revealing that I had already brought a little white tarsier from India to Japan. At the time, I had no inkling of its supposed mystical significance. Had I known, would I have acted differently? Would I truly believe that this tiny creature could lead me to a supernatural monkey god?

I chuckled inwardly at the thought. Of course, I wouldn't have believed it.

As I pondered, I waved my hands, dismissing the notion.

The expert watched me for a moment, sensing perhaps that our conversation had reached its end. He gestured subtly, indicating it was time for me to leave. I was about to take my leave when a tall servant entered, bowing to the expert. "Professor, Prince Yeri is waiting for you in the living room."

I had no idea who Prince Yeri was, but the expert's reaction spoke volumes. He leapt up, clearly flustered, repeating, "How long has he been here? I'll go right away!"

As he spoke, the expert glanced at me, and I took the hint. "Sorry to have intruded, I'll be on my way," I said politely.

The expert hurried out, and I followed, as I had to pass through the living room to exit. Despite India having no monarchy, the title "Prince Yeri" didn't surprise me. India was home to numerous local kings who ruled small states, wielding significant power and wealth. Even though the official system of local kings had been abolished, their influence and affluence ensured they remained respected figures.

As we entered the living room, I was met with a striking sight. A man stood with his back to us, tall and resplendently dressed. He wore a white cloth on his head, its edges woven with gold thread, and a white robe with similar gold embellishments. He was studying a painting on the wall, exuding an air of authority and elegance.

As soon as the expert saw the man, he stepped forward, waving me away discreetly to signal my exit. I understood that this man was likely Prince Yeri, and I had no intention of mingling with dignitaries, given my pressing tasks. I began to leave but halted abruptly as the visitor spoke.

The expert greeted him with polite apologies for any delay. "Prince, I'm sorry to have kept you waiting for so long!"

The visitor's response was casual, "It's nothing, don't mind it."

It was those simple words that froze me in place. While ordinary, the voice carried a familiarity that was impossible to ignore. It resonated within me, a voice etched into my memory from an encounter in a Tokyo bar. I had been with Kenichi when this voice had first intruded upon our conversation, uttering, "Oh, Chiwodaka!"

The voice was distinct—low and imbued with a haunting, shadowy presence. There was no mistaking it. The man speaking was the Indian who had played that peculiar leaf flute, the one who had spirited away the little white tarsier.

In a staggering twist of fate, here he was—the very individual I had traveled across continents to find among India's vast populace.

My heart raced as I realized the enormity of the coincidence—or perhaps destiny—that had brought us to the same place.

CHAPTER 13

The Primacy of Self-Discovery

Finding an unknown Indian among 900 million seemed an impossible task, and yet here I was, hearing his unmistakable voice. I was stunned and immediately turned around. At the same moment, the guest turned to face me, and our eyes locked.

It felt like a bolt of lightning had struck us both. Despite his regal appearance—dressed in splendid attire with a meticulously groomed beard that added to his majestic presence—I recognized him without a doubt as the same Indian who had spoken to me in that Tokyo bar. The transformation from a wanderer to a prince was astonishing.

I never imagined this mysterious Indian held the title of a prince, and his appearance and demeanor confirmed that his princely status was no fabrication. His shock at seeing me was palpable, likely even more profound than my own surprise.

The expert, noticing our intense gaze, hurried over and attempted to usher me out rudely, willing to avoid offending his esteemed guest. But I was determined not to let this opportunity slip away. The expert's brusque behavior only fueled my resolve, and I pushed him back without hesitation, causing him to stumble several steps.

With the expert momentarily out of the way, I approached the Indian—Prince Yeri. "Unexpected, really unexpected!" I exclaimed.

Prince Yeri's face twitched slightly as he replied, "Yes, really unexpected."

I was thrilled, rubbing my hands together in excitement. Discovering this Indian meant I could finally unravel many mysteries. I walked right up to him, ignoring the expert's angry protests. "So you're a prince? We need to have a good talk."

Before I could continue, the expert made another attempt to remove me, but I was prepared and pushed him firmly aside once more.

Prince Yeri's face twitched again. "Actually, there is nothing to talk about," he stated.

I retorted, "The Japanese police are very interested in you!"

Yeri sneered, "This is India!"

Though anger bubbled beneath my calm exterior, I remained composed. "Criminal cases can be pursued through international police cooperation."

Yeri offered a dark smile, pulling the corners of his mouth into a smirk. "I don't know what you are talking about!"

I took a decisive step forward, pressing my finger against Yeri's chest. The expert, having suffered two setbacks, approached again but refrained from further aggression, opting instead to glare at me with animosity. Ignoring him, I focused on Yeri, "You still remember Takeo, right?"

Yeri visibly flinched. I continued, "He helped you carry the bricks and mortar. I believe that's linked to the building manager's death, isn't it?"

Yeri's face darkened, yet he regained his composure swiftly. "Who are you?" he demanded, glancing at the expert. "Must I entertain such a lunatic?"

The expert, exasperated, shouted, "Get out! Get out! If you don't leave, I'll call the police!" He made his way to the phone, picking it up with intent.

Realizing the situation, I knew staying would only result in being detained by the Indian police—something I was keen to avoid. Moreover, as a prince, Yeri was a prominent figure, making him easier to track down than an ordinary citizen.

Stepping back, I raised my hands placatingly. "Alright, I'm leaving." I backed away, maintaining eye contact with Yeri. As I reached the door, I added, "How is Chiwodaka? Consulting him is futile," I gestured toward the expert, "I probably know more than he does. You'd do better to speak with me."

Yeri's expression remained cold, but I gave him my hotel name and room number before turning on my heel and exiting.

As I left, I overheard the expert offering hurried apologies to Yeri, who responded with silence.

Feeling an unexpected sense of relief, I marveled at my fortune in finding Yeri so effortlessly. Kenichi had deemed it impossible to locate an Indian in India, yet I had succeeded without even trying.

Back at my hotel, I called Nadsim to inform him I'd be in touch later. Then, I reflected on the day's events. Discovering Yeri was a significant breakthrough, and I was confident he would seek me out.

Given Yeri's unique status and his clandestine activities in Japan, he undoubtedly wanted to keep them hidden from prying eyes and further scrutiny. Regardless of whether his visit would be advantageous or adverse for me, he would come.

People generally dislike having their secret endeavors exposed, and Yeri was no exception.

I was exhausted and lay down on the bed, my mind still alert despite my fatigue. The past few days had been draining, and even though I considered the possibility of Yeri being a threat, I couldn't let my guard down. Just as I was about to drift off, the phone rang.

I jumped up, answered it, and heard Nadsim's voice: "There's a long-distance call from Japan for you. I've asked them to contact your hotel directly."

I immediately assumed it was Kenichi. My excitement was palpable since I had located the Indian, something Kenichi would never have anticipated.

Nadsim didn't keep me long. I hung up and informed the hotel operator to connect any calls from Japan directly to my room.

After a tense 30-minute wait, the phone rang again.

I grabbed it, prepared to share my breakthrough with Kenichi. As soon as I heard someone say "Hello" in Japanese, I blurted out, "You'll never believe it—I found that Indian! He's possibly a descendant of a fallen dynasty, and people call him a prince!"

I spoke rapidly, but there was silence on the other end. After calling "Hello" several more times, a voice finally responded, "I'm sorry, are you Mr.Morris? I don't know what you're talking about."

Stunned, I realized it wasn't Kenichi. Though the connection was faint, the voice was unfamiliar. I hesitated, then asked, "I'm sorry, who is this?"

The voice replied, "I'm Naka! Do you remember me? Yunko's good friend!"

I froze. Naka! This unexpected call from someone like him was perplexing. He had reached out to Nadsim first, which meant Kenichi must have shared my contact details, as Kenichi was the only one I had informed. So why hadn't Kenichi called himself?

Sensing something was amiss, I quickly said, "Yes, I remember, Mr. Naka!" Fearing he might take too long to explain, I urged, "What's going on? Please, quickly!"

Naka paused briefly. In that silence, I heard his rapid breathing, confirming something was indeed wrong.

Before I could prompt him again, he spoke, "Mr. Morris, Kenichi, he—he—"

Naka was struggling, his voice choked. Despite the distance, I could almost visualize his sharp, angular face contorting with urgency.

I shouted, "What happened to Kenichi?"

Naka finally managed to say, "Kenichi suddenly resigned and left Tokyo. He only left a note for me—"

On hearing this, I felt a wave of irritation. It seemed like Naka was overreacting. Kenichi's sudden resignation was unexpected, but hardly reason for emergency contact.

I retorted, "Is it just that Kenichi resigned?"

Naka hastily explained, "Yes, but he left me a note, asking me to inform you immediately and provided a way to contact you! He also wanted me to read the note to you over the phone!"

I felt a surge of impatience and urged, "Then please read it quickly!"

Naka's voice was filled with confusion and a hint of frustration as he prefaced Kenichi's note with his own thoughts: "What exactly does Kenichi's note mean? I don't understand it at all!"

As Naka began reading Kenichi's note, I listened intently:

"Ash, I saw myself. I saw myself where you saw yourself. After I saw myself, I realized that I was not myself at all over the years. I don't want to continue playing a role that is not myself, so I left. I want to make myself the real me. I returned to where I should belong. I didn't have time to say goodbye to you. Also, no matter how mysterious the matter is, I think you don't need to pursue it anymore. You don't need to look for that Indian. Find yourself quickly. That is more important than anything else. Listen to my advice, my friend."

Naka read each line carefully, and when he finished, he added, "I really don't know what he is talking about. However, he really resigned and left Tokyo immediately."

I sat there, stunned, processing Kenichi's cryptic message. While I didn't grasp everything, I understood the significance of "I saw myself." It referred to the room where Kenichi had accompanied me, the same room where Itagaki and Yunko had met.

Kenichi had experienced something profound in that room. He had seen himself.

My mind was racing, eager to piece together the details. Kenichi must have contacted Naka prior to leaving the note, and I needed to know more about what had transpired.

"Naka, please, I need you to tell me everything, in as much detail as possible," I urged.

Naka's voice turned hesitant, "I—I can tell you, but I don't have long-distance call fees, I—I—"

I quickly reassured him, "Hang up and call me back. I'll cover the charges."

Naka agreed, his voice brightening at the offer.

After Kenichi and I had left Yunko's ward, thanks to Kenichi's arrangements and the fact that Yunko was calm among the other patients, the doctors determined she posed no threat. Naka was permitted to spend time with her.

Naka, deeply devoted to Yunko, spent every available moment with her. The hospital later observed that Yunko seemed to improve with

Naka's presence. If not for her repetitive speech, she appeared almost normal.

Naka was heartbroken over Yunko's condition. He frequently whispered her name, urging her to share her thoughts with him, promising to shoulder any burden she revealed.

Naka's constant presence and his apparent distress led one intern, unaware of the situation, to mistake him for a patient and Yunko for a visitor.

Yunko remained unresponsive to Naka's pleas. That night, Naka requested a canvas bed to sleep beside Yunko, an exception the hospital allowed due to the severity of Yunko's case. They hoped his presence might jog her memory.

In the middle of the night, according to Naka's account, he was jolted awake by the sound of sobbing.

Naka, despite his exhaustion, couldn't ignore the heart-wrenching sobs that filled the room. The sound was so profoundly sorrowful that it stirred a deep empathy within him. Even if the person crying had been his worst enemy, he felt compelled to offer comfort.

Rubbing his eyes, he sat up and saw Yunko sitting on the edge of the bed, tears streaming down her face. Her sobs were so filled with despair that they seemed to draw the light out of the room, leaving a void of overwhelming sadness.

Naka was taken aback, unsure how to react. Yunko had cried in front of him before, often when life in the bustling city became too much to bear. Her cheerful exterior was a facade she maintained, and whenever tears fell, Naka would try to lighten the mood. "What's wrong? The sun is bright, and you have no worries about food or clothes. Why be sad?" he would say.

Yunko, strong-willed as she was, would always straighten up, brush away her tears, and insist, "Who said I'm sad? I'm very happy!" Her words were always a brave front, and Naka knew it.

Since the damage to her vocal cords, Yunko had more moments of vulnerability, crying in front of Naka. Yet she always managed to pull herself together, claiming she wasn't sad.

Naka found himself deeply affected by Yunko's tears. Despite his best efforts to remain composed, he was on the brink of tears himself. As he watched her cry, his voice cracked with emotion, "Yunko, please stop crying. Everyone struggles, but crying won't change things. Please, stop crying."

Yet, Yunko continued to sob, seemingly impervious to his attempts at comfort.

Frustration and helplessness swelled within Naka, prompting him to exclaim, "Fine, cry if you must. See what good it does!"

He hadn't anticipated a response, but Yunko surprised him. Through her tears, she spoke with a clarity that caught him off guard: "At least I can cry. You can't even cry when you need to. You want to, but you don't dare."

Her words pierced through him, stripping away the pretense he had maintained. In that moment, Naka was forced to confront his own suppressed emotions. Life's hardships and the facade he wore to navigate the big city's challenges had left him emotionally repressed, as Yunko had pointed out.

The truth in her words nearly brought him to tears. He realized how much he had been holding back, how much he had denied himself the vulnerability of expressing his own sorrow. Yunko's insight not only highlighted her regained clarity but also exposed his own emotional struggles.

As he processed Yunko's words, he nearly broke down himself. But then a revelation hit him—Yunko must have regained her senses. Her lucid speech was a sign of her returning consciousness.

Overjoyed, he exclaimed, "Yunko, you're awake!"

Yunko responded, "I was never asleep!"

Naka's excitement grew. "That's not what I meant. I mean, you're awake from your unconsciousness!"

Yunko's sobbing subsided slightly. "Unconscious? I was never unconscious. I wish I were, but I feel this despair vividly. I don't know how to live, I feel lost, and I truly don't know what to do—"

She continued speaking, but Naka was already taking action. He gestured for Yunko to stay put, then dashed out of the room to find a phone.

Kenichi was jolted awake by Naka's phone call in the middle of the night. As soon as he heard Naka's voice, his initial impulse was to curse at being disturbed, but a yawn delayed his outburst. Before he could say anything, he heard Naka shouting, "Mr. Kenichi, Yunko is awake! Yunko is awake!"

Startled, Kenichi swallowed his curse and urgently replied, "What? Please say it again!" The urgency in his voice was clear, and it was unusual for him to use "please" when speaking with Naka.

Naka repeated, "Yunko is awake!"

Kenichi jumped out of bed, securing the phone receiver between his shoulder and ear as he grabbed for his coat. "Where did you call from? Go back and stay with her. Don't let her wander off. I'm coming right now!"

He hung up, quickly donned his coat, and headed out, half-dressed and slipping on mismatched shoes—one yellow, one black.

Naka, retelling the story, noted, "Mr. Kenichi arrived so quickly. He didn't even notice his mismatched shoes. I was waiting for him at the ward's entrance."

Returning to the ward after the call, Naka found Yunko still in tears. He gently tried to reassure her, "Wait a moment. Mr. Kenichi will be here soon. He's a police officer, but a good man. He mentioned you're involved in an important case, something about Mr. Itagaki's death—"

Naka watched Yunko closely, hoping for a reaction to the mention of Itagaki. He never believed Yunko was involved in Itagaki's death; Itagaki was crucial to Yunko's life, and she couldn't afford to lose him. But Yunko showed no reaction, merely continuing to cry.

Naka encouraged her softly, "When he arrives, just tell the truth. Trust me, nothing bad will happen."

Yunko responded faintly, "What will happen?"

Naka hesitated, unable to answer.

Without waiting for a response, Yunko added, "I don't care about anything anymore." She glanced toward the barred window, the moonlight casting a ghostly glow across her tear-streaked face.

"What else do I care about? What could possibly bring me more pain and sadness? I don't know why I'm alive or what I should be doing," she murmured.

Naka felt a pang of panic at her words, struggling to find the right thing to say. He wanted to comfort Yunko but was at a loss. Yunko gazed at him with a look that was almost sympathetic, her voice calm and clear, "Naka, you should also think about yourself."

Naka was deeply affected by Yunko's earlier display of emotion and was taken aback by her sudden clarity. In his confusion, he had quickly called Kenichi, but Yunko's latest words left him feeling lost again. What could he say except to sigh in response?

Contemplating his own situation, Naka realized that someone like him had little to plan for. He believed that luck wouldn't simply fall into his lap. Any attempts to plan seemed futile compared to the ambitions of more influential people, akin to watching an ant labor tirelessly over a crumb.

Unable to find the right words, Naka simply reached out and gently stroked Yunko's face. She suddenly asked, "When will the police officer named Kenichi you mentioned arrive?"

"He should be here soon," Naka replied.

Yunko requested, "Can you wait for him at the door? I want to be alone."

Naka studied her face, then reached out to stroke her hair—a gesture of affection and care. Though he considered himself insignificant, he somehow felt a protective strength over Yunko, often expressing his feelings as if he were an elder figure.

Yunko responded with a slight tilt of her head, a gesture that Naka found endearingly beautiful. He mused that she had the potential to be a renowned singer. Perhaps, after this ordeal, all of Japan would come to know Suzuki Yunko. If she reentered the music scene, she could become a star, and he—Naka—might become the manager of a popular singer.

Buoyed by this thought, Naka left the ward as Yunko requested. He closed the door behind him and stood watch outside.

Standing there, Naka had no idea what Yunko was doing inside. According to his account, Yunko remained calm during that brief period, as he heard no sounds from the room.

It was midnight, a time of stillness even in a mental hospital. Had there been any noise, Naka would have heard it.

Naka didn't have to wait long before Kenichi arrived.

Kenichi rushed down the corridor, the mismatched shoes on his feet making an odd rhythm as he hurried along. His footsteps echoed through the silence, and when he reached Naka at the door, he immediately asked, "Where is Yunko?"

Naka pointed towards the ward, and Kenichi grabbed the door handle. Before entering, he paused and asked, "You said she is completely awake?"

Naka nodded, "Yes, completely awake." He hesitated, adding, "Too awake, she even advised me to think about myself. She never spoke so clearly before."

His last words were spoken softly, and Naka wasn't sure if Kenichi caught them. Kenichi opened the door, and as Naka moved to follow, Kenichi blocked him, saying, "I'm sorry, Miss Yunko and I need to talk privately. Please wait outside."

Reluctantly, Naka stepped back, feeling a twinge of resentment. "I could have insisted on going in," he recounted later, still feeling slighted. "But I have my pride. If they don't want me there, I won't force it." The door closed, leaving him outside, while Kenichi entered the ward.

Looking back, Naka thought he should have gone in, to know firsthand what transpired rather than just hearing the sounds.Denied entry, Naka could only listen to what happened inside. The muffled sounds and snippets of conversation offered clues, but they were often perplexing and incomplete.

Once the door was shut, Kenichi's voice came through, filled with surprise, "Oh my God, what's going on, you guys—"

His words were abruptly cut off by a loud "bang," which Naka identified as the chair falling—likely knocked over by Kenichi in his haste.

Kenichi's voice followed, more urgent, "You guys—what's going on with you guys? You guys—"

Naka was taken aback, noting that Kenichi, in just two sentences, had repeated "you guys" four times.

Naka stood outside the ward, grappling with confusion and curiosity. He knew that Yunko was alone inside, yet Kenichi's repeated use of "you guys" suggested otherwise. If Kenichi's earlier tone hadn't bruised Naka's pride, he might have barged in to see what was happening. Instead, he hesitated, simply listening.

Then he heard Yunko's voice, calm and low. Familiarity allowed Naka to decipher her words: "You're here? Don't worry, I can tell you everything you want to know."

Kenichi's urgency was palpable as he pressed, "Who contacted that professional killer? You guys—" Again, his words were cut off, followed by a series of whispers.

Naka recognized Yunko's voice but couldn't make out the whispered conversation, despite his familiarity with her. His curiosity intensified, and he was on the verge of opening the door when he heard a sound from Kenichi, a groan as if he had been struck.

Startled, Naka paused, unsure of what had happened. Before he could act, the door opened, and Kenichi stepped out, closing it behind him. Yunko's voice immediately pierced through the closed door, her scream clear: "If you don't believe it, you can go and see it!"

Naka looked at Kenichi, momentarily speechless. Kenichi's demeanor stunned him; his face was etched with distress and confusion.

Despite his usual disdain for police officers, Naka found himself feeling a rare sympathy for Kenichi. The sight of Kenichi's troubled expression elicited an unexpected empathy. It was clear that whatever had transpired inside the ward had deeply affected Kenichi, leaving him visibly shaken.

Kenichi's demeanor was so unsettling that even Naka, who had little regard for him, was taken aback. Kenichi's face was as pale as the hospital walls, his eyes vacant, and his body trembling. When he grasped Naka's arm, the chill in his touch was palpable, despite the fabric between them. The authoritative figure Naka had known seemed to dissolve, replaced by someone almost pitiable.

Naka was momentarily frozen by Kenichi's appearance but quickly snapped to attention. "Mr. Kenichi, you—" he began, only for Kenichi to interrupt, still in a trance-like state. "She—she told me—told me—" he stammered, then focused on Naka with a sudden intensity. "She told you too? She—she—told you?"

Confused, Naka asked, "What did she tell you?"

Kenichi's grip tightened painfully on Naka's arm, causing him to yelp. But Kenichi didn't release him, repeatedly insisting, "She told me, and asked me to go and see, she asked me to go and see!"

Staring directly at Naka, Kenichi's words demanded an answer. "She—she asked you to see what?" Naka inquired.

Kenichi replied, "She asked me to see myself, to look at myself!"

The cryptic statement left Naka bewildered. What could Kenichi possibly mean by "see yourself"? It was a concept that defied easy understanding.

Yet, I understood Kenichi's meaning. "Look at yourself" was literal. It was simple, just looking at yourself—something I'd experienced myself.

Naka, unsure of how to respond, watched as Kenichi's agitation mounted. Kenichi began shaking Naka's arm more vigorously, declaring, "I must go and look at myself!"

In pain from Kenichi's grip, Naka conceded, "Okay, then go, go and look at yourself!"

Releasing Naka, Kenichi stumbled forward a few steps, then turned back. "Naka, are you going? Go and look at yourself! People don't have many opportunities to see themselves!"

Naka's skepticism was evident in his expression, though he kept his thoughts to himself: the mental hospital might need to admit another patient. Despite Naka's unfriendly demeanor, Kenichi wasn't offended. He merely sighed, shaking his head with an air of regret.

And with that, Kenichi left, leaving Naka to ponder the cryptic encounter and the unsettling transformation he had witnessed in the once-commanding figure of Kenichi.

As Kenichi disappeared down the corridor, Naka couldn't shake his curiosity. He turned back and pushed open the door to Yunko's room, eager to understand what had transpired between her and Kenichi. Inside, he found Yunko seated on the edge of the bed with an expression that was both strange and unsettling.

"What did Kenichi ask you?" Naka inquired, hoping for clarity.

Yunko remained silent.

Persisting, Naka asked, "He said some inexplicable things to me. I don't know what he meant. What did you ask him to see?"

Still, Yunko did not respond directly but instead began to laugh—a laugh that was unsettling. "That's not me, it's her! It's another woman, that's not me!" she exclaimed, repeating the phrases amidst her laughter.

Her continued laughter was unnerving, and Naka, in his frustration and concern, grabbed her arm, shaking her slightly in an attempt to bring her back to reality. But Yunko continued to laugh and repeat her cryptic statements.

The situation mirrored previous episodes, but the laughter added a layer of distress. According to neurologists, a patient who laughs persistently can be more concerning than one who simply mutters to themselves.

As for Kenichi, after leaving Naka, his whereabouts were unknown to Naka at that time. However, others were aware of where Kenichi went.

It wasn't until later that I pieced together the events that unfolded after Kenichi left Naka. Though these events happened at different times, they are interconnected, so I will narrate them here for clarity.

Kenichi was seen at the entrance of a building by an agent. Ever since the incident involving Iron Smith, who had died under suspicious circumstances, agents had been stationed there.

The agent noticed Kenichi's hurried and erratic movements. His path was not straight, reminiscent of someone who had perhaps had too much to drink.

The agent approached Kenichi, offering assistance, but Kenichi brushed him off and made his way to the elevator.

"It was then that I noticed Kenichi's mismatched shoes—one yellow, one black—and his hurried demeanor," the agent later recalled. "I wondered if he had encountered some trouble. I considered following him, but knowing Kenichi's experience as an officer, I assumed he could handle himself."

Despite his reservations, the agent kept a watchful eye, concerned about Kenichi's peculiar behavior. When half an hour passed with no sign of Kenichi's return, the agent's concern grew.

As the agent contemplated entering the elevator, it ascended to the eleventh floor, paused momentarily, and then began its descent.

After Kenichi left the building where he had visited the rendezvous spot of Itagaki and Yunko, his next movements were uncertain. However, it's believed he returned home briefly due to the signs of hurried packing found later at his residence. This interlude lasted about an hour before Kenichi appeared at his office.

It was still early morning, with the sky dark and only one officer on duty. This officer, a friend of Kenichi's, greeted him with, "Good morning! Why so early? Is there any new progress in the case?"

Kenichi didn't respond. His demeanor suggested urgency as he moved straight to his office, leaving the door ajar behind him. The officer, curious, turned to see Kenichi through the open door.

Once inside, Kenichi sat down and began writing a letter. According to the officer, Kenichi composed two letters. The first letter he wrote swiftly and left on his desk. The second letter took three attempts before he was satisfied. This one he folded and slipped into his pocket.

Kenichi then picked up the first letter and exited his office, handing it to the officer on duty. "Please give this to the director as soon as he arrives," he instructed.

The officer on duty noted that Kenichi didn't linger for a response, departing swiftly. A quick glance at the letter revealed the word "resignation," which startled the officer. He considered calling Kenichi back for clarification, but Kenichi was already gone.

Following this, Kenichi made his way to the hospital to see Naka again. His movements and actions suggested a man in the midst of significant personal and professional upheaval, leaving those around him puzzled and concerned about his abrupt decisions and mysterious behavior.

The second letter Kenichi penned in his office was meant for me—a letter that Naka would later read to me during our first long-distance call.

When Kenichi and Naka met again, Naka noticed nothing out of the ordinary. Kenichi was uncharacteristically buoyant, his demeanor relaxed—a stark contrast to the usual furrowed brow that marked his constant contemplation, a byproduct of his demanding work. This time, however, he seemed unburdened.

Kenichi instructed Naka to contact me as soon as possible and to read the letter aloud. He handed Naka a small sum for the call, lightly patted his shoulder, and once more opened the ward door, peering inside. Naka seized the moment to glance in as well, observing Yunko's enigmatic grin as she repeated those cryptic sentences.

Reflecting on the encounter, Naka confessed, "I read the letter Kenichi left for you and thought it wasn't anything urgent. I considered keeping the money for other uses. But the next day, two agents came inquiring about him. That's when I learned he had not only resigned but also vanished from Tokyo. At the station, a colleague spotted him. Kenichi merely mentioned he was heading to where he 'should go,' offering no further explanation."

During the call, Naka recounted every detail of Kenichi's recent actions. After the call ended, I sat in stunned silence, my mind a whirlwind of confusion. Gradually, I began to piece together the fragments of this perplexing puzzle:

Yunko had awoken suddenly, her speech unusually candid and sorrowful when speaking to Naka. No one knew what she shared with Kenichi, except that she prompted him to "look at himself."

Taking her words to heart, Kenichi embarked on a journey of introspection. The outcome was a resignation letter, a symbolic shedding of his old life.

He also left me a letter, urging me to dismiss the strange occurrences and departed without farewell, heading to an undisclosed destination—the place he felt he "should go." I remain clueless about this mysterious destination.

The sequence of events, though straightforward, is astonishing in its implications.

One baffling detail persists: Kenichi's repeated use of "you guys" upon entering the ward. The room should have contained only Yunko.

After piecing together the fragments of this bewildering situation, I found myself contemplating a significant decision: Should I return to Japan to seek out Kenichi? Finding him could undoubtedly unveil countless answers, yet the challenge lay in the fact that he had vanished from Tokyo, leaving no trace of his new whereabouts. Searching for a single person in Japan felt as daunting as finding an Indian in India. However, unlike Kenichi, the Indian I sought had made his identity known to me, and I was confident he would reach out when the time was right. Given these circumstances, leaving India for Japan seemed unjustifiable. Thus, after nearly an hour-long call with Naka, I resolved to stay put, at least for the time being.

The night had left me restless, and as dawn began to break, I paced my room, lost in thought. I reasoned that if Prince Yeri managed to hold off until morning without seeking me out, it would demonstrate remarkable patience on his part.

His actions were shrouded in secrecy, the kind that typically repels outside scrutiny. Yet, I had already gleaned significant insights into his affairs, and knowing this, how could he resist approaching me?

CHAPTER 14

The Story of Prince Yeri

Though a flicker of anxiety lingered, I wasn't truly worried. Knowing his identity made finding Prince Yeri a simple task. I paced the room, stretching intermittently, when a peculiar sound drifted from the corridor—a whistle-like tune, slightly hoarse at the high notes. Instantly, I recognized it as the song of a leaf flute.

My heart quickened with the realization: Prince Yeri had arrived. I dashed to the door, opened it wide, and stood behind it. "Please come in," I called out, "I've been waiting for you."

Silence hung in the air for a brief moment before I heard a low hum. Then, a tall Indian man entered, his presence commanding yet serene. It was Prince Yeri, clad in traditional white attire, the leaf flute clutched in his hand. I closed the door behind him as he turned to face me.

We stood in mutual scrutiny. I had anticipated the potential for hostility, remaining on high alert. Yet, as I examined his dark features, I found no menace—only hesitation and a touch of helplessness. His demeanor suggested a man internally conflicted, unlikely to pose a threat to others.

He seemed poised to speak, but the words faltered on his lips. I gestured for him to take a seat. "How is our little friend?" I inquired.

He hesitated, placing his hands together in a respectful gesture before replying, "Our little friend?"

"Chiwodaka," I clarified.

A bitter smile crossed Yeri's face, an involuntary twitch betraying his worry. For a fleeting moment, dread seized me at the thought of the little white tarsier succumbing to another hunger strike. But he quickly reassured me, "Very good, our little friend is very good!"

Relief washed over me as Yeri took a few cautious steps back and sat down. His demeanor was a stark contrast to the expert I had encountered earlier. As expected, he murmured, "I can't believe you came to India just to find me."

I nodded silently, choosing to observe rather than speak, gauging his reaction.

Yeri offered another strained smile. "I admire your perseverance. My name is Yeri. It's a long name, so I won't trouble you with the details."

With that, he extended his hand, a massive green jade ring gleaming on his thick finger. I took his hand, the gesture a symbol of friendship and mutual respect.

Eager to unravel the mysteries clouding my mind, I welcomed Prince Yeri's offer of friendship without hesitation. As we shook hands, I addressed him, "Prince Yeri?"

He corrected me gently, "Yes, though my dynasty no longer stands. It's merely a title now."

I nodded, acknowledging my awareness of the ebb and flow of India's myriad dynasties and tribes. "And your territory—?"

Yeri replied, "The original land was in southern India. I still own property there, a palace now fallen to ruin—" His words trailed off, a bitter smile hinting at deeper reflections beyond the loss of mere bricks and mortar.

I gestured, perplexed. "Despite the dissolution of your dynasty, you clearly hold significant influence in India—"

Yeri interjected, "And substantial wealth."

"Exactly. So why venture to Japan and engage in such peculiar activities?" I pressed.

Yeri's lips twitched, hesitation evident. After a pause, he posed an unexpected question, "What do you think is the most alluring thing in the world, or perhaps, the universe?"

Caught off guard, I pondered. The answer seemed elusive, varying with personal perspective. Yet, as an insight struck, I offered, "Three wishes that can be realized!"

Yeri nodded in agreement, "Three wishes."

Confusion deepened. How did these three wishes connect to the white tarsier and the mystical monkey god, and why Japan?

Overwhelmed by the flood of questions, I found myself momentarily speechless. Yeri, perceptive as ever, noticed my bewilderment.

He clasped his fingers together, offering, "It's a long story, should you wish to hear it."

"Yes, please!" I urged eagerly. "No matter the length, I'm all ears."

Yeri straightened, attentive to my request. "I have many questions on my mind," I admitted. "I hope you'll allow me to interject as you narrate."

After a thoughtful pause, Yeri consented, "Alright."

Yet, he quickly added, "I have a request of my own."

I met his gaze, awaiting his terms. "After hearing my tale, I ask that you do everything in your power to help me."

I was momentarily stunned by Yeri's request, uncertain of what he might need from me. Yet, his expression made it clear—without my agreement, his story would remain untold. And without his tale, my myriad questions would remain unanswered. It seemed I had no choice. With a resigned sigh, I acknowledged, "You certainly know when to strike a bargain."

Yeri offered a shrug of helplessness, mirrored by my own. "Alright, I promise," I conceded.

Trusting my word, Yeri began his tale—a tapestry woven with history and intrigue.

India, a land of countless native kings, each with their own dynasty. Among them, Prince Yeri's ancestors had carved out a realm in southern India. Though small, their kingdom boasted a history of grandeur. Their palace stood as a testament to this legacy—a majestic fortress filled with jewels, beautiful women, and all the trappings of opulence.

In those days, power was often contested through war. The Yeri dynasty, nearly invincible, expanded its territory with each victory. Their influence grew until they claimed a vast expanse of virgin forest, a near-mythical domain even by today's standards.

The ruler of the Yeri dynasty had a single heir, a prince celebrated for his intelligence and bravery. Expectations soared that he would further elevate the dynasty's power, perhaps even unifying all of southern India under their rule.

But fate intervened. In his youth, the prince embarked on an expedition into the virgin forest with six handpicked warriors. Over a month passed with no word, and his father feared the worst, organizing a search party. Just as despair loomed, the prince returned—alone.

The mystery of his solo return deepened when he secluded himself in a room for three days before vanishing from the palace, never to return. His disappearance ignited a relentless search, driven by his father's hope and a substantial reward. Over time, reports trickled in: the prince wandered aimlessly, seeking conversations and posing the same question to all he met.

As Yeri recounted these events, a realization struck me. "I know the question he asked," I interrupted, my voice firm with certainty.

Yeri, skeptical, replied, "How could you possibly know?"

"I just do," I insisted.

Seeing my resolve, Yeri relented, spreading his hands in a gesture of acquiescence.

"The question was, 'Are you happy?'" I said, "And every answer was negative."

Yeri's reaction was immediate. He stood abruptly, then sank back into his chair, eyes wide and fixed on me. After a long pause, he asked, "How did you know?"

"In Tokyo," I explained, "I visited a gathering place for Indians because of you. An old man there, a harpist, shared a tale about a prince who sought three wishes from a magical monkey god. That's where I learned of it."

Yeri fell silent, absorbing this revelation. "So that's how it is," he murmured eventually. "That prince, the one who encountered the magical monkey god, is my ancestor."

I had anticipated this connection, so Yeri's admission came as no surprise. His story was a window into a past that intertwined with the present, a narrative of lost dynasties and unfulfilled wishes, leading us to this pivotal moment.

Yeri and I shared an unspoken understanding about the prince's fate. The old harpist's tale had left out the conclusion of the prince's journey, yet the outcome was an open secret—known but unspoken, a shared silence that neither Yeri nor I wished to break.

With a mutual reluctance to dwell on the prince's unresolved story, we shifted focus, and Yeri resumed his narrative.

As a child, Yeri witnessed the decline of local kingship. The Indian central government absorbed the regional powers, allowing former kings to retain only limited possessions. In this new era, most local rulers abandoned their ancestral lands for the allure of big city life, taking their wealth and families with them. Yeri's father was among them, embracing urban luxury despite the loss of political power.

As the local king moved away, the once-majestic palace slowly descended into desolation, its grandeur fading into whispers of the past. For Prince Yeri, the palace was but a distant memory, a relic of a heritage he scarcely knew. That might have remained so, if not for an unexpected encounter that rekindled his connection to it.

Prince Yeri had carved out a promising life in New Delhi, pursuing a degree in medicine. With his striking looks and bright future, he navigated a comfortable life filled with academia, social engagements, and a circle of admirers. His home near the university became a vibrant hub, often echoing with laughter and conversations of his classmates.

During one such gathering, the usual mix of voices was joined by a new accent. A classmate had invited a Japanese guest, whose presence was as intriguing as it was unexpected.

The Japanese, direct and earnest, introduced himself, "My name is Itagaki Mitsuyoshi, from Tokyo. I hope you can assist me."

Though puzzled, Yeri's innate hospitality shone through. He clapped Mitsuyoshi's shoulder warmly. "Tell me, what do you need?"

Mitsuyoshi explained, "I've studied the history of southern India's local kings. I understand you're a descendant of one."

A touch of pride flickered in Yeri's eyes. "Yes, I'm still addressed as a prince."

Mitsuyoshi pressed on, "And there's still a palace in southern India under your name?"

Mention of the "palace" evoked a bittersweet reaction from Yeri. When the central government stripped local kings of power, they permitted the retention of "residences," a dubious privilege. The grandeur of these estates became burdensome due to exorbitant upkeep costs. Many kings relinquished their palaces to the state, but Yeri's father, stubbornly, let theirs languish in decay. Two years prior, Yeri, on a whim, rented a helicopter to survey the neglected estate.

From that moment on, Prince Yeri preferred the comfort of his opulent New Delhi residence, shunning any desire to return to the dilapidated remains of his ancestral palace.

During his last visit, the so-called "palace" had been reduced to little more than rubble. Local villagers had stripped away anything salvageable, and the warm, humid climate of southern India had allowed nature to reclaim the structure. To access the former grand hall, Yeri had to hire ten locals to hack away the dense vines clinging to the entrance.Even then, he could only peer inside, his gaze met by a colony of bats with wings spanning nearly 40 centimeters. The sight startled him into a frenzied escape.

So when a Japanese man suddenly reminded him of his ownership, Yeri chuckled, "Yes, I have a palace. If you want it, it's yours!"

He meant it as a jest; to him, the palace was nothing more than ruins, devoid of any allure. To anyone who had seen it, the thought of interest seemed absurd.

Yet, upon hearing Yeri's words, Itagaki Mitsuyoshi's eyes gleamed with an unusual intensity. (At this point, Yeri offered a detailed description of Mitsuyoshi's appearance.)

Itagaki Mitsuyoshi was not a striking figure—standing around 160 cm, with a pronounced jaw and disproportionately large front teeth. His eyes darted constantly as he spoke, giving him the look of anything but a scholar of ancient Indian history.

Little did Prince Yeri know that this encounter with Mitsuyoshi would ignite a transformative chapter in his life.

Eyes alight with excitement, Mitsuyoshi rubbed his hands together, exclaiming, "Great! Great!"

After his jubilant exclamation, he adopted a more serious tone. "But even if you offered it, I wouldn't dare accept. My only request is to visit your palace."

Yeri laughed heartily, "Feel free! You have my blessing to explore it!"

Mitsuyoshi's excitement only grew. "Thank you! Thank you! Could you give me all the keys to the palace immediately?"

Prince Yeri erupted into laughter, a deep, rolling sound as if he had just heard the most absurd joke. He laughed for several minutes, leaving Mitsuyoshi blushing, feeling as though Yeri had been teasing him all along.

But Yeri's laughter had a reason. Once he composed himself, he explained, "Keys? You won't need keys. What you'll need are axes, knives, or maybe even dynamite!"

Mitsuyoshi blinked rapidly in confusion, prompting Yeri to elaborate, "That's how it was when I visited two years ago. Now, you'll have to contend with blood-sucking bats, cobras, and pythons. Good luck!"

Mitsuyoshi was taken aback, finally expressing his surprise, "I didn't expect it to be like this!"

Yeri assumed Mitsuyoshi would abandon his quest, but instead, Mitsuyoshi persisted, "But I know there's a full set of keys. Can you lend them to me?"

At that moment, Yeri's amusement vanished, replaced by a stern glare. This shorter Japanese man, standing before him, almost provoked Yeri to lash out in anger.

Curious, I asked Yeri, "Why did you react like that? His request seemed quite reasonable. Or was it because there were no keys at all?"

Yeri smiled bitterly. "Oh, there are keys, alright. And you'll understand my anger when I tell you. The palace has over 730 keys!"

I nodded, intrigued. "Indeed, it must be a grand palace."

Prince Yeri continued, "Each key is crafted from gold, with handles encrusted with various gems. This set of keys is a family heirloom. As the family's most important member, I'm entrusted with them. Their value is beyond measure. The Japanese man thought he could deceive me, claiming he needed them to access the palace."

I couldn't help but chuckle at the audacity. "I find it hard to believe he'd try such a clumsy trick."

Yeri studied me for a moment before letting out a sigh. "You're sharper than I gave you credit for. I thought he was trying to con me and nearly lost my temper."

Despite Yeri's refined education, the impulse to hit Mitsuyoshi had been strong, though he never acted on it. Instead, his demeanor turned icy. He waved a dismissive hand and said curtly, "Please leave. Even if I offered you this set of keys, you wouldn't be able to take them."

Mitsuyoshi quickly interjected, "I'm sorry if I wasn't clear. I understand the value of these keys. I only ask to sketch their shapes so I can recreate them. You can have as many people as you like supervise me while I do it."

Yeri was momentarily taken aback by this unexpected request.

After a pause, he exclaimed, "Oh my God! You really do intend to visit the palace!"

Mitsuyoshi responded with a peculiar expression, "Why not?"

Curiosity piqued, Yeri guided Mitsuyoshi to a secluded corner. There, he outlined the palace's decrepit condition, overrun with vines, bats, and venomous snakes, before posing the question, "Why are you so eager to visit a ruin fraught with danger?"

Mitsuyoshi's face flushed with embarrassment. "Originally, I should explain the purpose to you, because I wanted to go to your palace. But—but—but—"

He stammered, repeating "but" several times without further clarification. Yeri pressed, "You're still not saying!"

Mitsuyoshi's discomfort deepened. "Honestly, I'm not entirely sure, but if I do find something, I'll share it with you. I only need two, and I can give you one!"

Yeri was baffled. "Two of what? One of what?"

The exchange left an air of mystery hanging between them, hinting at secrets yet to be revealed and treasures or discoveries that Mitsuyoshi sought within the palace's walls. This puzzle, wrapped in enigmatic intentions and guarded by ancient relics, beckoned Yeri toward an adventure he hadn't anticipated.

At that moment, Yeri's room was bustling with classmates, their chatter filling the air. Two of his female classmates, growing impatient with his extended conversation with Mitsuyoshi in the corner, called out to him repeatedly.

Yeri, feeling the pull of youthful company, was ready to end his talk with Mitsuyoshi. After all, a middle-aged Japanese man with thinning hair hardly compared to the vibrant allure of two curvaceous and lively girls. But just as he was about to leave, Mitsuyoshi murmured, "Two wishes, and one wish, making a total of three wishes."

The words stopped Yeri in his tracks, his foot suspended in mid-air. He turned slowly, eyes locking onto Mitsuyoshi, who wore an expression of grave sincerity. It was as if the air had shifted, charged with the weight of myth and mystery.

Legends of "three wishes" were universal, transcending cultures and continents. What struck Yeri was the solemnity in Mitsuyoshi's voice, the suggestion of something more profound than mere folklore. As Yeri turned, he noted Mitsuyoshi's serious demeanor, dispelling any notion of jest.

Just then, the two female classmates reached him, tugging playfully at his arm. But Yeri gently but firmly pushed them aside, grasped Mitsuyoshi's arm, and without a word, led him upstairs to the privacy of his study.

Once inside, Yeri shut the door with a decisive click. "What did you mean by three wishes?" he demanded, curiosity piqued.

Mitsuyoshi met his gaze. "Yes, three wishes."

Yeri rubbed his chin thoughtfully. "Three wishes... What's their connection to my palace?"

Mitsuyoshi blinked, hesitant. "I'll only reveal that if you allow me to replicate the palace keys."

Without hesitation, Yeri nodded. "It's a deal."

Mitsuyoshi swallowed, his excitement palpable. "I came here to delve into ancient Indian history. In an old library, I found a document about one of your ancestors, a prince who encountered a supernatural monkey god."

Yeri felt a twinge of disappointment. As a member of this lineage, he had grown up on such tales. To him, the legend had lost its mystique through familiarity.

Still, he pressed on. "I know of that legend. What new insights have you uncovered?"

Mitsuyoshi hesitated, then confessed, "It's speculative, but I imagine that after meeting the monkey god, the prince secluded himself in the palace for days."

Yeri nodded, recalling the tale. "Yes, and then he began his travels."

Mitsuyoshi leaned in, his voice charged with excitement. "There's no clear record of the prince's encounter with the supernatural monkey god. But what if he documented it during those secluded days in the palace? If we uncover those records, we could find the monkey god ourselves."

His eyes gleamed with fervor, and he breathed with anticipation. "Imagine meeting the supernatural monkey god and being granted three wishes."

I couldn't help but chuckle at the notion.

Yeri's expression mirrored my amusement, murmuring, "You find it just as amusing as I do."

Ignoring his comment, I remarked, "Mr.Itagaki Mitsuyoshi certainly has an active imagination."

Yet, a thought struck me. Itagaki Mitsuyoshi was a common Japanese name, and Itagaki a common surname. Coincidentally, the lover of Suzuki Yunko, the businessman assassinated by the hitman Iron Smith, was also named Itagaki. Could there be a connection between Itagaki Mitsuyoshi and Itagaki Ichiro?

Curiosity piqued, I asked, "Is there any relation between Itagaki Mitsuyoshi and Itagaki Ichiro? Surely you know of Itagaki Ichiro?"

Yeri, rather than answering directly, cryptically replied, "You'll understand if you keep listening."

I let the question drop, and Yeri continued.

With a laugh, Yeri pointed at Mitsuyoshi. "You said you'd give me one of those wishes?"

Mitsuyoshi nodded earnestly. "Yes, and if that's not enough, you can have two. I only need one wish!"

Despite his curiosity and Mitsuyoshi's serious demeanor, the situation still seemed absurd to Yeri, who maintained a lighthearted approach.

"Forgive my curiosity, but what is your wish?" Yeri inquired with a playful smile.

Mitsuyoshi blushed, stammering before finally admitting, "I can only reveal my wish to the supernatural monkey god!"

Sensing Mitsuyoshi's sincerity, Yeri decided to ease up on the teasing. "Alright, I can't do it today, but tomorrow I'll arrange for you to access the keys."

Mitsuyoshi beamed, bowing repeatedly in gratitude. Yeri promised to meet him the following day and saw him out.

The following day, Mitsuyoshi arrived promptly, and Yeri accompanied him to the bank's safe deposit box where the set of golden keys was stored. Yeri carefully observed Mitsuyoshi's reaction to the priceless keys, expecting awe or greed. Instead, Mitsuyoshi remained indifferent to their material value, focusing intently on meticulously sketching each key's design on the paper he had brought.

As Yeri had mentioned, the collection comprised over 700 keys, and Mitsuyoshi's painstakingly detailed work took three full days to complete. Yeri stayed for the first half hour, but then left Mitsuyoshi under the watchful eyes of the bank guards to finish his task.

Once Mitsuyoshi finished, he returned to Yeri's residence to express his gratitude. During the visit, Mitsuyoshi proposed, "Prince Yeri, would you be interested in joining me to search for the possible records?"

Yeri declined with a shake of his head. "I'm not interested, but I do hope you'll inform me immediately if you find anything."

"Of course! Of course!" Mitsuyoshi assured him.

Yeri, intrigued, asked, "With so many rooms in the palace, most in ruins, how do you plan to start your search?"

Mitsuyoshi replied candidly, "I have a hunch about where the prince might have stayed. As the heir, he likely lived in the central part of the palace."

Yeri sighed wistfully, "If our dynasty still existed, I should be living there too."

With nothing more to say, Mitsuyoshi took his leave. Six months passed without a word from him.

Prince Yeri turned to me, his expression thoughtful. "Mitsuyoshi's been gone for half a year with no news. I nearly forgot about him until I suddenly wondered if he'd met a grim fate, bitten by a snake in that abandoned palace. Or perhaps he found the records and kept them secret, or even met the supernatural monkey god himself and secured three wishes, withholding one from me?"

I chuckled, "That's quite a wild imagination!"

Yeri shrugged. "The situation is strange enough to warrant such thoughts."

I furrowed my brow. "So, no news from Mitsuyoshi after that?"

Yeri smiled wryly. "Oh, I wish there wasn't, but there was news, alright. Not long after he crossed my mind, an airline employee approached me with a letter."

Yeri continued, "The employee said it was from a Japanese named Itagaki Mitsuyoshi. He'd left it before boarding a flight back to Japan, asking it to be delivered to me. Once the employee left, I opened the letter. As I read halfway through, I was utterly stunned."

I sat up, my pulse quickening with anticipation. The letter from Itagaki Mitsuyoshi lay before me, its significance almost palpable in the air. A sudden realization struck me: this letter could be the key to understanding why Yeri, a prince by birth, had led such a nomadic existence in Japan.

Without hesitation, I blurted out, "This letter—"

Yeri met my gaze, his eyes searching mine as if weighing a decision. Finally, he reached into his pocket and withdrew a wallet. Not just any wallet, but a finely crafted one, hinting at the value of its contents. After a moment's pause, he opened it and revealed the letter, old and fragile, its age betrayed by the faded envelope that had nonetheless been preserved by the wallet's craftsmanship.

"When Yeri first encountered Mitsuyoshi," I thought, "he was still in college. Given Yeri's current age, this letter must have been written over a decade ago."

Yeri held the letter with reverence. "This is the message Mitsuyoshi left for me. Please, read it."

With a mix of curiosity and trepidation, I accepted the letter, gingerly sliding it from its envelope. The paper was worn, the ink slightly faded, but the words were unmistakably penned in English.

And thus began the unraveling of Mitsuyoshi Itagaki's message to Yeri, a missive that promised to unveil secrets long buried by time.

CHAPTER 15

The Mysterious Death of Mitsuyoshi

Mr. Prince Yeri,

I am Itagaki Mitsuyoshi. I extend my deepest gratitude for your assistance, which afforded me unparalleled access to conduct an exhaustive search within your palace. My instincts were correct—the prince who once encountered the supernatural Monkey God did indeed document his experience. I have unearthed these records and, after meticulous study, have confirmed the existence of this entity. The Monkey God, as legend has it, possesses extraordinary powers, capable of granting three wishes to any who behold him.

Upon this discovery, I should have informed you immediately, honoring my promise to offer you one or two wishes. Yet, faced with the possibility of encountering the Monkey God myself, I succumbed to the temptation of greed. Noticing your skepticism regarding the feasibility of such wishes, I resolved to seek the Monkey God alone.

And so, I did see the Monkey God.

My encounter with the Monkey God yielded the opportunity to make three wishes, but the outcome was beyond anything I could have anticipated—beyond what you might ever imagine. Even if I recounted the details, I doubt you would believe them.

I have already deceived you once by not upholding my vow. I refuse to mislead you a second time, which is why I choose not to divulge my experience. However, I can offer you this: if the Monkey God truly intrigues you, come to Japan. My address is enclosed. Upon your arrival, I shall reveal how to meet the Monkey God.

I won't wait for you indefinitely. Should you choose to embark on this journey, do so swiftly.

My encounter with myself has left an indelible mark on my existence, reshaping my thoughts and altering the very course of my life. I now possess a clarity about my true purpose.

I sincerely apologize for my breach of trust.

Yours sincerely,

Itagaki Mitsuyoshi

As I finished reading, the letter left me reeling with disbelief. The Monkey God—a figure of ancient legend, dismissed by many as mere myth—had been authenticated by Mitsuyoshi himself. His letter asserted not only the Monkey God's existence but also its power to grant three wishes.

Most astonishing of all was Mitsuyoshi's cryptic mention of an "encounter with myself," a phrase that defies ordinary comprehension unless one truly experiences such a phenomenon.

In that enigmatic room, I came face to face with myself.

Kenichi, too, had witnessed himself in that peculiar space.

Suddenly, Suzuki Yunko's words echoed in my mind. She kept insisting, "It wasn't me, it was another woman." Could it be that she, too, had seen herself?

The thought sent a shiver down my spine, a chill so intense that it felt as though ice had settled in my veins.

I couldn't fathom what Kenichi saw, but my own encounter was more of a fleeting impression—deeply etched in memory, yet not manifesting into any tangible event.

Yunko's case, however, seemed different. If she had indeed seen herself, then the other "her" might act with a freedom and audacity she dared not claim. It was as if two versions of Suzuki Yunko existed, each a fragment of the original.

I recalled a conversation with Kenichi at Iron Smith's residence, as we puzzled over the second videotape. Kenichi had suggested "schizophrenia," where a person's psyche divides into dual aspects, A and B. My mind had entertained the bizarre notion that Yunko's experience was a physical split, a division of her very being into A and B.

Now, I felt more convinced that my hypothesis edged closer to the truth.

If true, the implications were terrifying. Imagine if every person harbors an A and B side, with one visible and the other obscured, yet both integral to the whole. If these dual natures could physically sever a person into two, it was an unfathomable horror—a singular identity cleaved into two distinct beings! Not merely a fracture of mind or spirit, but a corporeal duplication—a replica sharing the same visage but diverging in emotion, thought, and character, with the hidden aspect inhabiting the duplicate.

The realization sent cold sweat trickling down my back, a sensation like icy-legged insects scuttling across my skin.

What phenomenon was this? What force could manifest such an impossible occurrence?

What on earth was happening?

I opened my mouth, desperate to scream, but only ragged breaths escaped.

I flailed my arms wildly, grasping for comprehension amidst the chaos.

My thoughts were a tangled mess, my demeanor likely alarming, for Yeri watched me with a mixture of surprise and concern. Gradually, I steadied myself enough to speak, though the words came out dry and foreign to my ears. "You must have gone to Japan to see Mitsuyoshi as soon as you received his letter?"

Yeri seemed taken aback by my question, though it was perfectly logical. In his position, I would have sought out Mitsuyoshi immediately after reading such a missive.

Yet Yeri's response told me I had misjudged. He offered a rueful smile and asked, "Why would you think that?"

"Because Mitsuyoshi met the supernatural Monkey God," I replied. "A being that grants three wishes is an irresistible temptation for anyone. Aren't you curious at all?"

Yeri reached up, his fingers brushing across his face as if hoping to erase the fatigue and bitterness etched into his features.

"I never went to Japan initially," Yeri confessed, his voice tinged with frustration. "I didn't take Mitsuyoshi's letter seriously at all, because from the very beginning, I didn't believe in such nonsense!" He repeated, almost as if trying to convince himself, "I don't believe it at all!"

I spread my hands in understanding. To someone who dismissed such fantastical notions outright, Mitsuyoshi's letter held no value. Yeri's reaction was predictable.

Yet, I knew Yeri eventually found his way to Japan. He spent considerable time there, mastering the language and engaging in peculiar activities. What had changed his mind?

Before I could voice my curiosity, Yeri offered a self-deprecating chuckle. "You're wondering why I went to Japan later, aren't you?"

I nodded, urging him to continue. Yeri sighed, a sound laden with the weight of experience. "Life is unpredictable. When I first received the letter, I dismissed the idea of a Monkey God granting wishes. I had no desires unmet, no unfulfilled dreams. My life was content, and I wanted for nothing. So, I shoved it aside and forgot about it. Until nearly two years later—"

His voice trailed off, eyes clouded with a distant sorrow.

I could imagine what might have happened. Life has a way of throwing us curveballs, and when faced with dissatisfaction, people often turn to the divine for answers. Yeri, it seemed, was no exception.

"I fell in love with a woman," he stated plainly. "There's no need to embellish how beautiful or deserving of love she was. Suffice it to say, I needed her in my life and resolved to marry her. But she didn't reciprocate my feelings. No matter how fervently I pursued her, employing every conceivable tactic, she remained unmoved. I was driven to madness. At that point, my sole purpose in life was to win her heart."

Yeri paused, and I held my breath, not daring to interrupt. Though his recounting was straightforward, the raw intensity in his eyes and the urgency in his voice conveyed the depth of his passion for this woman. It was a love that had consumed him entirely.

"After six months of relentless pursuit, with nothing to show for my efforts," Yeri continued, his tone shifting from sorrowful to a detached calm, "it suddenly struck me: if there were a god who could grant me a single wish, all I would ask for is her love—to have her care for me as deeply as I did for her."

I nodded, understanding. "You needed a wish."

Yeri's expression tightened. "My mental state was in shambles at the time. Even then, the letter from Mitsuyoshi had faded from my memory. One night, drowning in wine and despair, I found myself curled up in a corner, my fingers intertwined, pleading with any deity who might listen. I screamed out for a wish, for her love to mirror mine."

Whether a god heard Yeri's desperate cries, no one could say.

Desperation nearly consumed him as he prayed for a miraculous wish. In that moment of utter hopelessness, the memory of Itagaki Mitsuyoshi and the legend of the supernatural Monkey God, who could grant three wishes, resurfaced in Yeri's mind.

He remained on his knees, no longer trembling or weeping, as his thoughts turned to Mitsuyoshi's letter.

Though he had dismissed the tale as fantasy, his longing for her love was powerful enough to make him consider any possibility, no matter how fantastical. Mitsuyoshi had been clear: the Monkey God could grant three wishes.

With renewed determination, Yeri sprang to his feet, retrieved Mitsuyoshi's letter, and began arranging his travel plans. For someone of his standing, the logistics were trivial, and Mitsuyoshi's address in Japan was precise.

Before departing India, he bid farewell to the woman he adored, promising that he would return to marry her. Her response was a dismissive laugh.

Yet, Yeri remained undeterred. He believed that once he reached Japan and located Itagaki Mitsuyoshi, he would follow the steps outlined in the letter. He would meet the supernatural Monkey God, obtain his three wishes, and return to India triumphant and ready to win her heart.

When Yeri finally reached Japan, the anticipated meeting with Itagaki Mitsuyoshi did not materialize.

Instead, he found himself in the company of a local police officer, a man who had taught himself rudimentary English. Together, they walked a narrow path flanked by dead grass, tinged with a mysterious purple-red hue, a color Yeri had never associated with grass. The cool, brisk air of late autumn, so different from the tropical warmth of his upbringing, nipped at his skin, adding a chill to the already enigmatic journey. The path meandered onward, seemingly without end.

Impatience prickled at Yeri, prompting him to ask repeatedly, "How far is it?"

Each time, the officer halted, responding with unwavering politeness, "Not far, we are almost there!"

Yeri tugged at his collar, a hint of irritation creeping into his voice. "I'm here to see Mr. Itagaki Mitsuyoshi. Can I meet him?"

Since his arrival in the quaint town, armed with the address Mitsuyoshi had provided, Yeri had posed this question to everyone he encountered. It was the first Japanese sentence he had mastered.

Yet, each inquiry was met with a look of surprise that puzzled Yeri. What was so bewildering about his quest to meet Mr. Itagaki Mitsuyoshi?

It wasn't until an encounter with a local elementary school teacher that he received a semblance of an answer. "Ah, you wish to see Mr. Itagaki Mitsuyoshi? He lives near the school, but he—he—"

The teacher's English was passable, but even he wore that familiar, strange expression. By now, Yeri was accustomed to it. "Please, just tell me Mr. Itagaki's address, and I'll find it myself."

The teacher advised, "I think you should contact the local police station first!"

"Why?" Yeri pressed, bewildered.

After a moment's hesitation, the teacher replied, "It's best to make contact first. You're from elsewhere, and you don't understand what's happened here."

Despite wanting to probe further, Yeri found himself directed to the police station, conveniently located on the town's only street. With repeated bows and a polite smile, the teacher bid him farewell.

Yeri stood in stunned silence, uncertainty gnawing at him. With no other options, he set off for the police station, acutely aware of the curious children and teenagers trailing him, pointing and whispering. It seemed Yeri was the first Indian to grace this small town with his presence.

Yeri stepped into the police station, his presence barely acknowledged by the two officers inside. One, an older man, was oblivious to English, while the younger officer had a basic grasp of the language. Yeri repeated himself, striving to remain composed, "I've come from India to see Mr. Itagaki Mitsuyoshi. A teacher advised I visit here first, but I don't understand why."

The young officer's demeanor shifted to one of gravity upon hearing Yeri's explanation. He exchanged urgent words with his senior, whose expression mirrored the seriousness.

Though the conversation was lost on Yeri, he sensed something unusual had befallen Itagaki Mitsuyoshi.

Impatience gnawed at him as he awaited clarification. After a lengthy exchange, the younger officer finally revealed, "Itagaki Mitsuyoshi is dead. He passed away six months ago."

The news hit Yeri like a physical blow, and he struggled to reconcile this with his memory of Mitsuyoshi—vigorous and alive when last they met. Mitsuyoshi's health had seemed robust, certainly not that of a man on the brink of death. But the officer's words bore the weight of truth, and Yeri's hope crumbled into ashes of disappointment. He had journeyed with the promise of answers, only to find them buried with Mitsuyoshi.

Detecting Yeri's dismay, the young officer offered, "You must have been a close friend of Mr. Itagaki. Would you like to visit his grave?"

In his confusion, Yeri barely registered the question but nodded absently, "Okay! Okay!"

The officer explained, "After Mr. Itagaki's passing, since his only relative was in Tokyo, and given the—strangeness—of his death, we buried him quickly. I was among the few attendees at his funeral."

"Strange?" Yeri echoed, his attention sharpening. "His death was strange?"

A flicker of discomfort passed over the officer's face. "Yes, it was—unusual—very strange."

Yeri scrutinized the officer, trying to decipher what could constitute a "very unusual" death. He intended to probe further, but the older officer cut him off with a sharp reprimand. The younger officer, visibly chastened, fell silent, merely offering, "I'll take you to Mr. Itagaki's grave."

The path they tread was lined with autumn's dying grass, turning a deep ochre red, as Yeri followed the officer out of the town. The walk stretched nearly forty minutes, yet the cemetery remained out of sight.

Yeri's mind churned with questions, each step compounding his confusion about Mitsuyoshi's mysterious demise.

Listening to Yeri recount this, my own curiosity mirrored his. What could possibly render Mitsuyoshi's death so peculiar? We had an understanding that I could interject with questions, and my mind was teeming with them.

My confusion was overwhelming, so I interrupted Yeri, asking, "What does it mean to die very strangely?"

Yeri met my gaze, his expression serious. "I can't sum it up in a few words. You need to hear the entire story. Mitsuyoshi's death was indeed strange. Despite efforts to keep it under wraps, the odd circumstances inevitably spread. It was so bizarre that even the townspeople, though skeptical, had heard whispers of the bizarre incident. That's why everyone reacted so oddly when I asked about Itagaki Mitsuyoshi."

His explanation only deepened my bewilderment. What could have been so peculiar about Mitsuyoshi's death? I realized I had no choice but to listen to Yeri's detailed account.

It took a full hour before Yeri finally reached Mitsuyoshi's grave.

The grave was unassuming, a simple mound of earth topped with flat stones. A wooden pillar stood before it, inscribed with a line of text that Yeri, unfamiliar with Japanese, could not decipher.

As the officer gestured toward the grave, Yeri stepped forward, crossing the wooden marker. Staring at the weed-covered mound, he was gripped by an unexplainable sadness. He murmured to himself, "Why did you die, Mitsuyoshi? Without you, how will I find the supernatural Monkey God? How will I fulfill my wish?"

He repeated his lament, then noticed the officer's horrified gaze fixed on the grave. Despite the encroaching darkness and the desolate surroundings, it seemed odd for a police officer to be so unnerved.

When Yeri caught his expression, the officer appeared embarrassed. "I'm sorry, sir. Mr. Itagaki's death was so strange that it unnerves me."

Yeri's frustration boiled over. "How strange was his death?"

The officer sighed. "There are two people buried in this grave."

Yeri was momentarily stunned, struggling to comprehend the officer's words. "Who is the other one?" he demanded.

The officer replied, "There is no other person."

Yeri's anger flared. In India, he might have lashed out physically, but he knew better than to assault a police officer in a foreign land.

Suppressing his irritation, Yeri decided not to press the officer further, realizing his incoherence. Yet, the officer continued, "Two—both are Mr. Itagaki!"

I leaped from my seat, my sudden movement causing Yeri across from me to recoil, his instincts urging him to defend himself. The shock on my face must have been palpable, my mind racing with the implications of what I had just heard.

I stammered, my voice rough with disbelief, "Two—two Itagaki Mitsuyoshi?"

As I uttered those words, the memory of "two Suzuki Yunkos" flashed vividly before me. I recalled a detail Naka had mentioned when Kenichi visited Yunko in the mental hospital. Naka had overheard their conversation through the door, noting that Kenichi repeatedly used the term "you guys."

Why would Kenichi use "you guys" if Yunko was alone in the room? There had to be someone else present—another Suzuki Yunko!

But who was this other person? If it was indeed another Suzuki Yunko, then there were two of her!

Moreover, I remembered the moment when Iron Smith, the assassin, entered the rendezvous point. He had exclaimed, "Who are you?" He must have encountered another person, prompting such a reaction.

Could he have seen another Suzuki Yunko? It seemed unlikely. Before his death, Iron had struggled to face the study and asked, "Who are you?"

This suggested the figure he saw must have shocked him profoundly. Who could this person be? It was Iron Smith himself—another Iron! He had seen his own doppelgänger!

And I, too, had faced myself—there were two of me! The realization sent shivers down my spine, the enigma deepening with every revelation. What force was at play here, duplicating identities, merging realities with such chilling precision?

At that moment, Yeri hadn't grasped the full meaning behind the officer's words, but the instant he recounted the story to me, the implications clicked into place like the final piece of an intricate puzzle.

My breath quickened, the sheer incredibility of the situation sending a chill down my spine. This was truly bizarre.

Yeri, watching me with a haunted expression, said, "From everything that's happened since, you can probably piece together what's going on."

I gestured wildly, unable to contain my confusion. "No, I don't fully understand. All I know is that there seem to be duplicates—Yunko has two versions, Iron the assassin might have two, and I've seen myself. Kenichi... I don't know about him, but he might have a double too."

Yeri remained silent, his gaze steady and inscrutable.

I pressed on, "It seems like everyone has their double!"

Yeri corrected me, "Not seems—everyone actually has a double."

My eyes widened, the weight of his words hanging heavily in the air. Unsure how to proceed, I fell silent, sensing Yeri's desire to continue without interruption.

Taking a deep breath, I settled back into my seat.

Yeri echoed incredulously, "Two Mr. Itagakis?"

The officer, visibly perturbed, replied, "Yes, we were unaware that Mr. Itagaki had a twin. One brother killed the other, or perhaps it was the reverse. They were indistinguishable, and no one could determine which was which. The two of them—"

Yeri interjected swiftly, "Wait, what are you talking about?"

The officer explained, "I was on patrol that night. Mr. Itagaki's house is near the elementary school. As I rounded the school's fence, I heard a quarrel from his home."

Yeri, stepping back from the grave, gestured for the officer to continue. The officer obliged, "It was peculiar because Mr. Itagaki lived alone, a fact known throughout the town. He was respected for his research, unrivaled in knowledge, and possessed an impressive library."

Yeri cut in impatiently, "Spare me the irrelevant details!"

The officer hesitated, clearly reluctant to recount the strange events, but resumed, "I approached the house, and the argument grew clearer. Two men were quarreling, but here's the odd part—the voices were identical. One was aggressive and furious, the other frail and sorrowful."

The officer had stood at Itagaki's door, listening intently to the heated exchange. Though alone, his testimony was later corroborated by no one else, yet it was deemed credible and archived by his superiors following the murder investigation.

The quarrel that the police officer overheard was both chilling and surreal, a cacophony of conflict echoing through the night.

A harsh voice bellowed, laced with a dreadful roar: "You're utterly useless! Why do you insist on staying hidden away in this obscure little town? If you weren't so pathetic, why resign yourself to obscurity?"

A feeble voice responded, laden with helplessness: "I must do this. I have no choice. Please, don't push me!"

The harsh voice continued, punctuated by a barrage of curses and accusations: "Nonsense! You can make your wishes come true! You can have whatever you desire! You could be the most famous, powerful, and wealthiest person alive! You could own everything!"

The feeble voice replied, "So what?"

"'So what'? You fool! Even farm animals know better than you! You shouldn't have given up or slunk back here!"

The weak voice sighed, "Even if I had everything, there's one vital thing missing."

The harsh voice sneered, "I suppose you mean happiness! Since no one truly finds happiness, why forsake what you can attain?"

The weak voice pleaded, "Without happiness, what good is everything else? Please, stop!"

"I won't stop! I must say it!" the harsh voice insisted.

The police officer then heard the sounds of a physical altercation, like bodies colliding, someone being forcefully shoved. Feeling compelled to act, he pounded on the door, shouting, "Mr. Itagaki! Mr. Itagaki!" Yet his urgent knocks went unanswered, the argument inside oblivious to the noise. A nearby teacher, roused by the commotion, emerged in his nightclothes. By then, the quarrel had escalated into a violent struggle.

Together, the officer and teacher forced the door open, and what they witnessed left them aghast.

Before them were two Itagaki Mitsuyoshis, locked in a deadly grapple. One had his hands around the other's throat, while the one being strangled scrabbled blindly across the floor, fingers closing around a sharp knife.

The officer and teacher screamed in horror, their cries mingling with the scene unfolding.

The strangled Itagaki thrust the knife deep into the side of his attacker, the blade sinking to the hilt. The stabbed Itagaki let out a bloodcurdling roar, his grip tightening in a final, desperate act. The sound of a trachea being crushed echoed grotesquely in the room.

By the time the officer and teacher rushed in, the tragedy had already unfolded, a tableau of violence and despair. The two Itagakis were so entwined in death that separating them proved impossible, leaving the witnesses paralyzed by the horror of it all.

CHAPTER 16

The Enigma of the Ancient Box

As dusk settled over the city, Yeri stepped into a dimly lit bar, a place where he was a familiar face. The bar had just opened for the evening, with only a handful of patrons scattered about. The barmaid was absent, and the proprietress stifled a yawn behind the counter. Out of sheer boredom, Yeri picked up a newspaper dated for the previous day. His eyes widened as he spotted a missing person notice—a notice for him.

The notice read:

"Attention, Indian gentleman: Many years ago, a Japanese individual requested to borrow your palace to find something. He found it and died shortly after returning to Japan. I wish to meet with you now. I have numerous questions that need answers. I attempted to locate you in India and have learned you are in Japan. Hence, I've published this notice. Please contact me via the 38th mailbox of this newspaper upon seeing this."

Yeri read the notice repeatedly, ensuring that it was indeed meant for him, an Indian adrift in Japan. A strange sensation stirred within him, a premonition that something significant was about to unfold.

After all these years, why had someone suddenly placed an ad to find him? Could it be linked to Itagaki Mitsuyoshi? The Japanese man in the notice who borrowed his palace was undoubtedly Mitsuyoshi!

Without hesitation, Yeri left the bar and headed to the newspaper office, leaving a note with his current address and contact information. The following day, he received a call.

A man's voice came through the receiver: "Mr. Yeri, I received your message. We must meet. Some things are truly mysterious."

Yeri asked, "Who are you?"

The voice replied, "It's not convenient to discuss over the phone. I'll introduce myself when we meet. I'm busy during the day, but after work, I'll provide you with an address where we can meet."

The man's tone was hurried, cloaked in mystery, but Yeri felt no fear. Regardless of the man's intentions, Yeri was confident he had nothing to lose.

He jotted down the address and awaited the end of the workday.

When Yeri later relayed the address to me, it was my turn to be taken aback.

The address was none other than the rendezvous spot where Itagaki Ichiro and his mistress, Suzuki Yunko, would meet.

Typically, a man would not invite another to such a clandestine location unless the person or the matter to be discussed was of utmost secrecy.

Given this address, I didn't need Yeri to spell it out for me; I realized instantly that "the man on the phone" was Itagaki Ichiro!

I refrained from interrupting Yeri's tale, offering only a soft sigh of realization and gesturing for him to continue.

Yeri waited patiently until the workday drew to a close, then made his way to the building specified in the mysterious address. Despite having lived in Japan for some time without financial worries—his agent in India regularly sending substantial remittances—Yeri had let himself go, his appearance disheveled and his clothes unkempt, reflecting a state of psychological self-abandonment.

As he stepped into the building, he was immediately confronted by the administrator, who approached him with a shout.

It's worth noting that this administrator, named Takeo, would later meet an untimely demise in the hunting area.

Yeri, once accustomed to a life of privilege, had, over time, grown indifferent to such treatment. He brushed off the administrator's brusque demeanor and simply informed him of the person he intended to meet and the unit number. The administrator eyed him with skepticism but relented, saying, "Wait a minute!"

Using the building's internal phone, the administrator made a call. Yeri overheard snippets of the conversation: "Yes, Mr. Inoue, yes, Mr. Inoue!"

After hanging up, the administrator gestured for Yeri to proceed upstairs.

Yeri entered the elevator, and when it stopped, the doors opened to reveal a middle-aged Japanese man standing expectantly. The man, though polite, exuded a sense of urgency. He was momentarily taken aback by Yeri's appearance but quickly recovered, saying, "Come in, Mr. Yeri, please come in!"

Stepping into the unit, Yeri noted its modest size yet elegant decor. He settled into a seat and faced the man. "Mr. Inoue, what's the matter?"

He addressed him as "Mr. Inoue" based on the administrator's phone conversation.

The man paused, then corrected, "Inoue is an alias. My real name is Itagaki, Itagaki Ichiro."

Yeri was momentarily stunned, an "ah" escaping his lips. The name Itagaki immediately brought to mind Mitsuyoshi. He quickly interjected, "There's a Mr. Itagaki Mitsuyoshi—"

Itagaki Ichiro cut him off, "He was my cousin, albeit a distant relative. Yet, given that Mitsuyoshi had no other family, I am effectively his only kin."

Memories flooded back to Yeri—his quest to find Mitsuyoshi, the visit to the grave, the police officer's eerie account of Mitsuyoshi's death. The officer had mentioned a cousin, a businessman based in Tokyo, who hadn't attended the funeral. At the time, Yeri hadn't given this "cousin" much thought, but now he understood that Itagaki Ichiro was Mitsuyoshi's sole surviving relative.

"You didn't attend your cousin's funeral," Yeri remarked, his tone neutral but probing.

Itagaki Ichiro appeared visibly uncomfortable as he explained, "I was swamped with work and couldn't leave my commitments. When I heard the news from the countryside, it said two cousins had fought to the death. I only knew of one cousin, so I assumed it was a mistake and decided not to go."

Ichiro's explanation was flimsy at best, but Yeri had little interest in delving deeper. He simply asked, "So, why did you want to find me?"

Ichiro hesitated, casting a cautious glance at Yeri. "Are you truly the Prince Yeri that Uncle Mitsuyoshi mentioned?"

Without a word, Yeri reached beneath his collar, unclasping a necklace, which he tossed to Ichiro. "See for yourself."

Ichiro snatched the necklace out of the air. The silver chain was tarnished and grimy, but as Ichiro examined the pendant, his eyes widened in astonishment.

Though a seasoned businessman familiar with fine jewelry, Ichiro had never encountered anything like this. The pendant was a massive sapphire, easily over 80 carats, surrounded by a flawless circle of jadeite, each stone over three carats.

Swallowing hard, Ichiro gingerly returned the necklace to Yeri, his hands trembling. Even as a successful entrepreneur, he realized that his entire fortune couldn't match the value of this pendant.

Yeri slipped the necklace back around his neck nonchalantly. "I'm sorry," Ichiro stammered, "I doubted your identity earlier. It was foolish of me. Please forgive my ignorance."

Yeri waved away the apology and pressed on, "Why did you want to see me—"

Ichiro rubbed his hands together nervously. "Well, after my cousin's death, the local police handed me a box of his belongings, claiming it was his bequest to me."

Hearing this, Yeri's heart raced.

His journey to Japan had been driven by the quest to find Mitsuyoshi and inquire about the supernatural Monkey God. Mitsuyoshi's death had seemed to close that door. But now, Ichiro's revelation of a box left behind reignited Yeri's hopes.

What could this box contain? Could it hold the key to finding the supernatural Monkey God?

Yeri sprang to his feet, then sat down again, visibly agitated. "That box of things—" he began, his voice faltering as his throat tightened with tension, making him unable to continue.

"When the box was delivered," Ichiro began, "they simply mentioned it was my uncle's belongings. It was old and battered, so I didn't give it much thought and stored it away."

Yeri's hands tightened with anticipation. "That box—what about it?"

Ichiro continued, "Just a few days ago, while searching the storage room, I stumbled upon it again. Curiosity got the better of me—I wondered what my uncle had left for me. The box was locked, and I had misplaced the key, so I forced it open. Inside, I found another wooden box."

"Another box within the box?" Yeri interjected, his interest piqued.

"Yes," Ichiro confirmed, "the remaining space was filled with books and notes penned by my uncle."

Yeri couldn't suppress a groan of excitement. He had traveled to Japan precisely for these items, believing hope was lost. Recently, he had heard that the woman he loved was about to marry. If he could encounter the supernatural Monkey God and secure three wishes, he could win her love.

His patience wearing thin, Yeri blurted out, "That's exactly what I came for! I must have them—name your price. I'll pay anything. My lineage includes royalty!"

Ichiro blinked at Yeri's fervor, sensing his desperation. "Mr. Yeri, please, calm down and hear me out."

Though eager to speak, Yeri saw Ichiro gesturing for silence and reluctantly sat back. Ichiro continued, "As a pragmatic businessman, I'm uninterested in the fantastical. Initially, I had no intention of reading those notes, but after opening the second box, I encountered something peculiar."

Yeri recalled mention of Mitsuyoshi's discoveries in the letter he had left him, hinting at an encounter with the supernatural Monkey God. It was possible Mitsuyoshi had documented his findings.

But what was this "peculiar thing"? Yeri was at a loss. "A strange thing? What do you mean?"

Ichiro admitted, "I still can't quite grasp what it is, nor can I fully describe its form. It's just... odd. I've moved it here; you should see it for yourself."

He gestured toward a door leading to the study.

Yeri was more interested in Mitsuyoshi's notes than any "strange things." Those records held the key to encountering the supernatural Monkey God, which was his true goal.

He tried to steer the conversation back. "Whatever it is, let's set it aside. Mr. Mitsuyoshi's notes—"

But Ichiro was insistent, interrupting once more. "You really should see this thing first. It's unlike anything you've ever seen."

With a sigh of resignation, Yeri glanced at the door. Ichiro had already moved toward it, opening it in an unexpected way. Instead of pulling the handle, Ichiro pushed it from another angle. Yeri stood, a noise of surprise escaping him.

Ichiro turned back, explaining, "Since I brought this here, I've had a feeling it's incredibly important. So, I installed the door backward as a precaution. If someone tried to break in, they wouldn't be able to open it and steal the item."

Yeri chuckled. "You don't even know what it is, so who would want to steal it?"

Ichiro shrugged. "It's strange and mysterious. You never know what might happen."

As they stepped into the study, Yeri noticed a small room dominated by an ancient wooden box in the center. Ichiro approached it and lifted the lid.

Just as Ichiro had described, another wooden box filled most of the space inside. This inner box, crafted from dark red wood, appeared older, its lid adorned with peculiar reliefs.

Yeri froze at the sight of the relief. It depicted a deity unmistakably of Indian origin. India was a land of countless gods, each with unique forms, and Yeri couldn't immediately identify this one.

Ichiro opened the inner box. "Take a look."

Yeri moved closer, peering inside, and was left speechless.

The box's contents were indeed the "strange thing" Ichiro had mentioned. Its nature defied explanation, leaving Yeri at a loss.

The object was about 50 cubic centimeters in volume, an irregular mass of black, oddly-shaped material that emitted a faint sheen. Its form was indescribable, resembling nothing so much as a haphazard mass of molten tin suddenly cooled in water—chaotic and without discernible purpose.

Despite its bizarre appearance, the object wasn't particularly heavy. Yeri, intrigued by its form, reached out to pick it up.

As Yeri lifted the enigmatic object, he was struck by its unexpected lightness. Its size and dark metallic appearance suggested a weight of over twenty kilograms, yet it hovered in his grasp, scarcely weighing a single kilogram. He'd anticipated a struggle, but instead, it rose effortlessly.

Technically, Yeri had only partially raised the object. What appeared to be a solid mass revealed itself as a complex assembly of countless ultra-thin layers, interconnected by delicate filaments no longer than a centimeter. The structure was a marvel, like a stack of ethereal sheets meticulously aligned, each layer distinct yet part of an intricate whole.

Standing at 180 centimeters, Yeri's reach extended about 80 centimeters. As he lifted, the object unfolded into over 800 shimmering layers, with more remaining in the box. Fully extended, it might span over 2,000 layers—a baffling sight akin to gossamer fabric maintaining its form despite being manipulated.

Unlike anything he'd encountered, the layers retracted seamlessly, falling back into their original configuration as if guided by unseen hands. Breathless, Yeri released his hold, watching the layers realign perfectly. "What is this?" he gasped, the words escaping before he could stop them.

Ichiro, equally mystified, shook his head. "I don't know. All I understand is that it can expand and retract, forming a vast sheet before returning to its initial state, as if there's an invisible bond between the layers."

Intrigued, Yeri gently separated a few slices, discovering they were thinner than paper, nearly invisible unless positioned just right under the light. When aligned with a light source, they revealed countless shimmering points, an unseen constellation.

Yeri turned to Ichiro, his voice urgent. "Mitsuyoshi's notes must mention this. Where are they? Where have you hidden them?"

Suddenly impassioned, Yeri grabbed Ichiro's arms, his grip firm. Startled, Ichiro recoiled, "The notes, they're here! I called you to study them together."

Yeri released him, and Ichiro, still shaken, stepped back. "I'm lost with these notes. I've consulted countless references but still can't decipher them. They allude to an Indian deity, the monkey god—"

"The supernatural monkey god," Yeri interjected, the name resonating with ancient lore.

"Yes," Ichiro continued, "a god rumored to grant three wishes."

"Precisely," Yeri nodded, urgency in his eyes. "Retrieve Mitsuyoshi's notes. We must unravel this together."

Ichiro's eyes gleamed with a cunning glint as he regarded Yeri, the unspoken words dancing on the tip of his tongue. His hesitation was palpable, yet enticing in its mystery.

Yeri, sensing the unspoken tension, urged him on with a low growl, "What is it you want to say?"

Ichiro's lips curled into a sly smile. "I just wonder," he mused, "does every witness of the monkey god receive three wishes, or are there just three wishes total?"

Yeri's impatience flared. "What difference does it make?"

"If everyone gets three wishes, then there's no issue," Ichiro continued, his eyes twinkling with the allure of untold possibilities. "But if there are only three wishes in total—"

Yeri cut him off, comprehension dawning. "Fine! I only need one wish. The rest are yours. Happy now?"

Ichiro's face lit up, his satisfaction plain. "Of course! Thank you, truly!"

With a decisive nod, Yeri gestured for the notes, eager to delve into Mitsuyoshi's discoveries. Ichiro obliged, revealing a trove of documents from a cluttered cabinet. "They're all here," he announced.

Yeri's gaze fell upon several brown paper bags, each bulging with content. He eagerly extracted them, his fingers brushing against the promise of secrets within.

Mitsuyoshi's notes unfolded in layers.

The first section chronicled his exploration of ancient Indian legends surrounding the elusive monkey god—tales already familiar, yet rich with intrigue.

The second section detailed his meticulous search through a forgotten palace, an endeavor steeped in historical resonance but largely irrelevant to their immediate quest. In short, Mitsuyoshi had unearthed a vast collection of writings in the ruins of a bygone dynasty.

These writings, housed in another paper bag, were inscribed on delicate silk scrolls, the material yellowed with age, the script an ancient Indian dialect.

Ichiro, unable to decipher the archaic language, had sought Yeri's expertise through a newspaper appeal—a desperate move that now bore fruit. As Yeri perused the texts, Ichiro's curiosity was insatiable. "What does it say?" he pressed, peering over Yeri's shoulder.

Only after he had absorbed the entirety of the scrolls did Yeri finally exhale, the weight of revelation lifting. "This is the account of an Indian prince from centuries past, detailing his encounter with the supernatural monkey god."

Ichiro's anticipation was tangible. "So, it's true?"

"Yes," Yeri confirmed, excitement threading his voice. "At least two people have witnessed the monkey god. One was a prince from long ago, and the other was Mitsuyoshi. Let's see what Mitsuyoshi's records reveal next."

The room seemed to pulse with the gravity of their discovery, each document a stepping stone toward unraveling a mystery that bridged the realms of myth and reality.

Yeri carefully extracted another brown paper bag, revealing a jumble of papers laden with dense, handwritten text. Despite his time in Japan, the cursive script proved challenging—Mitsuyoshi's handwriting was notoriously haphazard, a blend of hurried strokes and cryptic annotations.

"What does it say?" Yeri murmured, flipping through the pages, frustration evident in his voice.

Ichiro, persistent and probing, interjected, "And what about the prince's account?"

Yeri sighed, "I've explained it already."

"A vast collection of ancient Indian writings condensed into mere sentences?" Ichiro queried, skepticism dripping from his words.

Yeri paused, realization dawning on him. Ichiro's pointed gaze suggested an unspoken challenge; they were partners in this mystery, not adversaries. "I'm a businessman," Ichiro asserted, "and I dislike being shortchanged. Let's keep it honest—you translate the ancient script verbatim, and I'll handle the Japanese."

Despite inwardly bristling at Ichiro's bluntness, Yeri conceded, knowing the necessity of cooperation. Ichiro's eyes gleamed with suspicion. "No tricks, understood?"

Yeri withheld his irritation. "Ancient records are mere preludes to Mitsuyoshi's firsthand accounts. Surely you see their value?"

Ichiro merely blinked, his expression inscrutable. Resigned, Yeri began translating the prince's detailed narrative about the supernatural monkey god, recounting each line to Ichiro.

The ancient prince's encounter was vivid, meticulously chronicled. Yeri relayed the story with fidelity to the original, yet the details mirrored those found in Mitsuyoshi's own record—a tapestry woven from past and present threads.

Mitsuyoshi's account, however, was exhaustive, a diary capturing the minutiae of his experiences. It promised deeper insights than the prince's tale, utilizing modern language to convey subtleties the ancient script could not.

Having completed the translation of the silk scrolls, Ichiro turned to Mitsuyoshi's journals, reading aloud to Yeri. Each entry was a window into Mitsuyoshi's world—rich in detail, vibrant in emotion.

You might expect me to divulge Mitsuyoshi's notes in full, to unravel their secrets here and now. Yet, I choose restraint, for the events that followed echoed those same records, bringing them to life in ways mere words cannot capture. What transpired surpassed any written account, breathing reality into the pages.

One element demands immediate attention—the "strange thing." Its significance eclipsed all else, serving as the catalyst for the chain of events that led to Iron's fateful confrontation with Ichiro in that shadowed hotel room, as mentioned at the start of the story.

Mitsuyoshi's diaries mentioned this "strange thing" across three separate entries. Though fragmented, these entries formed a coherent narrative, their importance crystallizing as Yeri and Ichiro delved deeper into the mystery that bound them.

* * *

On a specific day and month

I found myself too exhilarated to sleep. Witnessing the mystical Monkey God was an experience that defied the mundane; only a fool or a superhuman could close their eyes after such an encounter. I, Itagaki Mitsuyoshi, was neither, and my mind raced with the implications of what I had seen. The Monkey God—his presence was so overwhelming, it was as if he read my thoughts. "Do not question it," he boomed. "I am the Monkey God. That is all you need to know."

In his presence, defiance seemed inconceivable. There was something deeply compelling about the moment, a blend of awe and trepidation that made my skin prickle. Yesterday, words had failed me, but after a restless night of contemplation, I resolved to voice my desires.

I knelt before him, my voice a reverent whisper. "I have heard that those who see you are granted three wishes."

"Indeed," he replied, his voice a gentle lullaby, soothing yet commanding. "But before you speak your wishes, consider carefully—will their fulfillment truly satisfy you?"

I had pondered this countless times since learning of his existence. "I have thought of my three wishes more times than I can count," I declared confidently.

The Monkey God smiled, a knowing curve of his lips. "Perhaps you have not reflected enough. I want you to see yourself first, to ensure your wishes are true to your heart."

The request seemed unnecessary, yet I dared not defy him. "Very well," I agreed. "But what does it mean to 'see myself'?"

His laughter was rich and warm as he gestured to an ancient wooden box, its surface adorned with intricate carvings. "Open it," he instructed.

Following his command, I revealed a collection of indescribable artifacts within the box—objects so bizarre that naming them seemed impossible.

As I scrutinized the peculiar items, the Monkey God fixed his gaze upon me, his eyes aglow with an unearthly light. "Stand still," he ordered, his voice imbued with an irresistible command. I obeyed, unable to tear my eyes away from his.

Then, the Monkey God's arm extended, impossibly long, bridging the distance between us. With fluid grace, he plucked one of the strange objects from the box. As he lifted it, the object unfurled into diaphanous sheets, each one thinner than paper, utterly transparent, and devoid of color. With a flick of his wrist, the sheets adhered to the room's walls, forming an invisible mosaic.

The object, once a shapeless enigma, now lay dismantled, its pieces fitting together like a jigsaw puzzle—a tapestry of hundreds of irregular fragments coalescing into a singular vision. Immobilized, I watched as the Monkey God retreated, his voice guiding me to slowly turn.

With each rotation, my world shifted. As I completed a full circle, I froze, confronting the unexpected.

I saw myself.

On the first day, Itagaki Mitsuyoshi's diary stopped after introducing the "strange thing." Yeri, who had clearly memorized the diary, recounted it to me with the ease of someone reading from a well-worn book.

As I listened to the first day's entry, I was left in suspense. "What happened after he saw himself?" I asked, my curiosity piqued.

Yeri assured me, "You'll understand as the story unfolds."

Nervously, I twisted my fingers. "Mitsuyoshi's diary seems to strongly suggest that seeing himself was connected to those strange objects?"

Yeri nodded with a wry smile. "It's not just a suggestion—it's quite explicit."

I let out a soft "ah," choosing not to speculate further. I trusted Yeri to reveal the rest without holding back.

Yeri resumed his narration, delving into Itagaki Mitsuyoshi's diary on the second day:

On a certain day and month

I saw myself.

This wasn't merely a likeness. It was me. I was staring at my own self, not through the distorting glass of a mirror, but face to face, in flesh and blood.

The encounter defied reason. Unlike a reflection, untouchable and silent, this version of me was tangible, capable of speech and interaction.

There were two of me now. One had become two. This duplicate stood before me, alive and real. I could converse with this second self.

And so I did. I talked to myself for what felt like an eternity.

Itagaki Mitsuyoshi's diary on the second day was straightforward, yet profoundly unsettling. As Yeri recited it, I found myself holding my breath, captivated by the notion of "seeing oneself."

Indeed, Mitsuyoshi's account was vivid, capturing the surreal experience with striking clarity. I, too, had experienced a fleeting moment of seeing myself—two versions of me, existing simultaneously. The realization was both fascinating and unnerving.

I wanted to ensure Yeri grasped the full weight of Mitsuyoshi's diary, but he gestured for silence. "I understand completely," he assured me.

I swallowed hard, acknowledging, "You've experienced it too."

Yeri nodded, his expression serious. "Yes, I've seen myself split into two. But be patient. As you listen further, the truth will become clear. Right now, no amount of speculation will reveal it."

I conceded, "You're right. It's futile to guess because I can't comprehend it."

Itagaki Mitsuyoshi's diary on the third day:

On a certain day and month

I conversed with myself for a long time.

Through this dialogue, I gained an unexpected clarity about my own nature. The notion of three wishes seemed trivial, insignificant in the face of such revelation.

The Monkey God asked, "You may make your three wishes now."

My response was simple: "I have no wishes. I just want to return, to go back to where I belong."

In that moment, I realized that the act of confronting myself had stripped away my previous illusions and desires. The wishes I had once longed for now seemed hollow, replaced by a deeper understanding of who I was and what truly mattered.

The experience had shifted my perspective, revealing that fulfillment lay not in external desires but in the acceptance of my own identity and place in the world.

The Monkey God replied, "I won't compel you. Are you sure you have no desires at all?"

I had already decided. If the Monkey God hadn't questioned me, I might never have voiced my desire. But since he did, I felt no hesitation. "Can you give me this strange thing?" I asked.

By then, the peculiar object had been taken down from the walls and returned to the wooden box, still a collection of bizarre shapes.

The Monkey God seemed momentarily surprised, as though my request was unexpected. But without missing a beat, he replied, "I can give it to you. Yet, I'm curious—why do you want it?"

"I want to converse with myself more," I explained. "I want to see myself more often."

The Monkey God offered no further comment. "You may go," he simply said.

I approached, retrieving the box. Despite its bulk, the object was surprisingly light. As I reached the door, I paused and asked, "What exactly is this strange thing?"

The Monkey God uttered a term with many syllables, one too complex to remember. Noticing my confusion, he added, "Think of it as something that allows you to see yourself."

I nodded, indicating my understanding, but then he added abruptly, "Taking this thing may not be beneficial for you."

I responded with a bittersweet smile, "Benefits? What are benefits?"

With that, the Monkey God vanished, leaving me alone. I clutched the box and made my way out, pondering his words.

Now, the strange object was mine, and I could see myself whenever I wished. True, there might be no tangible benefit, but through it, I could gain insight into my own soul.

For if a person does not know who they truly are, isn't that a profound sorrow? What meaning does life hold without self-awareness? Moreover, lacking the courage to confront one's own identity or to even contemplate it is a deeper tragedy. I refused to be that kind of person. I sought to understand myself, hence my request for the object. It was a tool for introspection, a means to confront and embrace the essence of who I am.

Yeri and I stood there, locked in a mutual gaze, our minds equally tangled in confusion. For a moment, my thoughts were a jumble, and I couldn't quite grasp what to make of it all. After a long pause, I broke the silence, "What on earth is that thing?"

Yeri responded, "You and I were in the same place. When Ichiro read Mitsuyoshi's diary to me, I found myself asking the very same question after hearing that passage."

I quickly interjected, "But surely, Ichiro wouldn't know what that thing is either!"

To my surprise, Yeri shook his head. "No, Ichiro knows."

Seeing my bewilderment, he explained further, "In fact, you and I should know too."

I shook my head, still unconvinced. "So what did Ichiro say?"

Yeri recounted how he had once stood in front of the enigmatic pile of objects, pointing at them with a question on his lips, "What on earth is this?"

Itagaki Ichiro had responded without hesitation, "The diary clearly states that this thing has a long, complex name. But essentially, it's a tool that allows you to see yourself."

Yeri was momentarily taken aback, then burst into laughter. "Even if you can see yourself, what's the use?"

This question lingered in the air, resonating with a deeper meaning. It suggested that while the ability to see oneself might seem profound, its true value lay in how one used that insight. The utility of such self-reflection depended entirely on what one did with the knowledge gained. It was a reminder that introspection, while powerful, was only the beginning of a journey toward understanding and transformation.

CHAPTER 17

The Device That Can Duplicate a Soul

Itagaki Ichiro's demeanor was grave, a stark contrast to Yeri's amusement. Yeri couldn't help but chuckle at the solemnity, questioning the significance of seeing oneself. What purpose did it serve?

Ichiro's patience snapped. "Stop laughing!" he barked, his voice slicing through Yeri's mirth.

Startled, Yeri ceased his laughter, meeting Ichiro's intense gaze. Ichiro gestured for silence, insisting, "This is no joke. Haven't you noticed the crucial detail mentioned in both the prince's and Mitsuyoshi's accounts?"

Confused, Yeri murmured a noncommittal "hmm," not fully grasping Ichiro's point. Ichiro pressed on, "It's vital: both sought three wishes from the Monkey God, yet he first compelled them to confront themself."

Yeri nodded slowly. "Yes, that's true. And—"

Before Yeri could finish, Ichiro interjected, "And both relinquished their wishes after seeing themselves!"

Yeri inhaled sharply, realization dawning. "That is peculiar. Why abandon their wishes after such a revelation?"

Ichiro leaned in, urgency seeping into his words. "I've pondered it, but speculation is futile. To uncover the truth, we must experience seeing ourselves firsthand."

Yeri exhaled deeply, still skeptical. "I still don't understand. Even if I see myself, what does it achieve?"

Ichiro fixed him with a penetrating stare. "In business, understanding my adversary's psyche and strategies is key. Armed with that insight, I can anticipate and exploit their weaknesses."

Yeri remained silent, waiting for Ichiro to elaborate further. His curiosity was piqued, but he needed more to fully grasp Ichiro's plan.

Ichiro continued, "If two people abandoned their wishes after seeing themselves, there must be a compelling reason. Our ultimate goal is to meet the Monkey God, right?"

"Of course," Yeri affirmed, nodding in agreement.

"We need to prepare ourselves," Ichiro explained. "Our aim is to secure at least one wish that will be realized, regardless of what the Monkey God reveals when we see ourselves. We must remain resolute."

It was then that Yeri understood Ichiro's intent. Ichiro sought a trial run, a way to experience the revelation without succumbing to doubt like the prince and Mitsuyoshi. Yeri appreciated Ichiro's foresight. Pointing to the enigmatic pile of artifacts, he asked, "Do you know how to use this?"

"I don't, but Mitsuyoshi's records are clear," Ichiro replied. "After spreading everything out, he simply turned a circle and saw himself."

"You think we can replicate that?" Yeri inquired, pacing thoughtfully as he considered the strange things.

Ichiro nodded, "Exactly." Yeri paced back and forth, mulling over the idea. His gaze lingered on the mysterious objects. "This isn't difficult to do alone. Why involve me? Why share potential wishes?"

I couldn't resist asking, "Good question. What was Ichiro's response?"

Yeri took a deep breath. "His reasoning was sound. Firstly, he feared the unknown nature of the object and didn't want to face it alone. Secondly, he couldn't decipher the Indian script in the records and needed a complete understanding before proceeding."

I was taken aback. "You—you guys actually did it?"

Yeri nodded, his expression introspective. After a moment of silence, he chuckled wryly and resumed his tale.

Executing the plan wasn't complicated. They lifted the strange object, and it unfolded into thin sheets. These sheets clung to nearby surfaces, adhering invisibly to the walls with a mysterious suction. Though compact in the box, once unfurled, the sheets expanded to cover the study's three walls, ceiling, and floor, leaving only a small portion nestled in the box.

Ichiro's anxiety was palpable. "What should we do? The room isn't big enough," he fretted.

Yeri glanced toward the window. "If that side were a wall instead of a window, it might just fit everything."

"Yes," Ichiro agreed. "We could build a wall there."

Yeri hesitated. "But that would look odd and might draw unwanted attention."

Ichiro dismissed the concern. "We can do it at night. With both of us working, it shouldn't take long. I can't dedicate too much time because of family obligations, but you can focus on it. It's quiet here at night, except for the administrator. We could bribe him to keep silent."

Intrigued by the prospect of the wishes and the mystery surrounding the strange artifacts, Yeri agreed to build the wall. The task went smoothly. Ichiro arranged a discreet bribe for the administrator, Takeo, ensuring his silence. Yeri procured bricks and mortar, and within two nights, a new wall sealed off the window.

The newly constructed wall transformed the room into something peculiar. It would later cause an unfortunate accident—a would-be intruder crashed into it, rebounded, and tragically fell to his death on the street. This outcome was unforeseen by both Yeri and Ichiro.

Despite their efforts, the expanded room barely accommodated the full spread of the strange artifacts, leaving just a small portion unaccounted for. Once unfurled, the remaining sections adhered seamlessly to the new wall, becoming invisible.

With the preparations complete, Ichiro and Yeri were tense with anticipation. Ichiro, preoccupied with the project, had neglected his mistress Yunko, ensuring she remained unaware of this secretive venture.

Facing each other, Ichiro finally asked, "Who turns first, you or me?"

Yeri raised his hand, volunteering. "I'll go first."

He spun around, eager to witness the phenomenon, but when he returned to his starting position, he saw nothing. Puzzled, he spun again, only to find the room unchanged. Ichiro followed suit, both turning repeatedly, but their efforts yielded no results.

After dozens of dizzying turns, Yeri felt lightheaded, yet the room remained as it was—devoid of any miraculous duplication.

Breathless and bewildered, they ceased their rotation. Ichiro broke the silence, frustration in his voice. "There must be something we're missing!"

Yeri smiled bitterly. "Even if there is something we're missing, what can we do? We don't even know what that thing truly is!"

Ichiro retorted, "I've already told you—it lets you see yourself."

"And what did you see?" Yeri snapped back, frustration edging his voice.

Taking a deep breath, Ichiro admitted, "I saw nothing. But Mitsuyoshi could use it. He had two selves, each aware of the other, and he could somehow manage that."

Yeri was taken aback. He recalled the rumors and police theories surrounding Itagaki Mitsuyoshi's death. The authorities speculated about a twin brother—a supposed fratricide. But Ichiro proposed a radical idea.

Ichiro suggested that there were indeed two versions of Mitsuyoshi—both authentically him. One was the original, born naturally, and the other emerged due to the strange object's influence.

I interrupted Yeri's recounting, gesturing for him to pause. My mind raced. "Wait, are you implying that before Mitsuyoshi died, he had effectively become two people?"

Yeri shook his head slowly. "No, it was still one Mitsuyoshi. But he had split into two."

Exasperated, I shouted, "Damn it, what does that even mean? Was it one or two?"

Yeri held my gaze, his expression contemplative. "Consider a document. When you make a copy, you have two—an original and its duplicate. Is it one document or two copies?"

The question was deceptively simple. A copied document results in two physical items: the original and the copy. Yet, conceptually, it remains a single entity, as the copy derives from the original.

I was momentarily baffled, overwhelmed by the paradox. "Yeri, you've been wrestling with this longer than I have. Surely you have some insight. Stop holding out on me!"

Yeri lowered his head, silent and tense. I noticed a subtle tremor in his posture, a sign of the disturbing thoughts swirling in his mind. Clearly, he had stumbled upon a profound and terrifying realization that he was reluctant to voice.

I waited, hoping Yeri would share his thoughts. His silence stretched long, and I finally urged him, "No matter how strange your theory is, just tell me. This situation is bizarre enough as it is."

Yeri lifted his head, something resolved in his eyes. "You're right. After everything we've encountered, I've developed a chilling hypothesis. But it's based on several facts we've seen. If I continue recounting events, you'll grasp my theory more easily."

Though impatient for answers, I recognized the wisdom in his approach and nodded in agreement.

Yeri turned his attention back to Ichiro. "So, you're saying Mitsuyoshi became two people?"

Ichiro challenged, "Do you have any other explanation?"

Yeri stepped closer to the wall, reaching out to touch the thin, invisible sheet. "How can that be possible?" he questioned. "You can't just split a person into two complete selves. If you cut someone in half, that's just two halves, not two people."

Ichiro's frustration was palpable. "Don't argue semantics with me! I don't know how it works—I just don't know!"

He repeated "I don't know" over and over, his voice rising with each iteration until he muttered, almost to himself, "Maybe we can't do it because we don't have the white tarsier."

Though Ichiro's voice was low, the stillness of the night made it easy to hear. The room was silent, amplifying every word. Yeri caught the mention instantly. "What tarsier?" he pressed.

Ichiro seemed to falter, as if he'd said too much. His expression betrayed his discomfort, but Yeri recognized the significance. The white tarsier, or Chiwodaka in local legend, was known as the supernatural Monkey God's messenger. It was clear Ichiro was withholding more than he let on.

Yeri's anger flared, and he glared at Ichiro with a fierce intensity. His imposing stature as a tall Indian man only amplified the fear he instilled. Ichiro recoiled, stammering, "I—I didn't—there's a page of Mitsuyoshi's diary I haven't shown you!"

In a fit of rage, Yeri swung a fist toward Ichiro's nose. But just as his punch was about to connect, Ichiro hastily produced a torn page, halting Yeri in his tracks.

Ichiro read aloud from the page: to encounter the supernatural Monkey God, one must have a white tarsier as a guide. The tarsier was the Monkey God's messenger.

Despite his fury, Yeri's eyes remained locked on Ichiro, who quickly explained, "I have no idea where to find this white tarsier. When I do, I promise I won't hide it from you. We have to work together."

Trying to placate Yeri, Ichiro added, "Look, I don't use this place often—maybe once or twice a week. The rest of the time, it's yours to study as you wish."

Yeri slowly lowered his fist, muttering "despicable Japanese" under his breath, but he didn't object to Ichiro's offer.

That night, Ichiro departed, leaving Yeri alone in the room.

In the days that followed, Yeri frequently returned to the room whenever Ichiro wasn't meeting Yunko there. He spent countless hours alone, hoping to "see himself," but the revelation never came.

Yeri observed that Ichiro, too, occasionally spent time alone in the room, yet he also seemed unable to achieve the desired outcome.

This pattern persisted for a year.

Then came the devastating news from India: the woman Yeri loved had married someone else. Heartbroken, Yeri drowned his sorrows in alcohol and staggered back to the room, seething with unspent rage.

In his drunken state, Yeri pounded the walls, lost in his anguish. He'd forgotten the thin film that coated the walls, a remnant of the strange artifacts.

Amidst his fury, he suddenly heard a chilling laughter from behind him.

Over the past year, Yeri and Ichiro had mostly visited the room alone. Typically, Yeri might assume the laughter came from Ichiro. But this time, he knew immediately—it was his own voice.

His first reaction was almost comical. In a tipsy reflex, he pinched his cheeks with both hands, as if trying to stop himself from laughing.

But the sneer persisted, a chilling echo that seeped into Yeri's bones. Fear laced through him, freezing his muscles and evaporating the alcohol-induced haze into a cold sweat. He stood paralyzed, unable to muster the courage to turn around.

The mocking laughter continued for what felt like an eternity, until a voice—his own voice—cut through the air with icy clarity: "What's the use of escaping and drinking?"

Yeri trembled violently, the realization dawning that it was his voice speaking. Summoning all his strength, he spun around to face the source. There, standing opposite him, was himself!

As Yeri recounted the experience, his body quaked involuntarily. I could empathize with his reaction, for I knew the terror of confronting oneself in such a surreal manner. To steady him, I placed a firm hand on his shoulder, urging calm.

Yeri took a deep, shuddering breath and continued, "I saw myself standing there, staring back with a look of utter disdain. I'll never forget that expression—mocking and contemptuous. In my life, no one has ever looked at me with such derision. It turns out the person who despises me the most is me."

His words left me momentarily speechless. I could offer no solace, so I continued to pat his shoulder in silent support.

"I was completely paralyzed," Yeri admitted. "I couldn't speak. I just kept shouting, 'Who are you?' I must have repeated it six or seven times, driven by sheer terror."

His confession hit me like a thunderclap, the gravity of his encounter resonating with an unsettling familiarity.

"Who are you?" It's a simple question, yet it sent a shiver through me. Instantly, my mind flashed to the professional killer, Iron Smith. Four seasoned detectives had described Iron Smith's final moments to me with precision. They recounted how, with his last breath, Iron Smith had dragged himself toward the study and uttered that same question: "Who are you?" Could it be that Iron Smith, too, saw himself before he died? Though Iron Smith was gone and Suzuki Yunko had descended into madness, there was no definitive answer. But my instincts told me the speculation was right. What could be more shocking than confronting your own image?

Yeri interrupted my reverie, asking, "What are you thinking about?"

I waved it off, unwilling to delve into the complexities of Iron Smith's demise. Instead, I focused back on Yeri. "What happened next?"

Yeri took a breath, steadying himself. "At first, I was terrified—paralyzed by fear. But then, rage took over. I couldn't stand the disdain in my own eyes, not from anyone, not even myself. So, I charged forward, swinging wildly at my own reflection."

The absurdity of the situation struck me as both amusing and chilling. I wanted to make light of it, but words failed me.

Yeri continued, breathless, "I hit myself. It wasn't a hallucination or dream. My fist connected with flesh, and the figure staggered back, blood trickling from his mouth. But the disdain only deepened. I couldn't bear it, so I fled. I didn't even wait for the elevator—just ran down the stairs and out of the building."

I listened, absorbing his story in silence.

Quietly, I offered, "That must have been a heavy blow to you."

Yeri's face twisted with bitterness. "More than heavy—crippling. Deep down, I've always despised myself. I'm a descendant of kings, born into wealth, yet what am I? A playboy, wasting away my life. The woman I love is beyond my reach. In Japan, without India's money, I'd be destitute. What am I? Nothing."

I shook my head gently. "Everyone struggles with that question— 'What am I?' Few find an answer."

Yeri nodded. "True, but not everyone sees their contempt from oneself so clearly."

Silence fell between us. Yeri finally spoke, "That night, I drank myself into oblivion and slept in a park. The next morning, I reached out to Ichiro, asking him to meet me there."

"Did he come?" I asked.

"Yes," Yeri replied.

When Yeri and Itagaki Ichiro met in the park, Yeri was still reeling from the effects of his drinking binge. His eyes were bloodshot, and his demeanor was unsettlingly intense. Ichiro was taken aback by his appearance. "What's the matter?" Ichiro asked, visibly concerned.

Without warning, Yeri lunged forward, seizing Ichiro by the collar and pulling him close. His voice was a harsh growl. "Itagaki Ichiro, listen to me. Our association ends here and now! From this moment, I don't want to see you again, and I want nothing to do with your damned three wishes. Do you hear me?"

Yeri's voice was nearly a roar, his demeanor bordering on madness.

Ichiro, struggling to break free, hastily agreed. "Okay! Okay!"

Yeri released him abruptly and turned away. As Ichiro adjusted his collar, he called after Yeri, "What happened?"

Yeri took a deep breath, his voice tinged with finality. "Nothing happened! Nothing is going to happen!"

With that, Yeri strode away, leaving Ichiro alone in the park, bewildered and shaken.

"Since that day, I've never seen Ichiro again," Yeri confessed, his eyes reflecting sincerity.

I was filled with questions, scrutinizing him as I shook my head. "No."

Yeri insisted, "I know it sounds strange, but I haven't seen him since."

Though his conviction was clear, I couldn't easily dismiss my doubts. "No, maybe you haven't seen Ichiro, but you must have seen his mistress, Suzuki Yunko."

Yeri's eyes widened in disbelief. "Suzuki Yunko? Ichiro's mistress? I swear I've never met her."

I paced, recounting the videotape I found in Iron Smith's house and its revelations. As I finished, Yeri's face turned ashen, his expression haunted. He sat trembling, his lips quivering, repeating, "Oh my God! Oh my God!"

"You must explain this," I demanded.

Yeri's voice was shaky. "That's not me, that's someone else, that's not me!"

His words mirrored those of the deranged Yunko. "That's not me, that's another person, that's not me!"

Yeri gasped, struggling for breath. "Mr. Morris, you must know who went to see Yunko!"

I inhaled sharply. "It was—yourself you saw?"

Yeri groaned, "Of course. God! He really exists. He can do anything, he—he's just like me."

My mind spun, unable to grasp the full implications. I gestured helplessly, searching for clarity.

Yeri continued, "Since then, I can't even look in a mirror, terrified of seeing him again. But—that me, that me—"

His expression was so distraught I feared he might break under the emotional weight. Yet, an understanding was crystallizing within me, and I suddenly exclaimed, "There are two of you, just as there were two Mitsuyoshi."

Yeri's throat emitted a strangled sound.

I pressed on, "And I believe there are two Suzuki Yunko as well."

Yeri's voice was reduced to a gurgle, the reality of his double sinking in, leaving us both grappling with the implications of this eerie duality.

My voice rose in urgency, echoing the revelation. "Did you hear that? There are two! There are two!"

My emotions surged, and I grasped Yeri's shoulders, shaking him with intensity. "Yes," he echoed, "there are two! The other one was made by that strange thing, that strange thing!"

I halted abruptly, the realization crashing over me. I had only considered the existence of two Yeri, two Itagaki Mitsuyoshi, and two Suzuki Yunko, but it hadn't occurred to me that the "strange thing" was the catalyst for these duplicates.

I stared at Yeri, dumbfounded, as he regained composure. "Do you remember what the Monkey God told Mitsuyoshi? That strange thing is something that 'can make you see yourself.'"

I nodded. Of course, I remembered.

Yeri continued, "After I saw myself in that room and fled, I kept pondering this. I believe the strange thing is a copying device, a magical tool of the Monkey God. It can duplicate a person!"

My mouth hung open, and Yeri's words seemed to lift me into an ethereal realm, leaving me with a profound sense of emptiness and disbelief.

A device that can duplicate a person? Could it really turn one person into two?

Anyone confronted with this concept would feel the same bewilderment.

Sensing my need for clarity, Yeri elaborated, "Imagine it like a photocopier. You place an original document inside and produce a copy. The document remains a copy, distinct from the original."

I continued to gape, needing extra air to steady my nerves. Despite the shock, I managed to ask, "So, the one who met Yunko wasn't you, but merely your copy?"

Yeri nodded repeatedly. "I—I always thought the copy appeared only momentarily, but according to what you've described—" His face was etched with fear. "The copy has always existed and is active. This is horrifying!"

A chill swept over me. "You have no awareness of your copy's actions?"

Yeri pointed at me, his voice trembling. "You've encountered your own copy. Do you know what your copy is doing right now?"

His question sent a shiver down my spine, leaving me grappling with the terrifying possibility that a part of myself, unknowingly, could be out there, acting independently.

We sat in silence, wrestling with the terrifying implications of Yeri's hypothesis. Despite my attempts to find alternative explanations, I couldn't shake the unsettling truth of his theory. It was too plausible, too aligned with the bizarre evidence we had encountered.

Yeri's assumption, frightening as it was, seemed to be the only explanation for Mitsuyoshi's sudden duplication. It also clarified why Kenichi used "you guys" repeatedly: upon entering, he must have seen both Suzuki Yunko and her copy in the ward. Similarly, Iron Smith's desperate question, "Who are you?" suggested he had confronted his own duplicate.

Not only did I find myself agreeing with Yeri, I also began to develop further theories based on his premise.

Breaking the silence, I said, "Yeri, I've realized something else—something crucial." Yeri nodded, urging me to continue.

I took a deep breath and spoke with gravity. "The terms 'original' and 'copy' are just labels. I think the reality is more complex."

Yeri's expression was skeptical, but he listened intently.

I continued, "The strange device does create duplicates, but while the copy looks identical to the original, their inner personalities are opposites."

A sound escaped Yeri's throat, a mix of realization and dread.

I pressed on, "Everyone has a dual nature. The copy embodies the hidden aspects of the original's personality, an amplification of the subconscious."

My theory was grounded in the behavior of those we knew had duplicates.

Consider Yunko: publicly, she appeared content with her life as Ichiro's mistress. But beneath that facade lurked resentment and misery, a hatred for Ichiro for buying her silence with money. Her copy acted on these buried feelings, attempting to arrange Ichiro's demise.

Itagaki Mitsuyoshi was a historian, composed and rational. Yet, his subconscious harbored greed and malice. These traits, repressed in his conscious self, became dominant in his duplicate, leading to a fatal conflict between the two.

Yeri, outwardly timid, exemplified this duality. His fear of rejection kept him in Japan, unable to return to India to pursue the woman he loved. But his duplicate, embodying the strength he lacked, scorned him openly, highlighting his self-doubt.

As for myself, I project an image of optimism and resilience. Yet, deep within, I harbor fears and vulnerabilities. My encounter with my own copy revealed a face of despair and confusion, the embodiment of my hidden insecurities.

This new understanding was unsettling, but it provided a framework for comprehending the strange phenomenon we faced. It suggested that these duplications were not mere reflections, but manifestations of our deepest, most concealed selves.

CHAPTER 18

Quest for the Monkey God, Part 1

Yeri listened intently as I recounted the four examples, fear etched on his face. He swallowed hard, and with a trembling voice, he added, "I suspect that Itagaki Ichiro also had a duplicate. The Ichiro who convinced Yunko to plot against his wife was likely his copy! Normally, he was petrified of her, but his copy, tapping into his subconscious desires, dared to orchestrate her murder."

I nodded, taking a deep breath. "It's not just the physical duplication; it's a split of the personality. Everyone harbors dual aspects within them, and this phenomenon reveals those hidden sides, creating two people with opposing traits."

Yeri concurred, "And it all happened due to the mysterious influence of that strange object."

We fell into another contemplative silence.

Breaking it, I ventured, "I think I now understand why Mitsuyoshi stopped wishing to the Monkey God after his encounter with himself."

Intrigued, Yeri raised an eyebrow. I explained, "Mitsuyoshi saw his duplicate and conversed with it, as he documented in his diary. Confronted with his own avarice and malevolence, he was likely appalled.

Realizing that even three wishes couldn't satiate such greed, he chose to stop asking altogether. Instead, his sole request was to spend more time with his other self, to truly understand it."

Yeri considered this and nodded. "That makes sense."

After another pause, Yeri confessed, "Since then, I haven't seen Ichiro. I have no idea what became of him. I stayed in Japan until I unexpectedly encountered a little white tarsier in a bar."

That was the night I first met Yeri.

It's easy to imagine Yeri's shock upon seeing a white tarsier—the legendary messenger of the Monkey God—given all he had been through.

Indeed, Yeri expressed his astonishment, exclaiming, "Chiwodaka!"

I interjected, "I remember that night well. But surely you heard about Itagaki Ichiro's death—it was all over Japan, wasn't it?"

Yeri replied, "Yes, I was aware. In a way, it was a relief. The bizarre nature of his death meant that others wouldn't uncover the truth. I don't know the exact circumstances of his demise, but I also heard about the building manager's death. I suspect Manager Takeo was blackmailing Ichiro and was silenced for it."

Yeri hadn't seen Itagaki Ichiro for quite some time, so when he happened to pass by the place where Ichiro and Yunko used to meet and saw a light emanating from it, he felt a mix of curiosity and apprehension.

Was it strange or frightening for him?

If Yeri had seen his own duplicate, he would likely be scared, knowing that his other self might be engaging in unpredictable activities. However, if he hadn't encountered his duplicate, he might merely feel suspicious, questioning whether Yunko was betraying him.

I asked Yeri, "That strange object has remained in that room this entire time, hasn't it?"

Yeri confirmed, "No, it hasn't been removed."

I gave a bitter smile, realizing the redundancy of my question. "Of course not. Yunko's duplicate summoned Kenichi to that room, where he also encountered his own duplicate and faced his subconscious desires. It led him to act on them and even encouraged me to find myself. What happened after you saw the white tarsier?"

Yeri fell silent, gathering his thoughts before continuing.

Seeing the white tarsier immediately brought the supernatural Monkey God and the notion of three wishes to Yeri's mind. The white tarsier was known as the Monkey God's messenger; securing its presence was key to meeting the deity.

From that night onward, Yeri discreetly monitored Kenichi and me, although he refrained from direct action.

After trailing us for several days, Yeri returned to India, seeking guidance from experts on capturing the elusive white tarsier. Armed with a flute crafted from leaves, he returned to Japan and successfully captured the white tarsier.

Recalling Mitsuyoshi's notes, Yeri understood that possessing the white tarsier would lead him to the supernatural Monkey God. Yet, he craved more information about the deity, so he enlisted an expert to gather details. It was through this expert that Yeri and I eventually crossed paths.

There's no need to recount the events following our meeting in detail. Yeri sought me out at the hotel, and what began as mutual distrust transformed into a shared hypothesis. With Kenichi missing, Yunko driven mad, and both Mitsuyoshi and Ichiro deceased, we were the last two entangled in this strange affair, necessitating our cooperation.

As Yeri concluded his tale, he fixed his gaze on me.

I paced, reflecting on everything he had shared. "Before you began your story, you mentioned you'd reveal everything if I agreed to a request, right?"

Yeri confirmed, "Yes."

I pressed further, "What is your request?"

Yeri's response was straightforward. "I want you to accompany me to see the Monkey God."

The weight of his request hung between us, a daunting yet intriguing invitation that promised answers—and perhaps more questions—about the mysteries that had ensnared our lives.

I had somewhat anticipated Yeri's request, so I wasn't surprised when he finally voiced it. I replied, "According to Mitsuyoshi's notes, he started from the abandoned palace, first encountering a white tarsier in the dense forest, which then led him to the Monkey God."

Yeri nodded. "We can follow the same path. Unlike Mitsuyoshi, we already have the white tarsier. I've brought it to India and am taking care of it."

"That certainly simplifies things," I agreed.

"If I hadn't met you, I would have gone alone," Yeri admitted, rubbing his hands together. "I've prepared everything I need, and we're in a better position than Mitsuyoshi was."

I gestured for him to stop. "You don't need to convince me. After everything that's happened, I'd want to see this magical Monkey God myself, even without your invitation. But—" I hesitated, choosing my words carefully. "There are still many questions about what's happened. Should we try to clarify them first?"

Yeri seemed to ponder this. "You mean—?"

"For instance," I continued, "that strange thing that creates a 'copy'—not the best term, but it fits. The copy seems to have the ability to appear and disappear at will."

Yeri frowned thoughtfully but remained silent.

"I only saw my copy briefly after a hole was made in the wall near the window, and then it vanished," I explained.

Yeri nodded, understanding my concern. "And in the mental hospital, Kenichi saw two Yunko, one being a copy. But after he left and Naka entered, only one Yunko remained. The copy had vanished. And then there's Iron Smith—"

Yeri cut me off. "No need for more examples. I acknowledge the copies are elusive, like pencil marks easily wiped away. Why this is, we don't know, and perhaps we never will."

"I thought maybe we could return to Japan, retrieve that 'strange thing,' and study it further—"

Yeri shook his head firmly. "I have no desire to go back to Japan."

I shrugged, resigned. "Some mysteries can be explained, like the locked room door—probably a copy's doing. But what baffles me is the gun Ichiro gave Yunko, capable of shooting two bullets with one pull. That's not an ordinary weapon. Where did it come from?"

Yeri speculated, "I believe it was Ichiro's copy who gave Yunko the gun and ordered the killing, and it was Yunko's copy who received it. When Yunko was about to act, it was my copy who met her." I offered a bitter smile. The tangled relationships among the copies were complex, comprehensible only to those who'd witnessed the events unfold.

Yeri continued after a pause, "The copy not only disappears suddenly but might have other abilities. For example, Ichiro's copy having access to that strange gun. My copy knew secrets about a professional killer with an enigmatic identity and guided Yunko's copy to him!"

I stared at Yeri and asked slowly, "You really don't know Iron Smith at all?"

Yeri responded with a bitter smile, "I have never heard of this name."

I sighed, "We should remember something crucial. The copies can come and go as they please, appearing at various times and places. The most terrifying thing is that they can kill, even those identical to themselves." As I spoke, a shiver ran through me, leaving me unable to continue. Yeri's expression shifted, reflecting the gravity of our situation.

Mitsuyoshi's own copy had managed to kill him, and simultaneously, Mitsuyoshi had killed his copy. This resulted in two identical bodies at the scene of his death. It's an unsettling thought: someone who looks exactly like you, yet is your polar opposite. This person is your copy, someone you know nothing about. You don't know when they might appear, acting against your intentions. They embody the hidden side of your personality, and despite your identical appearances, your thoughts make you mortal enemies. The danger this poses is palpable.

Yeri was silent for a long time before he finally said, "We have no choice but to set this issue aside for now. Let's assume neither my copy nor our copies will appear."

I was silent too, acknowledging the truth of his words. We had no other option. "We must proceed on that assumption."

After a pause, I couldn't help but add, with a bitter edge, "The biggest enemy a person faces is often themselves."

Yeri's lips moved, but no words came out. After a long silence, he finally said, "Yes, it's a tragedy of human duality. The enemy isn't external; it's within."

He shook his head, unable to continue. I inhaled deeply. "There's no point in debating this further. Not even saints could resolve such a conundrum."

I looked at Yeri, shifting my thoughts to how we would journey to see the supernatural Monkey God. I said, "Yeri, from what we've seen, the original people remain unaware of their copies' actions."

Yeri watched me as I gestured, explaining further, "For instance, Yunko had no idea about her copy's actions; the same with Ichiro and his copy."

Yeri's face twitched, acknowledging the truth. "It seems so. You and I also have copies, but what are they doing now? Who knows what they're up to?"

The thought sent a chill through me. What were they doing? And why were we in the dark? I calmed myself and asked, "What I want to understand is, do 'they' know what we are doing?"

Yeri was taken aback by my unexpected question. After a pause, he replied, "How could I possibly know? We'd need to ask 'them'!"

I gave a bitter smile. "It seems the copies, created by that strange object, might be more powerful than us. I just hope they aren't so powerful as to know everything about us."

Yeri frowned, "Why does it matter?"

I waved dismissively, "It matters, Yeri. Don't forget, 'they' are our biggest enemies."

Neither of us spoke further. When it came to these "copies," our discussion had hit a wall. We knew almost nothing about "them," except for their existence, created by the mysterious power of that "strange thing." That object belonged to the Monkey God, and it was Itagaki Mitsuyoshi's request to the deity that brought it into this world.

To truly solve this mystery, we had to see the Monkey God ourselves.

After returning to India, Yeri had meticulously prepared for our journey. His wealth allowed for thorough planning, and despite my unexpected involvement, the resources he gathered were sufficient for an entire expedition team. We discussed our plans in detail and agreed to set off early the next morning.

Our first destination was his ancestral "palace," from which we would follow the path taken by Itagaki Mitsuyoshi into the forest to seek the magical Monkey God.

We boarded a small helicopter and headed south, making several stops along the way. By nightfall, we arrived at the palace, a relic from the early years of the Yeri Dynasty.

The sight that greeted us upon landing was breathtaking and somber. The palace, once a symbol of a flourishing dynasty, now stood in ruin. Where it had once shimmered under the sun, it now cast a shadow of former glory, evoking an indescribable sadness.

The palace's once-grand spherical dome had collapsed, resembling a once-beautiful figure now reduced to skeletal remains. The setting sun cast a crimson hue over the broken walls and tiles, giving the place a hauntingly bloody appearance. It was a sight that compelled one to look away after just a glance.

The open space before the palace, paved with large stone slabs, spanned roughly 1000 meters square. In its heyday, it likely saw elephants adorned in brocade and regal officials arrayed in jewels proudly parading through. Now, however, it was overrun with weeds and wild vines.

These vines, sprawling across the ground, had uprooted the stone steps and even crushed the arched pathways with their relentless growth.

Disembarking from the helicopter, I found the weeds towering over me, forcing me to part them to see ahead.

Yeri followed suit, his voice tinged with bitterness. "Behold, my palace," he said, pausing before asking, "Would you prefer to stay in the palace's VIP room tonight, or set up a tent outside?"

I offered a bitter smile in return. Yeri had warned me of the palace's dilapidation, but seeing it in such a state still came as a shock.

Yeri gestured to what once might have been a wall, now reduced to a heap of stones entangled with vines that resembled a multi-tentacled monster in the dim light.

He gave me a melancholy smile, and while I understood his sorrow as a fallen prince, I couldn't fully empathize with his plight. Instead, I moved forward, saying, "Mitsuyoshi has been here before. He explored nearly every room and discovered records from a prince hundreds of years ago. It seems the interior might not be as daunting as the exterior suggests."

Yeri remained silent, trailing behind me. Both of us had read Mitsuyoshi's diary, which detailed his exploration. Although Mitsuyoshi hadn't described in detail how he found the prince's records, he had noted their location. Since Mitsuyoshi had once navigated this overgrown palace, he likely forged a path that day, making it easier for us to retrace his steps and enter the palace once more.

At that time, I believed it to be true, but many days later, a conversation with a botanist made me realize otherwise. When I mentioned our visit, the botanist chuckled, "You clearly underestimate the growth rate of tropical plants! How long ago did you say you went there?"

"About three years," I replied.

The botanist laughed again, "In that warm, humid air, tropical vines can grow 60 centimeters a day and branch within 48 hours. In three years, even if someone cleared a path, it would have vanished long ago!"

Whether the botanist was right or not, I couldn't tell, but as I approached the palace entrance, I found no trace of the original gates.

Instead, a large opening led into a tangled mass of wild vines. Mitsuyoshi's path was nowhere to be found.

Yeri returned shortly, having fetched necessary gear from the helicopter. Seeing me hesitate at the entrance, he handed me a flashlight, a protective helmet, and a sharp axe. "Please, go ahead," he said.

I accepted the gear, donned the helmet, switched on the flashlight, and began cutting through vines as thick as my arm, making my way forward.

To my surprise, once inside the hall, progress became easier. Vines clustered at the entrance due to sunlight, but inside, they grew vertically toward the ceiling, leaving gaps wide enough for us to pass. We navigated through the hall and reached another chamber beyond it. Yeri halted and remarked, "The entire palace is like this. At night, poisonous snakes become active, and they're difficult to avoid. There's really no reason to linger here. Why don't we—"

He didn't need to finish; I understood. Staying in the palace served no purpose. Mitsuyoshi had already been here and found the prince's records, which we had read. Our true goal was to find the supernatural Monkey God.

Agreeing with Yeri, we retraced our steps, cleared a space beside the helicopter, and decided to spend the night there for safety.

The night passed uneventfully, except at midnight when the little white tarsier began making a series of strange cries.

Yeri had entrusted the care of the white tarsier to a local in southern India after bringing it back. Although I couldn't say whether this caretaker knew as much as Kenichi, when I first saw the tarsier, I noticed an unusual melancholy in its eyes.

It might sound odd to describe a monkey as melancholy, but that's the impression I got. Whether the tarsier missed Kenichi or not was unclear, especially since it had left him for the flute. This question remained unanswered, as I couldn't communicate with the tarsier.

We had locked the tarsier in a large wire cage before departure. It remained curled and inactive, showing no interest even when I attempted to engage it before bedtime. Yet, just as I began to drift off, it suddenly started its peculiar cries.

I was surprised by the volume and pitch of the sounds—something I only associated with howler monkeys of East Africa, known for their powerful roars carrying for kilometers.

Startled awake by the cries, both Yeri and I rushed to the cage. The tarsier was leaping frantically, sounding like a terrified child. We exchanged worried glances, realizing something was amiss. We tried to calm the creature, but its panic only intensified, thrashing against the cage and emitting sharper cries.

Before we could decide our next move, a gunshot shattered the tense night air.

CHAPTER 19

Gathering at the Abandoned Palace

The open space outside the palace was eerily quiet under the midnight sky. The little tarsier's cries pierced the silence, and the gunshot that followed was even more jarring. Yet, in retrospect, the gunshot paled in comparison to its aftermath. As soon as the shot rang out, the helicopter shook violently. My instincts from years of living on the edge kicked in, and I shouted, "Jump out!"

I had no clear understanding of the situation, but the sequence—a gunshot, then the helicopter's shudder—spelled danger. In a split second, I realized we were under attack. The most vulnerable target on a helicopter is the fuel tank; a bullet piercing it could only mean one thing—imminent disaster.

Acting on impulse, I shouted, shoved the cage containing the tarsier, and leaped out with it. The helicopter hovered about two meters above the ground. I landed hard, rolling and kicking the cage away, tumbling several meters across the ground. I saw Yeri leap out as well.

Yeri reacted swiftly, but he was a fraction of a second too late. The events that followed unfolded like slow-motion scenes from a movie, yet initially, I heard nothing. Only the sight of blinding flames erupting instantaneously as the helicopter became engulfed in a sea of fire. Yeri had jumped out, but the flames spread with terrifying speed, enveloping him almost instantly.

No matter how quick my instincts were, it was too late to save him.

Finally, the sounds caught up with me—Yeri's scream pierced the air, only to be overpowered by a thunderous explosion. The explosive force and shockwave hurled my body backward. Along with me, the iron cage was flung back, crashing into me before rolling further. Amidst the chaos, I saw gleaming shards of metal from the helicopter, sparking like grotesque fireworks.

Then, silence fell once more. The helicopter was no more, replaced by smoldering grass. My sole focus was Yeri's safety. I shouted his name as I sprinted forward, leaping over burning bushes to reach the wreckage's site.

The helicopter's remnants lay scattered, twisted beyond recognition. Among the misshapen metal fragments, I found Yeri.

In that moment, Yeri was no longer the man I knew but a charred figure barely resembling a human form.

I stopped abruptly, swallowing hard, my ears ringing. Everything had happened so fast.

Yeri was gone.

In the aftermath of the explosion, the reality of the situation settled in—a shocking, tragic end to his journey.

In my lifetime, I've faced numerous unexpected events, but nothing quite like this. It was a situation I could never have anticipated.

For a moment, I was frozen, staring at Yeri's charred remains, unsure of my next move. Then, a "click" echoed behind me, jolting me out of my stupor.

That sound could mean many things, but given the circumstances, I was almost certain it was the sound of a gun's bolt being drawn.

Instinctively, I wanted to turn around, but before I could, a woman's voice stopped me: "Don't move, please don't move!"

The voice was vaguely familiar, yet not enough to place it immediately. The use of "please" in such a tense situation was strikingly refined, bringing to mind only one person.

In that instant, my shock peaked.

I could imagine a host of potential attackers, but never her.

Just after she said, "Please don't move," I felt the gun muzzle press against my back. I raised my hands slightly to show I meant no harm and tried to keep my voice steady: "Mrs. Itagaki, I never imagined we'd meet again under such circumstances!"

Itagaki Sadagumi, with her refined upbringing, was known for her elegance and poise. Even while holding a gun, her manners remained impeccable, confirming her identity.

It was hard to fathom Sadagumi, typically clad in a kimono and exuding grace, standing in such a desolate place with a gun in hand.

Yet the bizarre continued. Behind me, a burst of laughter followed by Sadagumi's voice: "You're dead! This time, you're finally dead!" The venom in her words was unmistakable, her voice seething with hatred. This bewildered me further. Her attack had inadvertently caused a death, yet now she seemed transformed from a sophisticated woman into a cold-blooded killer. Despite everything, I had to ask, "What grudge do you bear against Prince Yeri?"

Her voice was angry, incredulous: "Prince Yeri? Who is Prince Yeri?"

I was taken aback, at a loss until Sadagumi spoke again, her anger unabated. "Do you think I don't know? Do you really think I'm in the dark?"

Realization dawned on me, and I cried out, "Madam, you've killed the wrong person!"

Sadagumi's voice rose, insistent behind me: "No mistake! I don't know what trick he's playing, but I wanted him dead, truly dead, and now he is!"

I sighed, lowering my hands slightly, gesturing ahead. "This body might be hard to identify, but if you take a closer look, you'll see he's not your intended target. You wanted to kill your husband, Itagaki Ichiro. But the man who died in the fire is an Indian, a man named Yeri!"

I heard a surprised voice behind me and placed my hands on my head to show I meant no harm. "Just watch, I won't do anything," I said calmly.

The moonlight was bright that night, casting clear shadows on the ground. I saw Sadagumi's silhouette move as she stepped toward the charred remains, a rifle in hand.

In that moment, I could have easily disarmed her. But I chose not to, thinking that once Sadagumi realized the person burnt beyond recognition wasn't Itagaki Ichiro, her sorrow would halt any further harm toward me.

Since the moment I was jolted awake by the tarsier's cries, everything had unfolded so rapidly that I hadn't had the chance to process all the questions in an orderly fashion. For instance, there was one particularly glaring question that hadn't crossed my mind at the time.

Of course, I reflected on it later, but there's a significant difference between thinking in the moment and reflecting after the fact.

The question was: Sadagumi knew Ichiro had died from an unknown sniper attack, so why had she traveled all the way to India to kill him herself?

At the time, this question eluded me, so I remained inactive. Sadagumi reached the body and paused, leaning down to examine it closely under the moonlight.

I was genuinely impressed by her composure in the face of such a gruesome sight.

Suddenly, Sadagumi's body trembled violently. She staggered backward, her eyes lifting to meet mine. Her face twitched uncontrollably, drained of color, and her hands shook.

Before I could say anything, she abruptly dropped the rifle, covered her face with her hands, squatted down, and began to sob uncontrollably.

Her reaction was a mix of shock, grief, and guilt, each emotion surfacing in her anguished cries as the reality of her actions set in.

I felt a deep sense of bitterness. Yeri's death was so unjust, a tragic consequence of mistaken identity. If not for the little tarsier's sudden cries, I might have been the one to face doom. Sadagumi's actions were clearly reprehensible, yet seeing her tremble and hearing the anguished groans from her throat, it was clear she was wrestling with guilt over what she had done.

I sighed and took a step towards her, intending to speak. "You—"

I barely got a word out before Sadagumi's head snapped up, her face contorted with a ferocious expression that startled me. She screamed, "He thought I didn't know, not at all! But I knew it long ago!"

It's often said that a perceptive wife can discern when her husband is having an affair. Despite Itagaki's meticulous planning and seemingly plausible excuses for his meetings with Yunko, Sadagumi, married to him for many years, could sense the subtle changes in his demeanor.

She noticed his growing disinterest in her. At times, when she attempted to entice him by posing provocatively, Itagaki's eyes would avoid her, betraying his lack of interest.

For a wife, realizing that her appeal has waned in her husband's eyes is often the first clue that something is amiss. If she doesn't recognize this, she might as well not be a woman at all.

Sadagumi had pieced together the truth about Itagaki's affair with Yunko after it had been ongoing for over six months. The affair lasted that long partly due to Itagaki's careful concealment and partly due to Sadagumi's overconfidence. She believed Itagaki's success was heavily reliant on her family's influential connections and never imagined he would betray her.

When she finally realized the truth, her suspicions gradually accumulated. As these doubts grew, she hired a private detective. Two weeks later, Sadagumi learned all about Itagaki Ichiro's actions.

Despite knowing everything, Sadagumi maintained a facade of ignorance. Her upbringing and her family's esteemed social status meant that a change in her marriage would lead to scandal, shaming her in society. So, she endured in silence.

Many nights, she lay awake, listening to Ichiro's loud snores, tormented by thoughts of his infidelity. She considered countless solutions, but each seemed implausible. It felt as though enduring her husband's affair was her only option.

Then, one afternoon, everything changed.

Things took a dramatic turn one afternoon.

Sadagumi was in the living room, arranging flowers on the coffee table. She was contemplating whether to swap one of the half-opened roses for a fully bloomed one when the doorbell rang.

Shortly after, the maid entered, announcing, "Madam, a lady outside introduces herself as Suzuki Yunko. She claims to have something important to discuss with you."

Sadagumi had to summon all her cultivated self-control to remain composed.

Having knowledge of all Ichiro's actions, she was well aware of who his mistress was. And now, the mistress had come to her doorstep!

Taking a deep breath, Sadagumi instructed, "Please show the lady in."

The maid nodded and left. Moments later, Yunko entered. Sadagumi, having seen Yunko's photos from the detective, was both furious and shocked. Yet, she maintained her graceful demeanor. Gesturing politely, she said, "Please, have a seat, Miss Yunko."

Yunko sat, and Sadagumi signaled the maid to leave. Wasting no time, Yunko began, "Mrs. Itagaki, you might not know who I am."

Sadagumi surprised herself with her own calmness. "No, I know. You're his mistress."

Yunko looked taken aback, lowering her gaze, seemingly at a loss for words. Sadagumi paced briefly, asking, "Why have you come to see me?"

Yunko raised her head, meeting Sadagumi's eyes. "He plans to kill you—and me too!"

When Sadagumi discarded the rifle and crouched down, covering her face, I moved closer. She lifted her head again, and from "He thought I didn't know, not at all ," she began recounting her story without waiting for my probing.

Hearing this revelation, I was internally alarmed, trying to piece together the timeline of Yunko and Sadagumi's meeting.

This encounter likely occurred after Yeri's meeting with Yunko, or perhaps as a consequence of it. It was definitely Yunko who had approached Sadagumi.

I couldn't help but wonder if Yunko had already encountered Iron by then.

As I pondered, Sadagumi continued narrating the events.

The revelation left Sadagumi reeling. Before she could respond, Yunko opened her handbag, produced a gun, and placed it on the table. "He gave me this," Yunko explained. "He wants me to kill you. But this gun fires two bullets in opposite directions simultaneously. If I shoot you, I'd die too."

Sadagumi's body trembled, her gaze fixed on the gun—an object she had never imagined could exist, embodying such a dreadful scheme.

After a long pause, her parched throat managed a sound: "What do you intend to do?"

Yunko's voice was steady, "I've hired a professional shooter to eliminate him."

Sadagumi's eyes widened, her breathing quickened, and she shouted, "Wait! Wait! He—he is my husband, he—"

Yunko's voice was cold and slightly aggressive, "He's your husband, but don't you hate him deep down? He has a mistress and plans to kill you. Haven't you ever hated him? Haven't you thought of killing him yourself?"

Sadagumi looked lost, unsure of how to respond. Yunko sighed, "You don't truly understand yourself. Let me take you somewhere to see yourself clearly, and then you'll understand."

At that moment, I couldn't help but feel uneasy. Yunko wanted to take Sadagumi to "see herself," a concept that seemed both intriguing and ominous.

I took a breath and studied Sadagumi. In our previous encounters, she had always worn traditional kimonos. Now, dressed in hunting clothes, her expression was full of resentment. This wasn't the Sadagumi I knew. It struck me that what stood before me might be a copy of Sadagumi.

The realization sent another wave of unease through me.

Yunko took Sadagumi to a room. When Sadagumi returned home, she appeared agitated, her servants visibly surprised by her state.

She locked herself in her bedroom, her actions a mystery to those outside. Later that night, several servants were roused by the sound of a heated argument. Gathered together, they were shocked into silence, recognizing their mistress's commanding voice. The usually composed Sadagumi, admired by her staff, had never been known to raise her voice.

Who was she arguing with? None dared inquire afterward.

"Who were you scolding?" I asked.

Sadagumi's voice cracked as she confessed, "That night, I cursed Ichiro loudly!"

I was taken aback, "But isn't Ichiro dead?"

Sadagumi fixed me with a long stare, "I thought you knew!"

I offered a wry smile. I should have known, but my thoughts were too scattered to piece it together. "Is it Ichiro's copy?" I ventured.

Sadagumi laughed—a chilling sound that made my skin crawl, prompting me to step back. Her eyes bore into mine, a strange light flickering within them, as if her thoughts were locked in a place I couldn't reach.

I steadied myself to speak, but her laughter grew ever more piercing, until it became almost unbearable. Abruptly, she stopped and said in a cold, flat voice, "He killed me, you know, he killed me!" She repeated, "He killed me," and the chilling truth settled over me.

A profound coldness gripped me. The situation was becoming increasingly convoluted.

What did Sadagumi mean by "he killed me"? If I replaced the pronouns with proper names, it would read, "Itagaki Ichiro killed Sadagumi." Yet, that didn't fit. A more accurate interpretation might be, "Itagaki Ichiro's copy killed Sadagumi."

If Sadagumi was already dead, then the woman before me had to be her copy. My mind swirled with confusion, so I asked numbly, "When did it happen?"

Sadagumi continued her unsettling laughter, recounting, "Just a few days ago, I watched him do it with my own eyes. He took me to a cliff by the sea and pushed me over the edge. As I fell, my hands flailed helplessly, trying to grasp something that wasn't there. I didn't scream—not because I wasn't terrified, but because my upbringing taught me never to scream in an unseemly manner, no matter the situation! Haha! Haha!" Her laughter was haunting, echoing around us, while I could only swallow the sobs that threatened to escape my throat.

She went on, "They might never find my body. Even if they do, they'll think I killed myself, unable to bear the loss of my husband! Haha! It turns out he always planned to get rid of me! He used his mistress as a pawn to do it, but she turned on him, hiring a professional to take him out instead! Haha, it's all so amusing, isn't it? Everyone's cards are on the table now. So interesting! Haha!"

To Sadagumi, this twisted turn of events was "amusing," but to me, it was horrific. The brutal honesty revealed by everyone's actions was terrifying.

Sadagumi continued, "I watched him commit the crime from the sidelines. He didn't know I was there. He even laughed afterward. When I found out he was heading to India, I followed. I thought he was with you, so I—"

She abruptly stopped, leaving the rest unsaid.

But I understood. She believed Ichiro was in the helicopter, and that's why she fired. Yet, her shot had tragically taken Yeri's life instead.

I straightened, turning away, unwilling to face her any longer. In that moment, Sadagumi moved swiftly, picking up the rifle again. She aimed it at me, her voice harsh: "From now on, you will follow my orders. I want you to lead me to the magical monkey god!"

A wave of inexplicable disgust washed over me, making me feel weary. I replied coldly, "I'm sorry, I can't be your guide. That's the job of the white tarsier. And I'm afraid it perished in the explosion."

Sadagumi's expression shifted to shock as she glanced at the iron cage. I looked too, and after a moment, I could only sigh. If I hadn't jumped with the cage, the little white tarsier would have perished in the explosion, and perhaps none of the following events would have unfolded. Everything would be in peace. Yet I did, and the cage landed a safe distance away. Now, as I looked at it, I saw the tarsier's tiny paws gripping the bars, its eyes wide and curious, watching us intently.

Sadagumi laughed, "Look, it's not dead!"

Despite the tension, my voice was weary, "It's alive, that's good. You can have it lead the way."

Sadagumi's expression turned sharp and cunning. "Do you think I'm an idiot? You're the one who brought it here, so you must know how to control it. You lead the way!"

She pointed the rifle at me, her finger hovering over the trigger. I had no doubt she would shoot if provoked, but the thought of accompanying her to find the supernatural monkey god was unappealing. After everything that had happened, the last thing I wanted was to encounter any more supernatural beings.

In a flash, I devised a plan to outmaneuver Sadagumi. "Alright," I said, "if you want it to lead, it can't stay locked in a cage. Release it, and I'll command it to guide us."

My suggestion was strategic. If the cage was opened, the tarsier would likely seize the opportunity to escape into the wild, where Sadagumi would have little hope of catching it.

Once the tarsier was gone, her leverage over me would vanish. The logic was sound—after all, a guide can't lead if it's confined.

Sadagumi regarded the cage, noting the lock. She hesitated, clearly wary of a trick. "No funny business," she warned.

I spread my hands innocently. "Does my suggestion not make sense?"

Sadagumi's eyes bore into me with a fierce intensity. After a long, tense silence, she finally relented. "Fine. Open the lock and let it out."

With deliberate slowness, I took out the key and approached the iron cage. Unlocking it, I reached inside, and the little white tarsier wasted no time climbing onto my arm. As I withdrew my hand, I flicked my wrist, sending the tarsier soaring like an arrow through the air.

Sadagumi erupted in a scream, unleashing a string of curses that seemed unbecoming of someone who prided herself on her stature. It was the type of outburst that people like her typically avoided to maintain their dignity.

Fearing Sadagumi might shoot in her frustration, I instinctively crouched down. Just then, a shadow darted from behind a nearby bush.

The figure, though not as quick as the tarsier, moved with impressive agility. He lunged toward the tarsier, and in a blink, the creature clung to his neck, wrapping itself around him like a living scarf.

In that instant, I realized who it was—Kenichi!

Encountering Sadagumi was unexpected enough, but Kenichi's sudden appearance was truly astonishing. I tried to call out to him, but my voice failed me, leaving my mouth agape in silence.

Kenichi acted swiftly. Cradling the tarsier with one arm, he drew a gun with the other, aiming it squarely at Sadagumi. Her weapon was trained on me, but when she saw Kenichi, she hesitated, too slow to redirect her aim.

"If you move, I'll shoot!" Kenichi barked, his voice like steel.

Sadagumi froze, her face a mask of twitching fear.

Kenichi, brimming with confidence, took a few steps toward me, seemingly ready to speak. But before he could, another voice cut through the night air. "You too, Mr. Kenichi. Move, and you're dead."

Kenichi stiffened, unable to see who was behind him. The cold, commanding tone left no room for doubt—this was no idle threat. After a moment of indecision, he stood still.

I, however, could see her clearly. Under the moon's glow, Yunko's features were sharp, her face pale yet striking, her figure slender and poised.

A wave of dizziness washed over me, but this was just the beginning. What unfolded next nearly knocked me off my feet.

Sadagumi had me under her control, Kenichi had Sadagumi, and Yunko had Kenichi. As Yunko advanced, a new figure emerged from the shadows behind her, brandishing a massive military pistol. "Yunko, it's been a while," he said coldly.

Yunko halted, visibly trembling under the moonlight.

It wasn't just her; everyone was caught in the same web of shock, myself included. I couldn't stop shaking.

The man behind Yunko was Itagaki Ichiro!

Though I had never seen him in life, only in death, there was no mistaking him now. The slightly balding man with a businessman's belly— the quintessential image of success—was unmistakably Itagaki Ichiro.

And so, Itagaki Ichiro had Yunko under his control.

Overwhelmed by the absurdity of it all, I broke into laughter. "Well, it seems everyone is here!"

In this labyrinth of treachery and alliances, the truth was as elusive as the moonlight that cast its deceptive glow over us all.

I hadn't expected any response to my sarcastic comment about everyone being present. It was merely a helpless jest about the tangled web of control we found ourselves in. But no sooner had the words left my mouth than a voice from a nearby tree chimed in, "I shouldn't be missing, right?"

Startled, I turned to the direction of the voice, but saw no one. Instead, a rifle protruded from the dense foliage, its muzzle aimed unwaveringly at Itagaki Ichiro's back.

The gun was held so steadily it seemed an extension of the tree itself, rooted and firm.

Then the voice, laced with mockery, drifted down from the leaves again, "I've already shot you once, Mr. Itagaki. Surely you don't doubt my aim?"

I closed my eyes briefly, recognizing the voice. It had to be Iron Smith. When I opened my eyes, I looked at Yunko. Her expression was one of sheer horror.

Iron Smith had now taken control over Itagaki Ichiro.

A surge of impulsive defiance rose within me, and I shouted into the night, "Yeri, are you there? If you are, make yourself known!"

From what I understood, there were seven individuals with "copies": Itagaki Mitsuyoshi, Itagaki Ichiro, Yunko, Sadagumi, Iron Smith, Yeri, and Kenichi.

Itagaki Mitsuyoshi was dead, both original and copy.

Itagaki Ichiro's original body was dead, but his copy remained.

Yunko's original had gone mad, yet her copy persisted.

Sadagumi had been pushed into the sea, leaving only her copy.

Iron Smith's original was killed in a hail of bullets, but his copy survived.

Kenichi's original had vanished, "gone where he was meant to," but his copy stayed.

From these patterns, I surmised that Yeri's original perished in the explosion, meaning his copy was likely still around.

If Yeri's copy was indeed present, surely it was his time to emerge. So, I called out.

My call was met first with a startled yelp from Iron Smith in the tree, followed by Yeri's voice, calm and authoritative, "Stay still. Your weapon may be a gun, but mine is a venomous snake. If you move, the snake's venom will paralyze you within half a second, leaving you no chance to fire. And in five seconds, you'll be dead."

The eerie silence was broken by Iron Smith's panicked noises and Yeri's triumphant laughter.

Summoning all my courage, I stood tall.

Yeri had truly arrived!

There we were, seven of us gathered amidst the remnants of the blasted helicopter before the abandoned palace.

In the chain of control, the order was: me, Sadagumi, Kenichi, Yunko, Itagaki Ichiro, Iron Smith, and Yeri.

Yet among these seven, only I remained my true self.

As for the other six individuals, I am certain they are not their true selves, but rather "copies" created by that bizarre entity.

What exactly is a "copy"? Is it a person? Not quite. More like a simulacrum, a monster in disguise. I struggle to find an apt term in our language, so for now, "copies" will have to suffice.

Here I am, surrounded by six of these copies.

Oddly enough, the feeling that washes over me isn't fear or unease—it's amusement.

It's almost comical. Sadagumi, who once struck me as the epitome of elegance, stands rigid, the muscles of her face twitching, rifle aimed at me. Behind her is Kenichi, the loyal police officer and my trusted friend, but now, he appears as unfamiliar as a stranger.

The white tarsier seems to share my sentiment. Though it clings to Kenichi's neck, it gazes up at him with curious eyes, as if questioning who this person truly is.

Not far from Kenichi stands Yunko. A girl from a small Japanese town who dreamt of making it big in the city, only to find herself adrift in seedy entertainment venues. Eventually, she became the mistress of a businessman.

The real tragedy lies with the original Yunko, a woman trapped in hopelessness, forced to sell her youth to a crass businessman with no other paths available.

Under the moonlight, Yunko's face is a study in clenched determination. She's not the passive woman she once was, but a figure brimming with hatred and despair. Hatred that fuels her with the power to kill, and despair that could lead her to self-destruction.

This isn't the Yunko I knew, but her copy. The repressed desires and fears of the original Yunko have now surfaced in this version, allowing her to contemplate and act upon things she once dared not even imagine.

I can't help but wonder what wishes she might make if she encountered the supernatural monkey god.

Behind Yunko looms Itagaki Ichiro. A man who looks every bit the successful businessman, his visage greasy and fierce. I doubt he would recognize himself if he peered into a mirror.

Iron Smith remains hidden in the tree. I can't see him, but I know precisely which branch conceals him by the faint sounds of movement it makes under his weight.

The branches trembled because Iron Smith, the otherwise unflappable assassin, was quaking with fear. Here was a man who had made a career out of ending lives, now rendered vulnerable and uncertain.

Yeri, too, was perched in the tree, a regal heir reduced to gripping a snake, eyes wide with desperation, ready to strike.

Six individuals, each restraining the other, yet none truly themselves—merely copies. The absurdity of it all struck me, and I couldn't suppress a laugh.

"What is the purpose of all of you being here?" I asked, my voice echoing in the tense night air.

Itagaki Ichiro was the first to respond, his breath heavy with exertion. "To see the Monkey God," he admitted.

I nodded, addressing the group. "I assume that's the goal for all of you. But with weapons drawn against each other, do you really think the Monkey God will grant you an audience?"

From the tree, Yeri's voice carried down. "Do you have any better suggestions?"

I shrugged, spreading my hands in a gesture of peace. "Lower your weapons. Seek the Monkey God together. After all, 'Chiwodaka' is here to guide you."

The forest fell silent as the six of them considered my words. Finally, Kenichi spoke up, his voice tinged with doubt. "Will the Monkey God meet so many at once?"

I shook my head, honest in my uncertainty. "I don't know. But I believe in his extraordinary abilities. You are all constructs of his creation. I think, deep down, you all understand this."

My words seemed to cast a shadow over them, their expressions shifting into something inscrutable. I fixed my gaze on Kenichi. "Kenichi, is that you?"

He looked startled, his reply a stammer. "I—I don't know. I don't know where I came from."

His admission hung in the air, a poignant reminder of their shared reality. They were lost, searching for a truth they couldn't yet grasp, in a world where the line between creation and creator had blurred beyond recognition.

CHAPTER 20

Quest for the Monkey God, Part 2

Kenichi's expression became one of utter confusion, his eyes darting wildly. "I have already existed, right? I have already existed, right? Right?" His questions escalated into an almost desperate shriek.

I responded calmly, "Only the supernatural monkey god can truly answer that. You need to see him."

From the tree, Yeri shouted, "Yes," his voice carrying an urgency that spurred a venomous snake to leap from the bushes. As the snake twisted in midair, the crack of a gunshot pierced the silence. Iron Smith, with precision, had aimed his rifle from the treetop and shot the snake, its body falling in two bloodied halves.

After discarding the gun, Iron Smith and Yeri descended swiftly from the tree. Itagaki Ichiro hesitated briefly before lowering his weapon, followed by Yunko, Kenichi, and Sadagumi, who all relinquished their arms.

I exhaled deeply. "Well, it seems the group seeking the Monkey God is ready to depart. Unfortunately, I won't be joining you."

I was weary of the company of these six "copies." As dawn approached, light crept into the sky, and I resolved to leave as soon as the day broke.

Itagaki Ichiro interrupted, "You're a fool! Seeing the Monkey God grants you three wishes!"

I shook my head. "I'm not the first fool. Your cousin was the first, and he was killed by his own hand."

Kenichi approached, a chill emanating from him that made me gesture for him to stop. "The second fool is my friend Kenichi," I continued.

Kenichi protested, "I am Kenichi."

I clarified, "The one I mean is elsewhere now, perhaps back in the forest with the monkeys."

Kenichi bristled with anger. "Yes, he chose to be a wild man in the forest over three wishes."

I sighed, feeling a bittersweet relief. Kenichi had discovered a life he truly belonged to. Yet, even a nature-loving soul like him harbored a shadow of greed, manifesting in his copy here.

I slowly shook my head. "In that case, I'm the third fool."

Kenichi declared, "We won't let you be a fool. We need your skills. You must stay with us and help us find the Monkey God. You can't just walk away!"

Yeri quickly added, "Yes, you promised to go with me to see the Monkey God."

I replied bitterly, "Did I promise you?"

Yeri asserted confidently, "Of course, it's me."

I half-turned, pointing to Yeri's charred remains. Words caught in my throat, unable to escape.

What could I possibly say? Does this Yeri standing before me realize that he's merely a copy? If every aspect of this copy mirrors the original, then indeed, he is Yeri. How could I point to a corpse and expect him to understand his own existence?

I raised my hand, contemplating the futility, and then let it drop. Iron Smith approached, his demeanor unexpectedly earnest. "Please, come with us," he implored.

I couldn't suppress my frustration. "You're a lone wolf, a professional killer. Why insist on dragging me along?"

His face showed genuine fear. "I'm terrified. Every moment, every second, I'm consumed by fear. Have mercy on me! If I could have three wishes, my first would be to never feel fear again."

His confession was disarming, and I felt a pang of sympathy. I recalled the brief moment when I encountered my own copy—Ash Morris, usually so fearless, was visibly anxious, as if sensing impending doom. Perhaps, even I harbored fears buried deep within my subconscious.

My voice softened, resigned to the situation. "Alright, I'll go with you."

Kenichi, invigorated, declared, "I'll have 'Chiwodaka' lead the way."

Yeri added pragmatically, "Equipment is sufficient, but we must use it carefully."

Itagaki Ichiro, standing apart from Sadagumi and Yunko—perhaps wary of their potential alliance—insisted, "All supplies must be shared equally."

How they managed this "fair distribution" was beyond me, as I retreated to a quiet spot, hugging my knees. I needed rest.

As daylight crept in, we set out. Kenichi carried the little white tarsier, exchanging odd noises with it, perhaps finding solace in the creature.

The rest of us followed. Iron Smith brought up the rear, pausing when anyone lagged behind. His position at the back stemmed from a deep-seated fear of having anyone at his back. This seasoned assassin, living in constant dread, truly was pitiable.

Itagaki Ichiro also preferred to linger at the rear, while Sadagumi and Yunko marched ahead, heads held high. Walking beside Ichiro, curiosity got the better of me.

I lowered my voice, asking, "Ichiro, I understand why you might want to kill Sadagumi, but why Yunko too?"

He raised an eyebrow, as if the answer was obvious. "I tasked Yunko with the crime. If I don't eliminate her, she could hold that over me forever."

I was taken aback by Ichiro's response, unable to suppress a sigh. The depths of human consciousness can be so enigmatic. Pressing on, I asked, "There's still something I don't understand. How did you come by the gun you gave to Yunko?"

The mysteries of these "copies" were numerous and perplexing. They could appear and disappear at will, like Yunko's copy in the mental hospital. They possessed unusual abilities: Ichiro with a two-headed gun beyond ordinary acquisition, and Yeri's knowledge of Iron Smith's existence.

From Mitsuyoshi's diary, I knew we had at least four days ahead of us. This journey could be my chance to unravel some of these mysteries.

I was particularly curious about the origin of the gun—perhaps it could shed light on the special abilities of the copies. So, I focused on Ichiro and his pistol.

Ichiro seemed taken aback by my question, as if searching for an answer that eluded him. Worried he hadn't heard me correctly, I repeated, "The gun, the one that fires from both ends—where did you get it?"

His confusion lingered, so I prompted him again, "You remember the gun, right?"

Irritation flashed across his face. "Of course I remember the gun."

"So, where did it come from?" I pressed.

He gave a bitter smile, "I don't know—I just don't know."

I refused to relent. "You don't know? You're saying you have no idea how you came by it?"

Ichiro looked genuinely embarrassed, but the confusion persisted. "I truly don't know. I just wanted a gun like that—and somehow, there it was."

I was stunned. "Explain that more clearly."

He seemed to dig deep into his thoughts, but his explanation remained vague. "I wanted a gun that would ensure if Yunko killed Sadagumi, she'd die too. I was in my study, thinking about it, and suddenly, there it was on the table."

I was dumbfounded. "So, you wished for it, and it appeared?"

Ichiro seemed to struggle with his own recollection, his expression earnest yet baffled. "Of course not; if it were that simple, I wouldn't need to meet the Monkey God."

Growing impatient, I asked, "Then how did the gun come into your possession?"

He blinked slowly. "As I said, I reached out, and suddenly, I had the gun. I was familiar with its function, so I handed it to Yunko."

Despite my probing, I couldn't extract a clearer answer. There was undoubtedly a missing piece, something crucial I was failing to grasp. But without more from Ichiro, I had no choice but to let it rest—for now.

I quickened my pace to catch up with Yeri. He looked at me and offered a strained smile, the kind that suggested familiarity tinged with a hint of betrayal.

I returned his smile and asked cautiously, "Yeri? Is it alright if I call you Yeri?"

He seemed mildly irritated. "Of course, I am Yeri."

Raising my hands in a gesture of goodwill, I continued, "In Tokyo, did you ever meet Yunko?"

Yeri glanced over at Yunko. "Yes."

I pressed on, "How did you know Ichiro gave Yunko a gun and instructed her to kill Sadayumi?"

Yeri hesitated, a look of confusion crossing his face—the same look I'd seen moments ago on Ichiro. After a moment, he replied, "If I know, I know. Why should there need to be a reason?"

I didn't let up. "Surely there must be a reason. Ichiro's actions were very covert—"

Cutting me off, Yeri said, "No matter how secretive, things will eventually be known!"

"But you and Ichiro hadn't seen each other in ages—" I began.

He interrupted with a laugh, "It wasn't me who hadn't seen Ichiro in a long time, it was—"

His words trailed off, a mysterious smile playing on his lips. I understood: it wasn't this Yeri, but his original self, who had been absent.

This brought me to another question about these "copies": they seemed to have the uncanny ability to appear and disappear at will, unseen even by those closest to them.

I pondered this and asked, "Even if you could uncover Ichiro's secret, how did you know about someone like Iron Smith? He's a top-tier professional killer, operating under the radar. Global intelligence agencies haven't been able to track him down. How did you learn about him?"

Yeri adopted that same look of confusion again. After a moment of contemplation, he said, "I—I just thought that if I could eliminate Itagaki Ichiro, I could control the secrets of the supernatural monkey god. Then—suddenly, I knew about the secret involving Yunko."

His words were tentative, and he glanced at me as if seeking affirmation. I nodded, urging him to go on. "I'm afraid I'm not explaining it well," he admitted.

His explanation was indeed unclear, but the pattern was becoming evident—just like Ichiro's desire for a gun, which magically appeared, Yeri's desire to dispose of Ichiro led him to inexplicably know Ichiro's secrets.

It seemed that whatever these "copies" wished for or focused on, it manifested into reality. Yet, the individuals themselves remained oblivious to their own extraordinary abilities. This revelation left me both intrigued and unsettled, pondering the implications of such a power.

I urged Yeri to continue, and he recounted, "Once I knew Ichiro's secret, I realized it was the perfect opportunity to eliminate him. I devised a plan to incite Yunko's jealousy, pushing her to kill Ichiro. But Yunko wasn't accustomed to murder. I needed a way to have her act without implicating myself."

I lowered my voice, piecing it together. "So, as you considered this, you naturally thought of Iron Smith."

Yeri nodded eagerly. "Yes, exactly."

"And you knew how to leverage Iron, ensuring he would aid Yunko," I added.

Yeri seemed relieved, as if unburdened by confession. "Yes, that's right. With Iron's help, Ichiro was killed, and I remained blameless."

A shiver ran through me. In my brief conversations with these copies, I realized their cunning and danger surpassed that of their originals.

Human hearts are inscrutable, often restrained by moral codes that prevent acting on dark impulses. Many harbor desires they lack the ability or audacity to fulfill.

But the copies are different. They have no such restraints and possess special abilities. Whatever they envision, they can realize.

And here I was, among six such entities—an unsettling thought.

This sparked further questions. The "copies" were products of a bizarre phenomenon linked to the supernatural monkey god. The god's influence seemed to create these copies and perhaps, still control them through mysterious means.

Were the copies' sudden appearances, disappearances, and inexplicable knowledge due to the monkey god's manipulation?

Who or what is the supernatural monkey god? Why does he wield such power? What are his intentions? My mind swirled with questions, devoid of answers.

Confronting the supernatural monkey god seemed the only path to understanding.

For two days, we traversed the dense forest. The copies remained silent, avoiding eye contact, their relationships fraught with unspoken tensions.

Despite their wariness of each other, they were willing to converse with me. I spent this time probing for insights, though it yielded little beyond what I had gleaned from Yeri and Ichiro.

On the third day, the final leg of our journey, only Yeri, Ichiro, and I knew—thanks to Mitsuyoshi's notes—that we were nearing the monkey god. Although Ichiro had urged secrecy, I revealed this to the group. Everyone, except a disgruntled Ichiro, was buoyant with anticipation.

By noon, we emerged from the forest to a swift, shallow river. We waded across, and on the other side, the little white tarsier let out a cry. I heard an unfamiliar sound, reminiscent of the leaf flute Yeri had played.

Realization dawned—it wasn't a flute, but the wind through branches in the tarsier's homeland. We were near.

I kept this to myself, despite the group's surprise and Iron's evident anxiety. We were on the cusp of discovering the truth behind the supernatural monkey god and the mysteries that had drawn us into this tangled web.

We pressed onward, following the river upstream as it led us into an even denser forest. The wind through the treetops created an eerie, thrilling sound that seemed to vibrate through the air.

Ichiro and I exchanged a knowing glance. "This forest is mentioned in Mitsuyoshi's diary," Ichiro said solemnly.

I nodded. "Yes, it is."

Yeri joined us, curiosity evident in his eyes. "Mitsuyoshi's diary talks about a 'glowing path' after passing through a roaring forest. What do you think that 'glowing path' means?"

Ichiro scoffed. "It's just a path that glows. Isn't that obvious?"

Yeri bristled. "Only someone as simple-minded as you would think it's that straightforward."

Ichiro turned to me for my opinion. "What do you think it means?"

The concept of a "glowing path" puzzled me. A path, sure, but one that glows? That seemed fantastical. As Yeri and Ichiro continued their debate, an irritation rose within me. "Why argue? We'll know what it is when we see it."

My words quieted them for a moment, but Yeri soon added, "Mitsuyoshi's notes mention that at the end of the glowing path lies the palace of the monkey god."

"That means the palace is at the end of the path," Ichiro declared loudly, igniting excitement among the group. After three days of trekking through the oppressive heat and humidity of the forest, this was the hope everyone needed to quicken their pace.

Kenichi's little white tarsier was restless on his shoulder, its cries growing more frequent and frantic. As the sun began to set, we emerged from the dense forest, eager to find this luminous trail. Especially for Ichiro, Yeri, and myself, every landmark had matched Mitsuyoshi's meticulous descriptions, so surely the glowing path awaited us.

Yet, as the trees thinned and gave way to open land, anticipation turned to confusion. Spurred by hope, someone broke into a run, and the rest of us followed suit, sprinting out of the forest. But instead of a glowing path, we were met with a vast expanse of tall, dense grass—at least 80 centimeters high—stretching out before us with no trail in sight.

Across the grassland, about a kilometer away, another dense forest loomed. We halted at the grassland's edge, bewildered. Iron Smith voiced the question on everyone's mind, "Where is the trail?"

Ichiro's voice cut through the thick jungle air like a blade. "There must be a trail! Mitsuyoshi wrote about it in his diary. What are you all standing there for? Find it!"

His words ignited a spark of urgency. His logic was sound—if it was a trail, it would be narrow, easily swallowed by the voracious undergrowth. Ichiro feverishly pushed aside clumps of weeds, his determination infectious, as others joined him in the search.

I, too, searched briefly. But my mind lingered on the legend of the white tarsier, believed to be the emissary of the supernatural monkey god, destined to guide seekers. Why exhaust ourselves when destiny itself would lead the way?

With this revelation, I turned to Kenichi, who stood frozen, the white tarsier nestled silently in his arms, its eyes shut in serene slumber. A chill ran down my spine as I approached him. "What happened to Chiwodaka?"

Kenichi's smile was a mixture of resignation and irony. "Asleep. We've journeyed under its guidance, nearing the monkey god... and now it sleeps."

The tarsier's closed eyes betrayed no intent to move. Meanwhile, Iron Smith's voice pierced the thick air. "No trails, just wild grasses!"

Sadagumi's voice rose in a calm suggestion. "This is grassland. No need for trails. We can cross it to reach the forest beyond."

Her logic was irrefutable, and laughter rippled through our group, a release of tension. Of course, we simply needed to traverse the open plain. Why fixate on a trail? Forward was the only direction.

Kenichi led the charge, stepping boldly into the tangled sea of green. We followed, each step sinking into the soft, decaying earth beneath the suffocating foliage. The sun surrendered its light as we emerged from the forest, the grassland swallowing us as twilight descended.

The diary's promise echoed in our minds: "At the end of the luminous trail, you can lead to the palace of the monkey god." Though the trail remained elusive, the path across the grassland seemed certain. As night cloaked us, the ground grew uneven, our progress slow. Iron Smith, gripped by fear, clung to my clothing, his eyes wide with terror.

I sought words to reassure him, but before they formed, Sadagumi and Yunko's screams shattered the night. They pointed ahead, their voices rising in unison.

I turned, my breath catching in my throat. We all stood transfixed. Before us, at the grassland's edge, a strip of light unfurled—a glowing path stretching from the forest behind us to the distant shadows of mountains ahead. A dark red luminescence, like fire tracing the earth.

Ichiro's triumph rang out. "The glowing path."

Yeri clasped his hands, voice a reverent whisper. "Oh my god! The glowing path—we're on the right track."

Ichiro's exuberance was infectious as he charged ahead, compelling the others to follow in an instinctive surge. Iron Smith lingered beside me, torn between caution and desire. His eyes pleaded, "Why don't we go?"

I offered a calm reassurance, "There's no need to hurry. With the glowing path before us, the monkey god is within reach."

Even as I spoke, my steps quickened, Iron Smith a shadow at my side. As we advanced, my mind churned with questions about the mysterious light band. It wasn't a path through the weeds, but rather a luminous ribbon hugging the earth. Its glow, faint yet persistent, only visible in the deepening night.

What force had crafted this spectral trail stretching for kilometers? What purpose did it serve? Mitsuyoshi's diary cryptically hinted that it "can lead to" the Monkey God's palace, but what did "can lead to" truly imply? Why not state outright that the path ended at the palace?

Lost in thought, I pushed forward, Iron Smith mirroring my pace. Kenichi, nimble as a monkey, overtook Ichiro, surging towards the enigmatic glow. Ichiro, undeterred, was soon outpaced by Yeri, with Yunko and Sadagumi close behind.

As Kenichi neared the light, a chill of apprehension gripped me. The light band exuded an eerie, malevolent aura. What lay beyond its threshold? What dangers lurked within its glow?

"Kenichi, wait!" I called out, urgency tinged with fear.

But my warning came too late. Kenichi, caught in the thrill, leapt into the light band, enveloped in a cloak of dark red fire. The glow flared brilliantly before settling back to its original state. In that instant, Kenichi vanished, as if consumed by the light itself. He and the white tarsier were simply gone.

Yeri, mere meters from the light, halted abruptly, his face bathed in the ominous glow. His terror mirrored our own, each of us frozen in disbelief. Ichiro, Yunko, and Sadagumi joined him, staring into the void where Kenichi had been.

I pushed past Iron Smith, reaching Yeri's side, my heart pounding with dread. Iron Smith, trembling, clung to me once more, his breath ragged with fear. We stood on the precipice of the unknown, the light beckoning yet foreboding, its secrets shrouded in darkness.

CHAPTER 21

Meeting the Monkey God

and Fulfilling Three Wishes

As I sprinted toward the commotion, Yeri's voice met me, laden with panic. "What happened? Where did he go?"

His finger jabbed toward the enigmatic light strip—a question echoing in my own mind, yet I had no answers to offer.

Yeri, unsatisfied, cried out again, "Where did he vanish? The Japanese guy! Chiwodaka! I's gone too. Who will guide us now?"

Amidst Yeri's distress, Yunko's expression hardened with resolve. She stepped forward, unwavering. Iron Smith, alarmed, called after her, "Miss Yunko, what are you doing? You—you—"

Yunko halted, her voice calm yet resolute. "I believe Mr. Kenichi has reached the palace of the monkey god."

Iron Smith protested, "How can you know? He—he just vanished!"

Her response was a challenge, cold yet daring. "If you're scared, stay back. But if you're not, join me."

Without turning, she extended her hand behind her—a silent invitation for Iron Smith to grasp.

To everyone's surprise, Iron Smith moved forward. Although his expression showed that he was extremely scared, he did walk forward. I firmly believe that he was not suddenly brave, but because he must have a special feeling for Yunko.

We watched Iron come behind Yunko and stretch out his hand. Yunko's hand and Iron's hand were tightly clasped together. Iron took another step forward and stood side by side with Yunko.

When they stood side by side, they both turned their heads and looked at each other. Yunko's expression was firm and a little reserved, like a girl who met her lover for the first time. Iron Smith, though terror-stricken, managed a tentative smile.

Then, the two of them continued to walk forward. Just at the edge of the light band, they stopped.

Like Kenichi's situation, at that time, they seemed to be covered with a layer of dark red light. They stopped for a very short time, then stepped forward again and stepped into the light band.

In an instant, the light enveloping Iron and Yunko flared, then vanished in less than a twentieth of a second. It happened so quickly, beyond the eye's ability to fully capture, leaving only a lingering sense of uncanny speed.

As they disappeared, Ichiro instinctively stepped back.

Sadayumi, standing just behind, steadied Ichiro with a firm hand and a biting remark. "Your mistress left. Why didn't you follow?"

Ichiro's throat emitted a strained sound, but he remained facing the light. Sadagumi's expression twisted with malice, her voice cutting through the tension like a blade. "Ridiculous! She left without you, choosing another. What does that say about you?"

Ichiro spun around, his face flushed with anger. "Shut up!"

Sadagumi's laughter was edged with malice. "Blame me? You, a coward? Have you forgotten who built your success, who allowed you to keep a mistress?"

Alarm bells rang in my mind; this confrontation was spiraling dangerously.

Ichiro's rage erupted; he lunged at Sadagumi, grabbing her hair with a ferocity that belied his usual demeanor. The original Ichiro might have cowered under such provocation, but this was a different version—one unrestrained by past fears.

He not only seized her hair but struck her sharply. Had Sadagumi been in her original form, her noble upbringing might have left her stunned. But this was a replica, and she retaliated with a scream, driving forward into Ichiro's chest.

The impact sent Ichiro reeling toward the edge of the light band. In the chaos, Sadagumi's hair still clenched in his grip, they both tumbled into the light.

As before, the light flashed, and they vanished, swallowed by the mysterious glow.

Now, only Yeri and I remained, standing before the enigmatic path that had claimed our companions, each disappearance more baffling than the last.

We exchanged a glance, a silent acknowledgment of the strange reality before us. Yeri swallowed hard, his voice wavering. "Mitsuyoshi's diary... it doesn't mention people disappearing like this."

I managed a wry smile. "Well, if he vanished, he wouldn't have been able to write about it."

The humor was dark, but the logic sound. Mitsuyoshi had traveled alone. If he had disappeared upon stepping onto the "glowing path," there would have been no witness to document it. Naturally, his journal would be silent on such an event.

This reasoning led to a hopeful conclusion: those who vanished would eventually return, just as Mitsuyoshi had. After all, the diary existed.

Yeri's face bore the weight of indecision, his eyes searching mine for assurance. "So, you're saying their disappearance is... a way to travel somewhere?"

I nodded, conviction edging into my voice. "At the end of the glowing path lies the palace of the monkey god. That's what Mitsuyoshi's diary attests."

Yeri took a deep breath, steeling himself. "Shall we... shall we go together?"

I could sense the fear etched on Yeri's face, mirroring my own anxiety. Witnessing our companions vanish one by one, so swiftly and mysteriously, was unnerving to say the least.

When Yeri suggested we move forward together, I agreed without hesitation. "Okay, let's do this together," I replied, trying to inject some confidence into my voice.

He swallowed hard, extending a trembling hand toward me. Though I wasn't as visibly shaken, I took his hand, understanding the comfort of shared courage. It felt like two children holding hands while wading through an unknown, deep stream.

As we neared the "luminous path," uncertainty loomed large. My mind was a whirl of possibilities, none of them reassuring. What awaited us beyond that glowing boundary was anyone's guess.

We paused at the edge, exchanging a glance that spoke volumes. With a deep breath, we stepped forward together.

The moment we entered the light, Yeri's grip tightened reflexively. The light enveloped us, and suddenly, I was alone.

I turned, expecting to see him, but was met with blinding brightness. The light was so intense that it forced my eyes shut. Yeri was gone, vanished the instant we crossed into the glow.

I tried to call out, but a powerful gust of air stole my voice, propelling me forward with dizzying speed. Whether it was the light band moving or myself, I couldn't discern. The velocity was such that my body felt on the verge of disintegration.

Panic surged as I wondered, what was happening? Yet, there was no time for answers. Abruptly, darkness fell, and I was thrown from motion to stillness. The transition was jarring, my insides rebelling against the sudden halt. I reached out instinctively, my hand finding purchase on a flat surface. It grounded me, allowing me to regain my composure.

Then, a light appeared, growing rapidly as if someone had flicked on a flashlight in the void. In its beam, the little white tarsier bounded toward me, its eyes large and expressive. It stopped just before me, letting out a soft, almost reassuring cry.

I stood there, heart racing, as the tarsier watched me, its presence both mysterious and comforting in the strange new world I found myself in.

I took a deep breath and addressed the tarsier, "Chiwodaka, are you here to lead me to the mystical monkey god?" It chirped twice in response, then turned and bounded forward. I hurried after it, moving toward the source of the light. Beyond its glow, everything was shrouded in darkness.

The ground beneath was smooth, seemingly paved with massive stone slabs, which added to the surreal experience. After about three minutes, the light vanished, leaving me enveloped in darkness. In the stillness, I heard the subtle sound of something sliding open.

My instincts told me it was a door. My suspicion was confirmed when a soft, melodious voice drifted through the blackness: "You are here, please come in."

Mitsuyoshi's diary had mentioned that the voice of the magical monkey god was enchanting and gentle. Hearing it now, my heart raced with excitement and trepidation. I was in the presence of the legendary monkey god.

"I can't see anything!" I exclaimed, my voice echoing in the void.

The gentle voice replied, "For everyone, the path ahead is dark, but we all continue forward."

His words intrigued me, and with cautious steps, I moved forward. After a few steps, I heard the faint sound of a door closing behind me.

The realization that I was now sealed in darkness heightened my anxiety. What lay ahead was unknown and unpredictable.

Trying to steady my nerves, I asked, "Are you the legendary supernatural monkey god?"

The voice responded warmly, "Yes."

My pulse quickened as I strained to make out the figure in the darkness. Despite the soothing tone, I could see nothing, my senses heightened by the impenetrable blackness.

"You are the fifth person to see me," the voice continued. "You must have come for the three wishes. What is your first wish?"

The statement caught me off guard, sending my thoughts into disarray. Why was I the fifth? There should have been six people before me—Sadagumi and the others. But in the overwhelming presence of the monkey god, there was no time to ponder this anomaly. My mind raced to formulate a wish worthy of this extraordinary encounter.

In that moment, I wasn't truly prepared for the reality of the situation. When the voice asked about my first wish, my mind was elsewhere, fixated on uncovering the appearance of this so-called supernatural being. Without much thought, I blurted out, "I want to see you."

The monkey god seemed taken aback, letting out a surprised sound. Then, a beam of light materialized before me, illuminating a small, square area like a spotlight on a stage. Within this light sat a chair, and on that chair was a figure.

The figure was indeed unusual. Tall and slender, it wore a light grey garment made of an unrecognizable material. Its hands rested on the armrests, revealing astonishingly long fingers—twice the length of a human's. The elongated arms matched the fingers in proportion. But what truly struck me was its face: a monkey's visage, covered in thick, golden fur.

I actually saw the legendary Monkey God! It was a sight that both amazed and confounded me. I recalled laughing at the crude portrait I'd once seen at an expert's office, yet here was a being that matched the depiction with uncanny accuracy—an entity that was both man and monkey.

As I absorbed this astonishing sight, my mind a whirlwind of questions, the monkey god's voice broke through my thoughts. "You have seen me. What is your second wish?"

He had granted my first wish almost instantly, yet my mind was too muddled to appreciate the gravity of it. In front of this enigmatic creature, I struggled to find clarity, even as the opportunity for another wish beckoned.

I stared intently at him and blurted out, "I want to know what you are."

The Monkey God's smile was an odd yet captivating sight. A monkey smiling is not something one encounters every day, and while peculiar, it exuded a certain warmth. He replied, "I am the Supernatural Monkey God."

"No, no," I pressed, "I mean, what exactly is the Supernatural Monkey God?"

With another enigmatic smile, he explained, "A fair question. My form resembles an animal called a monkey, and I possess great abilities, thus I am the Supernatural Monkey God."

His answer left much to be desired, a mere scratching of the surface of my curiosity. I quickly followed up, "Where do you get that ability? Where are you from?"

The Monkey God gestured gracefully, "Look over there."

In the direction he pointed, a deep blue light curtain materialized, its hue indescribably profound. Amidst this abyss, a light orange-yellow emerged.

"This is where I come from," the Monkey God declared.

"A distant planet?" I ventured.

"Yes," he confirmed, his voice calm.

I inhaled sharply, "What constellation?"

He sighed, a sound filled with the weight of untold knowledge. "I can't explain it to you fully. From your perspective, it may be incomprehensible."

"Please try," I urged. "I might understand."

After a contemplative pause, he continued, "You asked which constellation I hail from. That question is fundamentally flawed. You look to the stars, or peer through telescopes, believing you can unravel the universe's mysteries."

"Of course," I interjected, somewhat defensively.

His sigh was one of gentle exasperation. "No, it's not so simple. Your astronomers claim to observe planets millions of light years away, but they miss a crucial point. Beyond those light years lies a temporal distance. They're seeing ancient history, the state of things eons ago. It's akin to viewing a photograph from seventy years past, and realizing that the infant in the picture is now actually a seventy-year-old."

I gasped at the revelation. "Are you suggesting some of the stars we see might not exist anymore?"

The profundity of his insight left me reeling, opening a window to the vast, enigmatic truths of the cosmos.

The Monkey God's expression brightened, "Yes, some stars have ceased to exist, others have transformed. What you see is the universe's past, not its present. You cannot perceive the universe as it is now because you haven't surpassed the speed of light."

My mind swirled with the implications, as I stared at the orange-yellow orb amidst the deep blue. This was the Monkey God's home planet, a place beyond human understanding, shrouded in the vast mysteries of the cosmos.

Despite my mental fog, clarity dawned upon me. The Monkey God continued, "My power stems from my origin."

I sighed, "It's like a modern person with advanced technology visiting a primitive tribe, becoming a god to them."

The Monkey God nodded, "Precisely. In such a scenario, that person would indeed be revered as a god."

Understanding washed over me, and I nodded. His voice retained its soothing quality as he prompted, "Now, what is your third wish? This is your final one."

My second wish had been granted. I grasped that the "Monkey God" was a being from an unfathomable planet, his abilities the result of extraordinary scientific advancement.

Faced with the prospect of my final wish, I was driven by curiosity. "I want to know everything about you," I declared.

The Monkey God regarded me with a penetrating gaze, his eyes alight with an enigmatic glow. He smiled, "You are different from the four who came before you."

Instantly intrigued, I asked, "Who were they?"

He lifted his head slightly, "The first was an ordinary young man. His wish was for supreme power on Earth, and I granted it."

Stunned, I inquired, "What happened?"

The Monkey God's tone turned slightly mocking, "What happened? Like anyone else, he met his end."

The answer was stark, a reminder of the perilous nature of power and the fleetingness of life. I braced myself for more revelations, eager to uncover the truths that lay hidden within the Monkey God's story.

I flinched at the implications. "What about the second one?" I asked.

The monkey god replied, "The second wished for wealth, and I granted that wish as well."

I couldn't help but groan, "And in the end, he... he died too?"

The monkey god nodded solemnly.

I exclaimed, "They have three wishes. One could ask for power or wealth, and the second should be for immortality."

The monkey god said, "Indeed."

Confused, I pressed on, "Then why—"

He interrupted gently, "Remember, they had three wishes. Their third wish was to die quickly."

I inhaled sharply, momentarily at a loss for words. The monkey god's voice remained soft, "So when the third person, a prince, sought happiness, I couldn't fulfill his wish. I truly don't know how to make someone happy. I can create a hundred tons of gold from seawater or air for those seeking wealth, but happiness... that eludes me."

I pondered this, nodding slowly. "Yes, happiness isn't something one can simply be given, nor is it something you can chase. It's a complex, elusive state."

The monkey god spread his hands, his long, supple fingers seeming almost ethereal. "The fourth person, after seeing himself—"

I interrupted, "I already know about the third and fourth visitors. What puzzles me is how you let people see themselves?"

The monkey god appeared surprised, "That's quite simple. There's a device—a copying instrument—"

I nodded, recognizing his description. "Yes, that peculiar device. I've seen it. That thing—"

The conversation hung in the air, the implications of the monkey god's revelations settling in, each answered question leading to a deeper understanding of his powers and the human desires they unearthed.

The Monkey God explained, "With just a single cell as the foundation, the factors within can cultivate a complete being, identical to the original."

I was taken aback, my eyes wide with astonishment. The Monkey God continued, "This shouldn't surprise you. Earthlings achieved single-cell reproduction long ago, growing entire frogs in labs using this method."

"I'm aware of asexual single-cell reproduction," I replied, "but the speed of your process—"

He gestured dismissively, "Speed is merely a technical issue. My device can replicate a person from a single cell in a hundredth of a second."

I inhaled sharply, "So, can we call this replicated being a 'copy' of the original?"

The Monkey God paused, as if the thought had never crossed his mind. "A copy? Yes, that's a fitting term!"

I offered a wry smile, "You might not realize, but the copy from asexual reproduction can differ greatly from the original. The original's subconscious often emerges as the dominant consciousness in the copy."

The Monkey God nodded, "I'm aware. That's why I have those who wish to look at themselves first, to understand their true nature and needs before making their wishes."

I couldn't help but smile bitterly, "But what's the point of that?"

He replied, "When a person truly understands themselves, they can better discern what they actually need."

I sighed, "But can anyone really fully understand themselves?"

The Monkey God sighed alongside me, "That's the very topic I'm exploring. Yet, even now, I must admit I haven't found the answer. Human personalities are so complex. People struggle to understand each other, and often can't even comprehend themselves."

Our shared contemplation highlighted the profound mysteries of identity and self-awareness, underscoring the challenges of truly knowing oneself, even in the face of extraordinary possibilities.

I wiped sweat from my brow, puzzled by why I was perspiring so much. "Do you know about Itagaki Mitsuyoshi?" I asked. "He was the fourth person to come to you for three wishes."

The Monkey God nodded, "Yes, he killed himself."

"No," I corrected, "it was his copy who killed him, and he killed his copy."

The Monkey God shrugged, "It's the same thing. He killed himself, just as many people without copies end up harming themselves."

I pondered this for a while, slowly grasping the deeper truth in the Monkey God's words. Before I could respond, he continued, "I came here to study the most advanced creatures on Earth. My research, however, has yielded no results. I'm planning to return soon. It was nice meeting you!"

The normalcy of his farewell amused me, given the bizarre circumstances. It seemed almost absurd.

After a moment's pause, I asked, "The six who came with me—"

The Monkey God interrupted with an "Oh!" and added, "They no longer exist!"

Stunned, I stammered, "No longer exist? What do you mean? They—"

He waved a dismissive hand, "I can transform them from a cell into a person in a hundredth of a second, and just as easily reverse that process."

The revelation sent a fresh wave of sweat down my face. The enormity of what he was saying rendered me speechless, grappling with the overwhelming implications of his power and the fate of my companions.

The Monkey God laughed as he pointed at me, "I've gathered many cells, including yours and those of the six who accompanied you. I plan to take them back for further study. I believe you won't mind? After all, your body contains hundreds of millions of cells, and each can become a copy of you."

I took a deep breath, quickly responding, "No objection! Feel free to take as many as you need!"

He chuckled, then his expression turned serious. "When the copies are active, they are under my control. They may seem to possess unique abilities or knowledge they shouldn't have, but it's just me fulfilling their desires according to their wishes."

I stared at him, bewildered. "But... from so far away, you're here in India, and they're—"

The Monkey God interrupted with a sly smile, "Don't forget, I am the Monkey God!"

Feeling a bit helpless, I spread my hands. "Is there anything else you're curious about?" he asked.

I sighed, "No, thank you. It was nice meeting you." I mirrored his casual farewell. He smiled, approached me, and extended his hand.

I shook it, his grip soft yet firm. Standing beside me, he was about two heads taller. I looked up, "I'd love to learn more about your planet."

He laughed heartily, "I came to study earthlings, not to be studied. Plus, your three wishes are fulfilled. You can't ask for more."

I sighed, realizing my wishes were indeed granted.

As his words faded, darkness enveloped me once more. I felt the familiar sensation of rapid movement. When the light returned, it was as dazzling as when I first encountered the "luminous trail."

Suddenly, I was back in the wilderness, watching the trail dim until it vanished completely within moments. I stood there, processing the extraordinary events until dawn broke the horizon, prompting me to head back.

For several days, I traversed the tropical forest, using primitive means of transport until I reached a small town. Life resumed its normal pace. Five days later, I returned home.

After a few days of rest, I found myself on a plane bound for Japan once more, carrying with me the secrets of the Monkey God and the mysteries of the universe yet untold.

In the tangled web of this mystery, all the players had either succumbed to death or spiraled into madness, save for a singular figure: Kenichi. The lone exception in this narrative that defied belief. And there, shrouded in secrecy, lay the device—a marvel capable of multiplying a single cell into a fully formed human in mere fractions of a second. Its draw was undeniable, a window through which I glimpsed my own frailty and vulnerability.

My journey to Japan this time had a single purpose: to uncover the truth hidden in the study of Itagaki Ichiro and Yunko's clandestine meeting spot. Yet, upon my arrival, I was met with devastation—a peculiar fire had ravaged the place, leaving nothing but charred remains and unanswered questions.

Naka and I eventually joined forces, our shared quest leading us to Yunko. Her transformation was stark—her jawline more pronounced, her face an alabaster mask. Madness clung to her like a shroud, rendering her a mere specter of her former self. Naka, steadfast and enduring, stood by her side with unmatched patience. Each time he beheld me, a sigh escaped him, laden with an unspoken lament.

Determined to uncover Kenichi's whereabouts, I focused my efforts on tracing his elusive path. Yet, as the days stretched into weeks and then months, my search yielded nothing but silence. Kenichi remained a ghost, his location as enigmatic as the mysteries we sought to unravel.

Just as I was on the verge of abandoning my search, news reached me from an unlikely source—a group of mountaineers returning from the northern wilderness. They spoke of an enigmatic figure dwelling in the heart of the mountains, living harmoniously among a troop of monkeys, exuding a peculiar contentment.

My instincts whispered that this mysterious recluse could be none other than Kenichi. After confronting the depths of his own soul, he had left behind the trappings of his former life, resigning from the police force to return to his roots. The mountains, his childhood sanctuary, called him home. Was it not natural for him to seek solace in the embrace of the wilderness?

In many ways, a life among the monkeys offered a simplicity far removed from the tangled complexities of human existence. There, in the wild, Kenichi might have found a peace that eludes those who navigate the labyrinthine corridors of the human heart.

People often find themselves ensnared in the enigma of understanding—not just of others, but of their own selves.

The tapestry of human personality is woven with threads so intricate that even the revered "Monkey God," with all his profound wisdom, confessed his research had led him to no definitive answers.

As for me, each time my reflection meets my gaze in the mirror, I am confronted by the same persistent question: What kind of person am I? Who am I?

What truth lies hidden in the depths of my soul?

The answer is—an unfolding mystery, an ever-evolving journey without a clear destination. In the labyrinth of self-discovery, perhaps the answer is not a single revelation but a lifelong pursuit of understanding.